BREAKING THE CIRCLE

BREAKING
THE CIRCLE

M.J. Trow

**SEVERN
HOUSE**

First world edition published in Great Britain and the USA in 2023
by Severn House, an imprint of Canongate Books Ltd,
14 High Street, Edinburgh EH1 1TE.

Trade paperback edition first published in Great Britain and the USA in 2023
by Severn House, an imprint of Canongate Books Ltd.

severnhouse.com

British Library Cataloguing-in-Publication Data
A CIP catalogue record for this title is available from the British Library.

ISBN-13: 978-0-7278-5070-6 (cased)
ISBN-13: 978-1-4483-0832-3 (trade paper)
ISBN-13: 978-1-4483-0831-6 (e-book)

All Severn House titles are printed on acid-free paper.

Typeset by Palimpsest Book Pr
Falkirk, Stirlingshire, Scotland
Printed and bound in Great Bri
TJ Books, Padstow, Cornwall.

ONE

The sounds of the city seldom found their way into this little room, chosen deliberately because it was at the back of the slightly run-down house. Sometimes, a shrill call of a coster would impinge, but today, not even commerce could break the suffocating silence. Two people sat at the table, opposite each other, one, dressed in a light coat leaning back casually, the other, in a flowered housedress, leaning forward, her head cradled in her arms, apparently asleep.

'Have you ever thought,' the lounging one said, 'whether if a tree falling in a forest with no one there makes a sound?'

There was no reply.

'Nothing to say? Well, of course, the correct answer is that God would hear, but I don't know whether you are of that opinion, are you?'

The visitor made a rueful face – it was always so rude when people didn't answer a civil question. The silence was briefly broken by the squeal of a chair being pushed back on worn linoleum.

'Well, I must be off. It has been, as always, an absolute pleasure. But you'll excuse me, I know, if next time I visit one of your colleagues. We just don't seem to be getting anywhere, do we?'

There was a sniff as sensitive nostrils snuffed the air.

'And I have never been able to abide the smell of mulligatawny.'

With a small sigh, the door opened and closed, leaving Muriel Fazakerley to settle down just a little further into her bowl of soup, cooling and congealing in the quiet, airless little room. Outside the blossom might be bravely shaking its petals in the spring breeze, the air singing with the joy of the reborn sun. But Muriel Fazakerley had passed beyond the veil, and would never smell a London May day again.

*   *   *

Early May in Bloomsbury. The fogs of winter had long gone and the trees around Gower and Malet Streets were heavy with blossom. Not that Margaret Murray had time for such irrelevance. Most ladies of her social class would be rising with the aid of a maid or three, taking breakfast in bed and considering the wardrobe for the day. In Margaret's case, she had already battled her way on the omnibus, wedged between a gentleman with shoulders like tallboys and a woman who was clearly a martyr to catarrh.

Margaret had an important meeting that morning, a confrontation, she feared, with Mr Bernard Quaritch of Bernard Quaritch, Publishers of that Ilk, regarding her new book, *Elementary Egyptian Grammar.* It had all gone very well at first. Mr Quaritch – 'Dear lady, *do,* I beg of you, call me Bernard' – had been most complimentary and had spun worlds of fame and fortune in the air. Then, it had started to go a little pear-shaped, and from being 'dear lady', she had become '*par hempt*' as the ancient Egyptians would have it, as in 'Keep par hempt away from me, she is driving me insane!' All she wanted was for the artist to rein himself in. The eagles, dogs, vultures and flies of the hieroglyphs did not, she had told him numerous times, need to have small, appealing faces. If she had wanted flights of fancy, she would have asked Ernest Shepard, who she happened to know was always on the lookout for work. In vain had she told Mr Quaritch that all that was needed was a simple line. The page proofs kept coming back looking like a galley for *Punch.*

Today was make or break. She would tell Bernard Quaritch, and brook no argument, that the world of academe was waiting with bated breath for the volume. Flinders Petrie himself had given her his seal of approval. Professor Virchov had written from Berlin to say how impressed he was – perhaps not unsurprisingly, as she had given him a shameless plug on the first page. But of course, from fellow archaeologist Arthur Evans, there was not a word. But first, she needed to have a word with Mrs Plinlimmon and have someone make her a cup of tea.

She flashed her dimples at Kirby, the man at the door who carried the keys of the dead and, hauling up her skirts, bounded up the stairs to her inner sanctum. Jack Brooks was there already, of course, except that his face was invisible behind the *Telegraph.*

Margaret flicked the paper with a practised finger and thumb and the young man nearly fell off his chair.

'Sorry, Professor,' he said. 'I didn't hear you come in.'

'Clearly not.' Margaret unpinned her hat. She was not actually a professor, but a quiet inner vanity stopped her from correcting the boy. 'At least it's the *Telegraph*, so I don't have to do that tiresome joke about you being behind the times.'

There was no fear of that. Jack Brooks was one of the Brooks of Hertfordshire, a family that had stood staunchly behind every Tory prime minister since the elder Pitt. There was absolutely no chance that Jack would be seen dead reading *The Times*.

'Tea, Professor?' He folded the paper carefully.

'I thought you'd never ask,' and she sorted her papers as he clattered the crockery. 'What was so riveting in the *Telegraph*?'

'Well,' Brooks set about warming the pot, 'it's quite intriguing, really. Something that might interest you.'

'Oh?'

'Lights,' he said, reaching for the paper and sitting down again. 'Strange lights seen in Wales.'

Margaret sat down too. 'Say on.'

Brooks found the relevant article. 'Merthyr Tydfil,' he read. 'Last Thursday. A clergyman – or at least, a Unitarian minister – was making his way home from a friend's house when he saw three or four circles of light in the night sky. There was no street lighting where he was and the lights were in the form of orbs that moved independently.'

'Was this near water?' she asked.

Brooks glanced quickly through the article – it was no use being inaccurate when it came to conversations with Dr Murray. 'Doesn't say,' he confirmed. 'Why?'

'Marsh gas,' she said, 'or something of that sort. Some ponds glow with an eerie light.'

'Yes, but marsh gas doesn't bob about all over the place, does it? Independently, I mean?'

'I suppose not,' she said. 'How large were these lights?'

'About the size of tennis balls.'

Margaret was as mystified as Brooks. 'If the reverend had been an Anglican,' she said, 'or a Roman Catholic, I would have suspected the old vino sacro, but I don't think the Unitarians

partake, do they? Still, who's to say how much he may have
consumed at the friend's house?'

'That's probably it,' Brooks said as the gas hissed under
the kettle.

'It probably is,' she smiled, 'and, if I may say so, those
hallucinations pale into insignificance alongside the edicts of
Amenhotep. How are your translations coming along?'

'I'll get right on to it, Professor,' Brooks smiled, folding away
his newspaper. 'As soon as I have made the tea.'

Detective Sergeant Andrew Crawford had already read it twice.
And he was still grinning from ear to ear when he hurtled down
Whitehall and took a sharp left into Clarence Place. The Yard
loomed above him, as it had for the last ten years now, never the
opera house it had been intended to be but the most famous
police headquarters in the world. France had the Quai d'Orsay;
Germany, Wilhelmstrasse; America more precincts than Ancient
Rome. But there was only one Scotland Yard and Andrew
Crawford was crossing its threshold once again.

He called cheerily to the desk man. 'Any joy on the lift,
Nacker?'

The desk man shook his head. 'Week Thursday,' he said.
'Apparently – and I quote – "There has been an unprecedented
upsurge in the demand for elevating machinery". And we're
twenty-eighth on the list.'

Crawford grunted and made for the stairs.

'Our business is important to them, though, they assured me
of that,' Nacker called after him and Crawford didn't doubt it
for a moment.

The Yard's staircase didn't faze a man like Andrew Crawford.
Older coppers knew it as the treadmill, but he was still the right
side of thirty and fit as a flea. He burst in to the offices on the
second floor, A Division, detectives for the use of. His boss was
already there.

'Good of you to call, Detective Sergeant,' John Kane said,
looking over his rimless spectacles at the lad. Kane didn't usually
do sarcasm, but there *were* limits.

'Sorry I'm late, guv,' Crawford chirped. 'Horse down in the
Aldwych.'

'Always,' Kane sighed. 'And the Tube?'

'Leaves on the line round Ealing Broadway.'

'In May?'

Crawford smiled. 'No one said how long they had been there.'

Kane tutted. Then he caught sight of the folded paper under the arm of his number two. 'Are you reading what I'm reading?' he asked.

Crawford grabbed a chair. 'The *Telegraph*, God bless 'em. The Stratton brothers! The Mask Murders. We did it!'

'That we did, lad.' Inspector Kane knew that neither of them had been involved in that case, but he knew what Crawford meant and they shook hands. The first felons to be sentenced to death based on the evidence of their fingerprints. It was a milestone and both men knew it. 'More work for the Billingtons, I suppose,' he shrugged, 'on a chilly morning in Wandsworth.'

'Forgive me, guv.' Crawford sensed his boss's mood. 'You don't sound as chipper about all this as I had expected.'

'Read the small print, son.' Kane stabbed the newspaper with his finger. 'That overpaid shit Curtis Bennett, for the defence, did his best to undermine the march of science. Luckily, the jury didn't fall for it, but that old fart Mr Justice Channel – why they named a stretch of water after him, I can't imagine – said he didn't think the jury should convict on fingerprint evidence alone. The assistant commissioner's having kittens.'

'Still, job done, eh?' Crawford held his ground. 'And two more murderous bastards will be walking the walk at Wandsworth any day now.'

'Indeed they will,' Kane nodded. 'Indeed they will.'

Edmund Reid looked out of his study window over the beach and the glittering sea. How long, he wondered, would this view survive? Kent, he had warned everybody since he had moved to Hampton-on-Sea, was falling into the water, inch by inch, foot by foot.

Where was he before he was distracted by the view? Ah, yes. He dipped his pen into the inkwell again and continued his sentence, the second-most-vitriolic in his latest missive to the Council – 'Hampton has no roads, paths, lights, sewer, water or dust collector, nor any residents receiving parish relief despite an annual payment of £40 in rates.'

How should he sign it? Ex-Detective Inspector, Scotland Yard? The man who hunted Jack the Ripper? The inspiration for the Inspector Dier series of novels? Balloonist? Conjuror? Tenor? No. He would just sign it 'Reid' and the Council could add any adjective they liked.

He put the pen away and stretched and yawned. He reached for the *Telegraph* lying untidily across his desk. The Stratton brothers – that was good; at last, an edge for the rule of law. That nonsense about weird lights in the sky – it could only happen in Wales. Then, his eyes fell for the first time on a little piece he'd missed. He read it aloud, as if to remind the gulls, screaming and wheeling outside his home, that they did not rule the air alone.

'Famous Sensitive Found Dead. Police Baffled.'

The whole thing sounded archaic. Nobody had called a medium a sensitive for years. And as for 'Police Baffled' – that sounded like one of the better lines of the ever-predictable Arthur Conan Doyle, whose ludicrous detective creation Sherlock Holmes was advertised as about to make a comeback. Joy! People like the violin-playing cocaine addict of Baker Street gave *real* private detectives like Reid a bad name. And as for the dead medium, old habits died hard and ex-Inspector Reid found himself drawn to the scanty details as if he was looking down at a body in a mortuary.

The Famous Sensitive looked neither famous nor sensitive, laid out on a slab in the mortuary of Vine Street Police Station. She had not been a beauty in life and the police mortuary attendant was not a mortician, but he had felt sorry for the poor soul, found face down in her soup at her solitary table, so he had done his best with her, washing her face and getting the worst of the mulligatawny out of her hair. Her sister, standing now looking down at her, her handkerchief a sodden ball clutched in her hand, appreciated it, he could tell.

'Mrs Whitehouse, is this your sister, Muriel Fazakerley?' the police constable in attendance asked. 'I know it's upsetting, but we need a positive identification, if you don't mind.'

The woman looked up at him, her eyes dark pools of tears and nodded, clamping her lips together. 'Only . . . she didn't go by Muriel, not these days,' she said.

The police constable narrowed his eyes and thought of the pile of paperwork he had amassed on the dead woman. 'Had she changed her name by deed poll?' he asked, tersely.

'Oh, no, dear.' The dead sensitive's sister couldn't help calling the constable 'dear'. He looked just like her youngest, only just out of short trousers. She gave another sniff; it was true what they said, about policemen looking younger the older you got. 'She just used her other name for business, you know. She said to me, "Maudie," she said, "Nobody's going to come to Muriel Fazakerley to get told whether Auntie is happy in the Beyond and what's going to win the 12.50 at Plumpton."'

The constable drew himself up. The woman may be dead, but he was still on the lookout for any misdemeanours. 'She claimed to tell the future?' he rapped out. 'That's illegal, that is.'

Maud Whitehouse was a patient woman, made so by the brood of children she had given birth to and waved from her door with varying degrees of pleasure or regret. It was just her and Alf, her husband, now, and young Alfred, off on an apprenticeship soon, or her name wasn't Maud Whitehouse. But she had had enough of this wet-behind-the-ears lad and his stupid questions. She took one final, enormous sniff and stowed her handkerchief up her sleeve. 'Illegal, is it?' she snapped. 'Illegal? Oh, goodness, we'll have to wake her up and arrest her. Are you going to do it, or shall I? She's sometimes a little hard to rouse in the mornings.' And to the horror of the mortuary attendant and the constable, she took her sister by the shoulders and shook her, hard. 'Come on, Muriel,' she shouted into the dead face. 'Wake up.'

Rigor mortis had long passed and the woman's head lolled back and forth, the jaw becoming slack as the binding cloth tucked under her chin slipped free. Maud Whitehouse let go the shoulders and stepped back, her hand to her mouth. A black feather emerged between the pale lips and lay, moist and bedraggled, on the mortuary sheet.

Maud Whitehouse and the constable slid gracefully to the floor in a simultaneous dead faint.

Andrew Crawford, being a happily married man and, moreover, a man happily married to a very rich wife, had a packed lunch which some others would give their eye teeth for. The delicate egg mayonnaise sandwiches, made freshly that morning by the cook, were cut into elegant triangles, the crusts removed and the cut edges garnished with finely chopped cress, grown for the purpose on a square of flannel on the kitchen windowsill. The package was wrapped in oiled paper and tied with a narrow length of raffia. The dessert was a slice of pie, filled to the brim with peaches grown last summer on the south-facing wall of his parents-in-laws' country home in Kent and bottled lovingly for Miss Angela's husband by her nanny, kept on long after she was needed simply because no one knew how to ask her to leave. A small glass jar accompanied it, filled with brandied cream. Crawford rarely ate in the office – he loved his job but needed the smell of the river, the bustle of the Embankment, at least once a day, to remind him why he still worked when he could be a gentleman of leisure. If any of his colleagues ever found out how much money his wife had, his life as he knew it would be over.

So he left the Yard going at a fair old lick on that lovely spring day. Almost unbelievably, there was a hint of the smell of blossom in the air, the plane trees were giving off their little puffs of golden dust which reduced so many to puffy-eyed automata but made not one jot of difference to Andrew Crawford's sense of bonhomie. He dropped the pack of sandwiches into the hand of a beggar on one corner, the pie was laid at the feet of another. Andrew Crawford and his packed snap was legend among the shiftless and homeless who hunkered down under Westminster Bridge, and he tried to spread his largesse evenly among them. The jar of cream he kept; cook would have his hide if he didn't return her cream jar.

Soon, he was in the damp fug of the coffee shop on the corner, crushed shoulder to enormous shoulder with Constable Freeman, of Vine Street Police Station down the road.

Freeman was a storyteller par excellence. His friends often told him he should write a book and he would duck his head, blushing. The truth was, he had tried, but always came to a dead stop after 'It was a dark and stormy night . . .' But today, he held his audience rapt as always, with the tale of Mrs Whitehouse and the constable, entwined on the mortuary floor, to all intents and purposes dead to the world.

'So, old Joe, the mortuary chap, he don't know quite what to do, see. Because Constable Bentinck, the daft young fool, he's fallen across Mrs Whitehouse's legs, y'see, and so he can't lift her up first, like he should, being a real gent and as nice a chap as breathed. But he don't want to move Bentinck, because it would mean, well, he'd have to touch the woman's legs and he didn't want her to wake up and find him with his hand on her fol-de-rols, as you might say.'

Crawford, his mouth full of bacon sandwich, the grease running down his chin, just nodded in agreement.

The girl behind the counter was agog. She didn't know the mortuary attendant, but the big lad with the greasy chin could put his hand on her fol-de-rols whenever he liked. She wiped the same patch of zinc over and over again with a none-too-clean cloth. 'What happened next?' she breathed.

'Well,' Freeman said, wiping round his plate with a hunk of bread and popping it into his mouth, 'luckily for all concerned, Bentinck woke up first and was up and trying to look as if nothing had happened as quick as winking. Poor Mrs Whitehouse wasn't far behind him, but she wasn't too chipper. We had to take her into the inspector's office for a lie-down. It was the feather what finished her off, I reckon.'

'Feather?' Crawford asked. 'I don't think you mentioned the feather.'

'Oh, yes,' Freeman said. 'A feather, a blackbird's wing feather old Cartwright on the desk reckons, him being a bit of a bird-watcher in his spare time. It was in her mouth. Fell out with the shaking.'

'A fevver?' The girl-behind-the-counter's level of agogness rose exponentially. 'What did she have a fevver in her mouth for?'

'Blessed if I know,' Freeman said, draining his tea. 'She died when she was eating her bit of supper, and there wasn't no poultry. Just soup and some bread.'

Crawford couldn't help it, he always needed to get to the bottom of any story. 'But . . . even if there *had* been poultry,' he said, 'surely, a feather wouldn't go into her mouth like that, not whole?'

'It's a bit of a mystery,' Freeman conceded.

'What does your inspector think?' Crawford asked.

Freeman shrugged and reached behind him for his coat. It was time he was back in the station. 'I dunno,' he said. 'The inquest's tomorrow. I think it's accidental death, from what I remember.'

'Accidental death?' Crawford was staggered. 'A woman of not too advanced years, found dead at the table, no marks of violence, no illnesses we know of, and it's accidental death?'

'Well,' Freeman said, on his way to the door, 'these sensitives, they take a risk, don't they? Meddling with the Other Side and everything. Must take a toll.' And with that, he was gone.

'Take a toll?' Crawford looked at the girl, still cleaning the same bit of counter. 'What does he mean?'

'Ooh, well,' the girl leaned forward, 'they speak to dead people and that, don't they? My old gran, she comes back to my auntie sometimes and auntie has to have a lie-down and some gin after.'

Crawford smothered a smile. 'So, it's hard work, is it, speaking to dead people?'

'Ooh, yes,' the girl said. 'And Madame Ankhara – that's the dead lady he was talking about, she lived down our street – Madame Ankhara, she worked all hours, helping people talk to their departed. It's a dying trade, you know.' She looked at Crawford portentously. 'A dying trade.'

'So it appears,' Crawford said, fishing some money out of his pocket and wiping his mouth with a spotless handkerchief. 'How much?'

'Five bob.'

'*How* much?' Crawford might have a rich wife, but he wasn't stupid.

The girl looked at the door, significantly. 'That includes Constable Freeman's.'

Crawford sighed and pushed three florins across the zinc. Why, along with Madame Ankhara, had he not seen that one coming?

'Keep the change,' he said.

Edmund Reid was a busy man. Not as busy as he had been back at the Yard, of course, but he kept himself occupied. It had not taken long in a town the size of Hampton-on-Sea, for news to

get around that he was a conjuror of some skill, and he had as
many children's parties and Ladies' Groups to attend as he could
wish for – the fact that he took no fee was not the only reason
he was so popular, but it certainly had a bearing. But this lovely
May day, he was at a loose end. No toddler needed to be entertained as it turned three. Ladies' Groups were taken up with
flower arranging again now that spring had definitely sprung. His
housekeeper was turning all the mattresses and airing the rugs
out in the garden, savagely beating them with a yard broom.
Wherever he went, there seemed to be clouds of dust or billows
of feather beds. He found his mind wandering to 'Sensitive Found
Dead. Police Baffled'.

He was in two minds about mediums. That they were fraudulent, he was in no doubt. But they brought comfort to many, in
exchange for hard cash though that may be. When his wife had
died, his friends had encouraged him to visit various women they
knew, who would put him in touch with the 'dear departed'. He
didn't need women in seedy back rooms to put him in touch
with his wife. She was in every breath he took, every step he
made on the path he was now treading alone. If her face was
now less clear in his mind's eye, that was not a sadness to him.
He knew he had aged, as she would not, so he just let her image
fade, in lieu of wrinkles.

But – Sensitive Found Dead? Was it just a bored journalist
who chose that headline or was the fact of her mediumship that
had caused her death? Edmund Reid sat behind his desk, looking
out over the sea and tapped his teeth with a pencil, a habit which
had driven colleagues in J Division to the brink of murder over
the years.

It was no good sitting here, mulling. Edmund Reid jumped
up and went out into the lobby to get his coat. He would do what
he always did when he had a conundrum wearing grooves in his
brain. He would go and see Margaret Murray.

Margaret Murray sat by the fire in the nursery at Angela and
Andrew Crawford's house in Bloomsbury. Their eldest child,
little Esme, sat curled in her lap, playing with the beads that
were looped carelessly around her neck. The child didn't know
that they were from Egypt's Middle Kingdom and should have

been in a museum – she just loved the feel of them, smooth and cool in her fingers. Her mother, sitting opposite, smiled indulgently.

'Should you really be wearing those, Margaret?' she asked, knowing the answer.

Her guest looked down and smiled back. 'If I wasn't wearing them,' she said, 'they would be in a packing case somewhere in the basement of the museum,' she said, 'waiting to be catalogued. And they have been restrung, it's not as though they will break and go rolling everywhere.' She bent and kissed the little girl's glossy head. 'Esme can feel the antiquity, look at her. An archaeologist already.' She gave her a squeeze and the child looked up with a smile.

'Nurse tells me that she wants to be a gingerbread man when she grows up,' Angela told her.

'A worthy ambition,' Margaret said, nodding. 'Perhaps we can leave it to Francis to be an academic.' She looked fondly to the cot in the corner, where Esme's brother slept soundly.

'Or Esme could be the first gingerbread man to graduate from university,' Angela said. 'If women can do it, then I don't see how biscuits can be far behind.'

'Speaking of which,' Margaret said, looking at her friend sitting across the hearth, her face glowing with the joy of motherhood, 'when will we be seeing you back at your desk? Surely, you haven't left us forever, have you?'

Angela Crawford dipped her head. 'Not forever, no. It's simply that . . .'

Margaret Murray cocked her head and waited for the excuse. She had never been one to let students down lightly, even students like Angela who had taken another path.

'The children, you know. They keep me busy . . .'

'With two nannies?' Margaret was unconvinced.

'I like to spend time with them. I *like* them. And Andrew . . . well, he wasn't brought up like I was. For him, parents look after their children.'

'Hmm, yes, Andrew. Why isn't he back at his studies too? You've been married, what is it? Four years, now?'

'Four years and two months.'

'How very precise.' Margaret's twinkle took the edge off the words. 'And how many children is it?' She knew the answer, but liked to keep up to date.

'Only two!' Angela laughed. Then she looked askance at her erstwhile mentor. 'All right, Margaret, since it's you, two and a third. But how on earth . . .?'

'Mrs Plinlimmon told me,' Margaret said, then added, 'actually, it was you. The way you stand, the way you sit. The glow. When are we to be blessed with another Crawford?'

'Well . . .'

Esme struggled off Margaret Murray's lap and ran to the door at the sound of boots on the stairs.

'Any moment now,' Angela said, as her husband burst through the door, bringing the fresh air of the spring day with him. 'Darling, you're early. Look, here's Margaret come to tea!'

Detective Sergeant Crawford swept up his daughter and leaned over to kiss his wife and his mentor in a smooth movement. Pausing briefly to check on his sleeping son, he subsided on the hearthrug, tucking Esme into his crossed legs, where she sat, playing with his watch chain. 'This child is going to be a pick-pocket, I am sure of it,' he said. 'How are you, Margaret? It seems ages since we saw you last.'

'At Francis's christening, I think,' Margaret Murray said. 'And now, it seems, I must start saving for another new hat.'

Crawford blushed and grinned. 'You spotted that. I thought you might. You don't miss much and actually . . . for that reason, it's good to see you today. Not that it isn't always good . . .' His blush deepened. 'Is it me, or is it hot in here?'

Angela nudged him with her toe. 'Stop, dearest, before you dig yourself too deep to climb out. Tell us what's bothering you.'

Crawford put Esme gently off his lap. 'Can we call nanny and decamp downstairs?' He turned to Margaret. 'We try not to talk . . . shop . . . in front of the children.'

'Very wise,' the archaeologist said. 'Although I assume you mean police business specifically, it isn't really very appropriate to talk archaeology either, when you consider some of the practices of the ancient Egyptians . . .'

Angela got to her feet and led the way downstairs, calling to the nanny as they went. A starched woman with a bust like a rolltop desk took their place in the nursery; there would be no racy chat on her watch, that was clear.

The drawing room had no fire on this warm afternoon, and a bunch of immortelles in a cloisonné vase filled the fireplace. Crawford rang for tea as to the manner born and Margaret suppressed a smile. He and Angela were from different ends of the spectrum, socially, but they had met seamlessly in the middle and she had seldom known such a happy home. She had no regrets, but spared a moment while they waited for tea to arrive for all the Crawfords she had let slip through her fingers.

'So,' Dr Murray said, balancing a plate on her knee, 'what did you want to ask me about?'

'It's awkward,' Crawford said, wolfing two egg sandwiches in one go.

'Dearest!' Angela put out a restraining hand. 'Not so much egg! You had them for lunch as well; you'll get bound up and you know what that means.'

Crawford was caught between a rock and a hard-boiled egg. He couldn't tell his wife what had become of his sandwiches, and yet . . . feigning constipation couldn't be that difficult, surely? 'Sorry,' he said. 'I forgot. And they are delicious.' He took two pieces of anchovy toast and put them carefully on his plate.

Margaret Murray smiled encouragingly. Domestic bliss was all very well, but she was sure that there was more interesting conversation to be had.

Crawford took a sip of tea. Egg sandwiches were so cloying. He cleared his throat and told her all about the feather in the dead medium's throat, how it had come to light and how the powers that be were putting the death down as accidental.

Margaret Murray had not got where she was by being slow on the uptake. 'Accidental sounds like another way of saying they can't be bothered to look into it,' she said. 'Surely, the feather alone . . .'

'You would certainly think so,' Crawford said. 'Sometimes I am ashamed of my colleagues. But the feather . . . it reminded me of something . . .'

Angela put down her teacup. 'It reminds you of death, dearest,' she said. 'Black birds presage death in many cultures, as you know.'

Margaret Murray smiled at her indulgently. So her brain had not quite atrophied, after all.

'Mostly they are ravens,' Angela went on, 'especially in European folklore. And we mustn't forget Poe, either. He gave it a bit of a boost.'

'Nevermore,' Crawford intoned, right on cue.

'Norse mythology has the two ravens of Thor . . . but this wasn't a raven's feather, was it?' Margaret just wanted the facts.

'Blackbird, or so some birdwatcher at the station reckoned. I don't think they even kept it. Poor Madame Ankhara, she's just one more of the legions of the dead, whichever mythology we follow.' Crawford pushed his plate away. Even he could be full up sometimes, and something about the way the conversation had gone had quelled his appetite.

'Ankhara?' Margaret Murray sat up and looked brightly at the policeman. 'As in "ankh"?'

Crawford thought a moment. 'I suppose so. I haven't seen it written down. It's what she went by, when she was mediuming. Her name was actually Muriel Fazakerley.'

Margaret Murray smiled, the smile that all her students, present and past, recognized. It was the smile that said she would not be letting this one rest. But she turned to Crawford and said, as if they had not been discussing dead women bringing forth feathers of birds of ill omen, 'So, Andrew, the Stratton brothers. You must all be so proud.'

'I have to admit,' he said, 'there are some trassenos – er, felons – we almost feel sorry for. The Strattons are not among them.'

'Burglary gone wrong, wasn't it,' Angela asked, 'the Mask Murders?'

'It's not often a burglary goes right,' Crawford said. 'And it certainly won't from now on, thanks to fingerprinting. Yes, the Strattons forced a strongbox at premises in Deptford High Street. They left their dabs all over it and the owners dead – Ann and Thomas Farrow, nice old couple by all accounts who wouldn't say boo to a goose. Sorry to sound harsh, ladies, but come the reckoning day, I'll be holding Mr Billington's coat.'

'I wonder,' Margaret said, 'if it's possible to take fingerprints of the dead, as well as the living. Who's in charge of all this at the Yard, Andrew?'

'Well, it's the assistant commissioner's baby, of course. Edward Henry insisted on it being implemented before he took up the post, apparently. The actual department is run by Stockley Collins, part of the Anthropomorphic Office.'

'Right,' Margaret beamed. 'Tell Mr Collins I may have a lot of extra work for him.'

TWO

Margaret Murray had two inner sanctums. The Classical Scholar in her knew that that should be sanctu, but she didn't like to boast, nor did she stand on ceremony. Her little eyrie above the boiler rooms at University College had a window that looked out over Gower Street and contained the stuff of most people's nightmares.

In particular, the head of a high-born Egyptian of the New Kingdom looked back at her now, through the one eye that remained open. The skin was the colour of Nile mud, the long strands of hair dull and copper-coloured. The teeth, though few, were surprisingly good for a man who had died nearly three thousand years ago. The archaeologist measured the space between the eye sockets, the occipital length and the drop of the lower mandible. She noted it all down and started to draw it. Photography had been available all Margaret Murray's life, but the camera would never replace the pencil when it came to accurate detail. And accurate detail was what archaeology was all about.

There was a knock at the door.

'Come in,' she called.

A burly man stood there, in passé Ulster and bowler hat.

'Mr Reid!' She crossed the room and shook his hand. 'What brings you to Bloomsbury?'

'I happened to be passing,' he said, sweeping off his hat.

'Liar,' she scolded him. 'Ex-doyens of Scotland Yard never happen to pass anything. Try again.'

'Hello,' he caught sight of the head on the archaeologist's desk. 'Anybody we know?'

'Ah, I wish I could tell you. He's from the Valley of the Kings, certainly, but not, I think, a pharaoh. Probably a high priest or a royal official of some kind. Unfortunately, by the time we got him, he'd long ago become separated from the trappings that might have given us a clue as to his name.'

'And from his body, presumably,' Reid nodded. He looked closer at the shrivelled face. 'I think we've got his twin brother at the Police Museum,' he said. 'Wedged between Charlie Peace's false arm and William Corder's left ear.'

Margaret Murray raised an eyebrow.

'Oh, on the skin cover of a Book of Common Prayer, of course.'

'Of course,' she smiled. 'Tea, Mr Reid?'

'Thank you, Dr Murray. It's been a while since we've seen each other, but I was sure we were on first-name terms by now.'

The little Egyptologist looked up at the big Kentishman. 'Very well,' she said, adopting the primmest pose she used on a student she believed was above himself. 'I shall call you Edmund if you tell me why you're here.'

'Madame Ankhara.' Reid accepted her gestured offer of a chair.

'Ah, Muriel Fazakerley.' She clattered her crockery.

Reid laughed. 'As always, Margaret, you don't miss a trick.'

'Did you know the lady?' she asked.

'Not personally,' he admitted. 'She was just the small print in the paper. I find myself drawn to that sort of thing these days. You?'

'No,' she lit the gas. 'She came up in conversation with the Crawfords yesterday at tea.'

'Ah. Andrew. How is he?'

'Detective sergeant nowadays, of course. Doing well at the Yard, I believe.'

'Hmm,' Reid nodded. 'Under John Kane. Good man, Kane – I'd have liked to have worked with him. Two kids now – Crawford, I mean.'

'Two and a third,' Margaret corrected him. 'But you didn't hear that from me.'

'Quite. Quite.'

'So.' She placed the Unknown Egyptian to one side, 'the late Madame Ankhara . . .'

'I popped into Vine Street on my way here,' Reid said. 'Old Joe Davenant, the mortuary attendant there, owes me a few. He mentioned the black feather.'

'Yes,' she said, nodding. 'Intriguing.'

'Even more intriguing is the mulligatawny.'

'Mulligatawny?'

'The woman was found, effectively drowned in the stuff, on her fortune-telling table at her home.'

'Good Lord. Where was this?'

'Bermondsey.'

'I've always been rather fond of mulligatawny,' she told him. 'Conjures up my Indian childhood.'

'Disguises a multitude of things, too.'

'Such as?'

Reid shrugged. 'Any poison that doesn't lead to convulsions. I chatted to Constable Bentinck, a wet-behind-the-ears kid who attended the crime scene. No signs of a struggle, apparently. Nothing upset or overturned.'

'Quick-acting poison, then?' Margaret queried.

'I'd say so,' he said, 'but it's all about the feather. That's the clincher.'

'Where was it found, exactly?'

'In her mouth . . . well, it fell out of her mouth.'

'You mean, she swallowed it?'

'No. Apparently, it was completely intact and undamaged, just damp.'

'So . . .' the professor's forensic brain was whirling, 'it must have been placed in her mouth post-mortem – or ante-mortem into the soup – by person or persons unknown.'

'That would be my reading of it,' Reid said.

The kettle whistled loudly and Margaret did the honours.

'Which brings me to the point of my visit. In your line of business, does a black feather have any significance?'

'A certain kind of woman gives a *white* feather to any man she considered a coward. We had a few of those during the war, didn't we?'

'We did,' Reid nodded. 'Two lumps, please, Margaret.'

'Black birds of all breeds are associated with death, of course. And with battle. In Gaelic tradition, the rooks pecking at battlefield corpses were believed to be Annis stealing their souls. In the Norse, the Valkyrie often ride horses with black wings. And we all know what will happen to the Tower if the ravens ever leave, don't we?'

She passed Reid his tea.

'I'm not sure you're taking this very seriously,' he chuckled.

'No, I'm sorry, Edmund,' she said, solemnly. 'I don't mean to be flippant. What's the official take on this? Andrew said something about accident?'

'Natural causes, the coroner's going for, apparently, in the absence of anything more definite. Even he baulked at accidental drowning in soup.'

'They're ignoring the feather?'

'They are,' he said. 'Of course, it's A Division's baby. They *might* call in the Yard, in which case it'll find its way to John Kane's desk. But with the inquest calling it natural . . . well, it's likely to be case closed.'

'But if it *isn't*,' she said, sipping her tea, 'the whole thing might have to be left to an ex-detective of police and an interfering amateur busybody.'

Reid leaned forward and carefully put down his cup. 'You may well be busy,' he said, nodding at the silent Egyptian, 'trying to identify ancient victims and all. You have certainly been known to interfere. But amateur, Margaret? Never.' He sat back, arms folded. 'Nobody could call you that.'

Flinders Petrie's left eye loomed large behind his Ross and Cavanagh magnifying glass. All his working life, whether in the swirling sandstorms along the Nile or here in damper London, he had been screwing up his face and straining his eyes to decipher the little squiggles that men long dead had etched in stone, or bone, or marble, or clay. Every quirk of the stylus, every tap of the chisel, he knew, would throw new light on the ancient world he loved. He had been wrestling with this particular scarab now for weeks, and the little black and gold insect was threatening to get away from him.

He didn't notice the knock on the door.

'William,' his visitor tutted, 'you never call. You never write . . .'

He looked up, irritated. 'Oh, Margaret, I know I promised to get back to you . . . It's this wretched inscription!'

She looked at him; he was crimson with frustration above his starched wing collar, his wild white hair less obedient than usual. 'Tea,' she said. 'That's the answer.' And she busied herself with the makings.

Flinders Petrie's rooms were as arcane as hers, except that he had no Mrs Plinlimmon watching his every move. 'I heard from Goubran the other day,' he called through to the woman clattering in his little kitchen, 'in the Valley of the Kings.'

'Oh, how are things?'

'Murderous,' he told her. 'Same as usual. There was some trouble with the fellaheen, but he shot a couple and all is well.'

'Shot a couple?' Margaret bustled through with a cake stand brimming with French fancies courtesy of both archaeologists' favourite pâtissier, Thomas, of the Jeremy Bentham tea rooms across the road. 'Not literally?'

'You know Goubran,' Flinders Petrie shrugged. 'Never met a hyperbole he didn't like. Probably involved a little mild thrashing on his part. The French are trying to muscle in on the digs again.'

'Par for the course,' she said.

'And Arthur Weigall's up to his old tricks.'

'Dear Arthur,' she smiled.

'Yes.' His mouth was a twisted line of annoyance. 'Isn't he, though?'

She patted his shoulder. 'You mustn't let it all get you down, William,' she said. 'Egypt has been there for the best part of five thousand years, give or take a dynasty or two. It'll outlive both of us.'

'Yes,' he sighed. 'I suppose you're right. Sorry, Margaret. What did you want my views on?'

She looked around the chaos that was Flinders Petrie's study. 'There,' she said, her eyes alighting on a package of papers. 'Mr Merrington's artwork.'

'Ah, for your book, yes. I thought Quaritch was supportive.'

'He was at first.' Margaret poured the tea. 'But as soon as I began to raise complaints, his support fell away, so to speak.'

'Bound to defend his own, I suppose.' Flinders Petrie took his cup. 'Thank you.'

'But he's not "his own", is he? As I understand it, Kirk Merrington is a freelance artist. He's not in-house as such.'

'And what's the problem, exactly?'

Margaret rolled her eyes, just a little. She and the Great Man went back to who knew when. He had been her mentor, her guide, occasionally more than that, but always her friend. What he was *not* was organized. She pointed to the first of the foolscap sheets. 'See this? Hieroglyph Four?'

Flinders Petrie adjusted his pince-nez. 'Is . . . is Nefertiti winking?' he asked.

'She is,' Margaret confirmed. 'But that's as nothing to Hieroglyph Nine.' She sorted the pages accordingly.

Flinders Petrie peered again, frowning. Then he reached for his Ross and Cavanagh. 'Good Lord!' he said.

'I personally had no idea that Rameses I was hung like a mule,' she observed.

'No more had I,' he said, 'especially considering all the incest. Is this man having a joke at our expense?'

'At the expense of scholarship, that's what concerns me.'

'I'll get right on to Quaritch. This isn't good enough.' He clicked his fingers. 'Pen. Pen.' Then he looked about him. 'I've got a secretary somewhere . . . haven't I?'

Margaret laughed. Surely not even William Flinders Petrie expected to find a living woman under a pile of papyrus in the corner. 'You have indeed, William,' she said. 'But it's her day off today. No, leave it to me, at least in the first instance. I need to beard Mr Merrington in his lair, ask him face to face what his game is.'

Flinders Petrie smiled. At five foot nothing, Margaret Murray was easily a match for any scribbling artist. He almost wished he could be there. 'Very well,' he said. 'But you'll let me know if and when I can be of further assistance?'

'Of course,' she smiled. She picked up the scarab and looked at it, the shaft of sunlight streaming through the window, translating as she read. 'Twenty barges,' she said, 'shall take the pharaoh to the hereafter. Back . . .' she peered closer, 'jackals?' She nodded. 'Yes, jackals. Back, jackals, for the pharaoh is mine.'

There was a stunned silence. 'Jackals?' Flinders Petrie thundered, after it was over. 'Barges?'

Margaret shrugged and held up the pot. 'More tea, Professor?'

*   *   *

It didn't take long for Margaret Murray to get the information from the girl on the desk at Bernard Quaritch, Publishers. No, she didn't know Mr Merrington personally, but she felt sure that he would welcome working with an author whose book he was currently illustrating, and she handed over the man's address.

'I'm Courtney,' the girl said on the elegant studio threshold at that very address.

What an odd name for a girl, Margaret thought. And how broad and tall she was for a receptionist. However, the archaeologist in Margaret Murray had been exposed to Egyptian courtship rites for some time now; she didn't judge.

'Mr Merrington will see you now,' and Margaret followed her through an arched passageway hung with questionable lithographs of the Aesthetic school, heavily embellished with lilies and phallic symbols. The stairs, which split in two halfway up, were thick with purple carpeting and the wallpaper burned a dull gold. Margaret was shown into a large drawing room, the windows of which gave a charming view of the British Museum and her own dear domain of University College.

Lolling on a chaise longue at the far end was the artist-in-residence, who got up at her arrival.

'Dr Murray, what an honour.' He bowed and kissed her hand extravagantly. 'Will you take tea?'

'Thank you, no,' she said. 'I'm afraid my visit may not, in the end, turn out to be a social call.'

'Oh dear,' Merrington said. 'That would be most unfortunate. Courtney, be a dear and bugger off, would you? I sense that Dr Murray is a little miffed.'

He patted the chaise longue and she rather reluctantly sat down beside him. Kirk Merrington was the wrong side of forty, like Margaret herself. His hair was black and glossy, combed forward *à la* Nero, and his grey eyes sharp and watchful. Margaret expected him to be at least a *little* daubed with paint, but he – and the whole house that she had seen – was spotless.

'It's the drawings, isn't it?' He looked concerned.

'It is, Mr Merrington,' she nodded and hauled the portfolio up on to the nearest table. 'For instance, this.' She pointed to Hieroglyph Four. 'As an historian and archaeologist, I am prepared to accept that the ancient Egyptians had many habits similar to our own. Nefertiti may have winked, just as I am sure that Rameses the Great probably broke wind. The point at issue is that, in what I hope is a scholarly work, we cannot have frivolities such as this. And as for Hieroglyph Nine,' she pointed to the pharaoh's private parts, 'this is simply obscene and Mr Quaritch could never publish it in a family book.'

Merrington had the decency to look shame-faced. 'Let me show you something,' he said and led her across the room. He slid aside a screen and pressed a button on the wall. Panels slid sideways with a gentle scrape and thud and a range of canvases hung there, like ballgowns in a lady's toilette. He flicked the first one round. 'What do you notice?' he asked.

Margaret blinked. 'It's the Mona Lisa,' she said. 'With a moustache.'

Merrington slid the canvas aside and produced a second. 'And this?'

'Leda and the swan,' she said. 'Except . . . oh.'

'Not a swan, but a cormorant. Or, as the more casual ornithologists call it, a shag. And then, there's this.'

He hauled a third canvas to the front. 'Lady with an ermine,' Margaret said, 'but the ermine is now a toad.'

'I could go on,' he said.

'I'd rather you didn't,' she said and whirled away, back towards the door.

'Let me explain,' he said. 'But first, tell me honestly, apart from the moustache, the cormorant and the toad, would you say the painting is good?'

'It's remarkable, Mr Merrington,' she said. 'I am not an artist myself, except in the strictly archaeological sense, but I know what I like. You have enormous talent.'

'Dear lady,' he gushed, 'you are *too* kind.' He ushered her back to the chaise longue, 'but I also have an extremely low boredom threshold. Oh, I can copy till the cows come home, create fresh canvases of my own, even illustrate archaeological tracts. But I quickly tire. My imagination takes over and I begin to doodle. God forbid that Frederic Leighton or Lawrence Alma-Tadema should find out, but I have lampooned them both outrageously. Are you familiar with Millais' *Princes in the Tower*?

Margaret was; two terrified little boys, awaiting murder below a dark and spiralling stair.

'Mine, I am ashamed to admit, has the lads playing diabolo. Holman Hunt's *Light of the World*?'

Margaret nodded.

'My version has the lantern with the flame just gone out with a gust of wind. It's completely black.'

For once in her life, Margaret didn't know what to say.

'I call it the Flippant School,' Merrington told her. 'And I can only apologize again. Please, Dr Murray, give me a second chance. Let me redraft the drawings – and supply the rest – and I promise you, there will be no more jokes.'

She looked at him, the earnest grey eyes, the worried countenance. 'Oh, very well,' she said, 'but I must see them all first.'

'Absolutely.' He took her hand and patted it.

She stood up, collecting her papers. 'Shall I leave these with you?'

'No, no,' he said. 'I shall be starting afresh.'

She took her leave and paused at the door. 'Oh, by the way,' she said. 'The Flippant School. Do what you like with anything by J.M.W. Turner. You could hardly make it worse, could you?'

'So, ladies and gentlemen, I remain convinced that there were a number of sun temples to the great god Ra. It's just that we haven't found them yet.'

Margaret Murray closed her notebook, her face lit from below by the flicker of the magic lantern. 'And perhaps one of you will find them in the not-too-distant future.'

There were hoots of approval, whistles and cheers. The throng of students in the auditorium were on their feet, crowding around their little lecturer, wanting to know more, as always, about her excavations along the most mysterious river in the world. She held her hands up. 'Please,' she said, 'Dr Tingle will be along shortly and you must be in your places. I believe his theme today is Medieval post-holes and their role in pan-Hellenic society – you won't want to miss that.'

Actually, most of them did and they shuffled out accordingly, leaving the tiny scattering who had mistakenly signed up with Tingle at the start of the university term sitting with a resolved look of boredom on their faces. One man, however, had not moved.

'Andrew!' Margaret's face lit up. 'I didn't see you there. Don't tell me you've come to rejoin my classes?'

'Ah, Dr Murray,' he smiled, keeping it formal. 'Would that I could. But you know how it is. In a busy world, a policeman's lot and other overworked phrases.'

'Precisely.' She understood. Then, a thought occurred. 'There's nothing wrong, is there? Angela? The baby? The babies?'

'No, nothing like that. I was just wondering – is there somewhere we can talk?'

Margaret fished her fob watch from under her mantle and looked at it, nodding. 'The Jeremy Bentham,' she said. 'You can buy me a Chelsea bun.'

A Chelsea bun it was, complete with tea and a cream horn for the detective sergeant. Margaret had her favourite table in the tea rooms across the road from the monolith that was University College, and woe betide anyone else who sat there. An accommodating Thomas, the proprietor, always placed a reserved sign on the table to deter interlopers.

'Sergeant Crawford,' the man gushed. 'Always a pleasure to entertain our brave upholders of law and order.'

'Always a pleasure to be entertained by one who has seen the folly of his former ways.' Crawford had seen Thomas's record. Were he of the blackmailing persuasion, he could make himself, as several of his colleagues did, a nice little bit on the side.

'My salad days,' the surprisingly erudite Thomas said, 'when I was green in judgement. Talking of which, if you are intending to extend your palates to lunch, we do have an exciting salmagundi on offer. Or there's the Waldorf . . .'

'Always,' Margaret smiled. 'We'll stick with the cakes for now, Thomas, thank you.'

When he had gone, into that mysterious darkness from which magical delicacies emerged, Crawford became serious. 'The Madame Ankhara case,' he said, dropping his voice to a mutter.

'So it *is* a case now?' She raised a quizzical eyebrow.

'No,' he scowled. 'And thereby hangs a tale.'

'Say on.'

'John Kane doesn't think foul play is involved at all. He's going with the coroner's verdict of "cause of death unknown"; something internal, something that now she's no longer with us to tell us her symptoms, the doctors can't quite put their fingers on.'

'But surely,' Margaret said, with a ghost of a wink, 'she *can* tell us her symptoms. Don't we just have to . . .' she spread her fingers on the table and rolled her eyes, '. . . ask?'

'Very amusing,' Crawford said, trying to work out the least messy way to eat a cream horn. 'She never said anything to her sister about feeling seedy and I just can't accept that verdict. The inspector and I have spent the last two days interviewing various people and I just can't shake the impression that something isn't right. But I think I have come to the end of Inspector Kane's tether.'

'Who have you interviewed? Friends of the deceased?'

'You might say that,' he nodded. 'They're all members of the Bermondsey Spiritualist Circle. Ankhara was a founder member, quite a few years ago now, when table-tilting was all the rage. Have you ever dabbled?'

'Séances?' Margaret smiled reminiscently. 'Oh, yes.'

'What's your view?'

'Séances are party games,' she said. 'Like hunt the thimble or pin the tail on the donkey. I understand the Germans have patented a Ouija board, to make spiritual sessions easier. Rather than endlessly scribbling letters on bits of paper, this gadget has a printed board with the alphabet, *ja* and *nein* and a needle that moves. Great fun, kept in its place.'

'So, it's all a con?' Crawford was poking a toe into the waters, testing the archaeologist's reaction.

'I didn't say that,' she said. 'You don't stand in a three-thousand-year-old pyramid and fail to feel it. The dead stay with us, Andrew, I am sure of that.'

'So, you believe?' He was probing further.

'I believe . . . I believe . . . I believe that you have a blob of cream on your nose. I believe what I can see and what I feel, when I see and feel it. Everything else, my mind is open.'

Crawford wiped the cream off with his handkerchief and presented his nose for inspection, just as his son would. Margaret nodded her approval and looked at him over her teacup.

'Andrew, where is all this going?'

Crawford sighed as if he had been holding his breath for the last half an hour. 'Kane and I have talked to every member of the Circle we could find. On the surface, they were all saddened and shocked by Ankhara's death. They all subscribed to the view that she wasn't dead at all, of course, just in a different plane, if you get my drift.'

'I do,' she said. 'There!' She pointed to a napkin that had just fallen from a nearby table. 'To you and me, that's an act of gravity, a whim of physics. To members of the Bermondsey Circle, it's Madame Ankhara trying to tell them something.' She looked up at the lights. 'If one of those breaks, of course,' she said, 'it'll be William the Conqueror trying to get in touch. Those who died long ago are on higher planes than the recently departed.'

Crawford leaned back in his chair. 'So, you're a sceptic,' he said.

'Always,' she told him. 'It goes with the job.'

'Well,' he finished his tea. 'That's exactly what I need – someone who is rational but involved, dedicated and open-minded.'

She laughed. 'And what is this mythical person required to do?' she asked. 'Although I'm not sure that I measure up.'

'Do?' he repeated. 'Oh, nothing much. Just join the Bermondsey Spiritualist Circle, that's all.'

'Is there anybody there?' The voice behind the door was old and querulous, asking a question it must have asked countless times before.

'Hello?' Margaret called back. Perhaps her knock had not been firm enough.

'Who are you?'

'Henrietta Plinlimmon,' Margaret lied. 'Did you get my letter?'

The door opened an inch or two after what seemed endless rattling of locks and bolts and a watery eye peered through the small gap.

'You *are* the Bermondsey Spiritualist Circle, are you?' Margaret thought she had better make certain.

'I am part of it, certainly,' the voice said, 'although I cannot claim to make up the entire circumference. Who did you say you were?'

'Henrietta Plinlimmon,' Margaret repeated. 'I wrote to the hon. sec. of the Circle at this address. Are you she?'

'No,' the voice said. 'I am Agatha Dunwoody.' She hauled the door open. 'You'd better come in.'

Stepping into the vestibule of Thirty-One Cavendish Street was like stepping into the past. Not the ancient past that Margaret Murray knew, but one with a vague feeling of yesterday, where nothing had changed since that nice Mr Disraeli was at Number Ten and General Baden-Powell wore short trousers the first time around. There were aspidistrae in the corner that made the botanical gardens at Kew look like a wasteland, and darker corners that had never seen a feather duster.

'I'm afraid the hon. sec. isn't here,' the old lady said. She was a whisker shorter than Margaret, but considerably older, with silver hair and obsolete clothes that gave her an air of Miss Havisham.

'Will he be long?' Margaret asked.

'He has crossed Beyond The Veil,' the old girl said, 'although of course we still converse at the meetings. And he still waters the plants, every other Wednesday, just as he did all our married life.'

'Of course,' Margaret said. 'So, you are . . .?'

'Out of mourning now, since week Thursday,' the woman told her.

'Er . . .'

'Perhaps I should explain.'

'If you would,' Margaret said, wondering anew whether she'd knocked on the door of the asylum by mistake.

'The hon. sec. of our Society was Alexander Dunwoody, of Dunwoody, Dunwoody, Pettigrew and Dunwoody, solicitors of this parish. He left this vale of tears over a year ago and I have assumed the mantle of hon. sec. Well, we had a lot of headed notepaper and it seemed profligate to waste it. I must say, I never *quite* appreciated how much paperwork was involved. My husband spent hours in his study and I always assumed . . .' she lowered her eyes modestly, '. . . well, gentlemen have needs, don't they?' She looked up again, brightly. 'But no, it turns out he really was dealing with paperwork. I am not as tidy as my husband, Mrs . . .'

'Miss.' Margaret thought that things were about to get complex enough without a phantom husband to muddy the waters.

'Miss Plinlimmon, but do come into the parlour. I have your letter here, somewhere.'

She rummaged among a mountain of correspondence and eventually found the missive in question. 'Here we are,' she said, turning round. Margaret had found a seat and was waiting expectantly.

'Oh, not there, dear!' Mrs Dunwoody said, slightly horrified. 'That was Alexander's seat.' She waved a withered hand over the oval table. 'This is our actual Circle. We all have our places, you see. Sadly, we have two empty chairs now.'

'Oh?' Margaret saw her opening. 'Another bereavement?'

'Another crossing of the bar, yes,' Mrs Dunwoody said. 'Poor Muriel was recently taken from us. Drowned in her mulligatawny.'

'Oh dear.' Now was not the time to pry – for now, Margaret tried to put mild sympathy into her voice, as anyone would hearing of the death of a stranger.

'If you wanted to, you could take her place.'

'I'd be honoured,' Margaret said.

'But first,' the old girl sat down and did her best to cross her legs, 'a few preliminaries. Forgive me, Miss Plinlimmon . . .'

'Henrietta, please.'

'Henrietta. There are so many charlatans in our world – and of course, in the world beyond. We have to be careful.'

'Indeed we do.'

'Your letter says that you have been a believer for a number of years.'

'Correct,' Margaret smiled and nodded.

'May I ask how old you are?'

'I am forty-two.'

'And what success have you had, in your contact with the Other Side?'

'Little, I'm afraid,' Margaret told her. 'Ambience is so impor-tant in these matters, don't you think? Somehow the atmosphere of previous Circles I have known has never been quite right. But *this* room,' she smiled up at the cobwebs and took in a deep, spiritual breath, 'this has such a presence.' She stifled a cough as the lungful of dust struck home.

'We think so,' Mrs Dunwoody beamed.

'I was saying to Oliver only the other day . . .'

'Cromwell?' The old girl looked excited.

'Lodge.'

'*Sir* Oliver Lodge?'

'Yes,' Margaret trilled. 'But he's such a dear. He hates to stand on ceremony.' This was not quite a lie, more an embroidery of the facts. She did indeed know that Oliver Lodge did not stand on ceremony – his brother and sister, who had wisely taken the path of historian, were often at dinners Margaret attended and could wax long and elaborately about how their brother had a fine mind, was a lovely man and excellent husband and father, did not stand on ceremony but nonetheless was as mad as a box of frogs.

The old girl's eyes were wide with admiration. 'You know one of the greatest advocates of our faith alive in the world today?'

'Why, yes,' Margaret said. 'Not to mention Arthur Conan Doyle.'

For a moment, Agatha Dunwoody sat there, mouth open. Then, with a suddenness that surprised them both, she clasped Margaret's hands with her own. 'Dearest Henrietta,' she said, 'when can you start?'

THREE

Unusually for him, Jack Brooks had his head down and was working on a particularly obtuse page of transcribed hieroglyphs when Margaret Murray came into her study with even more speed and gusto than usual.

He looked up, to see her brushing herself down with a horsehair fly whisk she kept in a vase on the mantelpiece. He let her get on with it for a moment, before he asked the obvious question. 'Can I help at all, Dr Murray?'

'Of course you can,' she snapped. 'Check me over for spiders, will you? I've been twitching like a horse in a heatwave all the way here. I just know there's one on me somewhere.'

'A horse?'

She fixed him with a baleful stare. 'Don't be flippant, Mr Brooks.' She glanced at the pile of untranslated papers at his elbow. 'There are plenty more of those where that lot came from. Now, for the love of Ra, check me over for arachnids. And don't spare your blushes – they could be anywhere.'

And so it was that William Flinders Petrie walked in some minutes later to find one of Dr Murray's graduate students beating her gently but thoroughly with a fly whisk. After a confused few moments, a flustered Brooks gathered up his papers and fled to the library. Margaret Murray put the kettle on and Flinders Petrie settled himself by the fireplace. The spring day was warm and the fire had been replaced for the duration by a silhouette of Bast – no home was complete without a cat on the hearth, according to those who should know.

'You're not afraid of spiders, though, Margaret,' Petrie said, picking over the biscuits she had put down on the low table in front of the hearth to find the garibaldi with the most squashed flies. 'You're not afraid of *anything*.'

'I know,' she said, suppressing a final shudder. 'But the whole place was full of *fresh* cobwebs. As opposed to the cobwebs of the ages, if you know what I mean. On the walk here, I could just *feel* a spider down my back. As if it were stalking me, on behalf of Alexander Dunwoody.'

'Alexander Dunwoody of Dunwoody, Dunwoody, Pettigrew and Dunwoody?' Petrie asked, biting into his biscuit. 'He's dead, you know.'

'Yes, I do know that,' Margaret said, puzzled. 'But how do you?'

'He left some bits and pieces to the museum,' Petrie said. 'Nothing much, it's not on display. A scarab, if memory serves. An ankh. Nice enough tourist pieces, I suppose.'

'Well,' Margaret put the cup down next to the biscuits and took a seat opposite the great archaeologist. 'What a small world it is, to be sure.'

'Very,' Petrie agreed. 'But with that as a given, why did you think that Alexander Dunwoody was chasing you?'

Margaret Murray looked at him, this man who had encouraged

her and so much more over the years, and opened her mouth to speak, then shut it again with a snap. 'Please don't take this the wrong way, William,' she said, 'but I'm not at liberty to say.'

He shrugged. He knew his Margaret. When she wanted to tell him, she would.

She narrowed her eyes at him. 'Aren't you going to press me? To insist I tell you?' she said.

'No,' he said, laughing. 'You'll just have to keep it to yourself, Margaret. Unless you want me to beat it out of you, something I had no idea you enjoyed.' He choked on a biscuit crumb and had to stop while he coughed.

'Don't think I'm going to so much as pat your back, William Flinders Petrie,' she said, from the back of her highest horse. 'And I'm not going to tell you, not even when it's all over and I am the heroine of the hour!'

'Margaret,' he managed to grate out, 'you're always a heroine to me.' The biscuit crumb finally dislodged itself. 'Any chance of another cup. I think I've overdunked in this one.'

Tutting, she washed out his cup and poured some more tea.

When she gave it to him, he was more serious. 'Margaret, my dear,' he said, putting his hand on hers. 'Will you promise me one thing?'

'Anything, William,' she said, smiling. He was hard to stay angry with for long.

'Before you go off chasing whatever hares you have in your sights, leave a note for me, will you? Or for Detective Sergeant Crawford. Mrs Plinlimmon. Anyone. Just don't disappear.'

She patted his hand. 'If you say so,' she said, sitting opposite him again.

'No, Margaret.' He leaned forward, his face solemn. 'Promise me you will.'

She looked deep into his eyes and felt her own fill with tears. Margaret Murray had not gone down the path of marriage and motherhood that her contemporaries had done. It wasn't in her to preside over a growing nursery while her intellect took second place, as Angela Crawford did. But she knew love when she saw it and she was looking at it now.

'I promise,' she said. 'I promise, William.'

*   *   *

The next morning, there was a note propped up on Mrs Plinlimmon's perch – the stuffed owl tolerated most things. Under the heading of 'A. Dunwoody, Hon. Sec.', it was short and to the point. 'Miss Plinlimmon,' Margaret chuckled as she realized why Brooks had propped it there, 'we have an extraordinary meeting this evening at the above address and would be delighted to see you. 8pm. Yrs AD.'

She sat down at her desk and drummed her fingers for a moment, thinking. Was this an important moment? Should she leave a message for William Flinders Petrie as she had promised to do in this very room only the day before? Surely not – an extraordinary meeting would simply mean a quick sit round the table, someone taking laborious minutes with a pen with a crossed nib and much stertorous mouth-breathing. Someone would propose her, someone else would second it and that would be that. She folded the invitation and slid it into her pocket. Time enough to report to Detective Sergeant Crawford when she had met everyone. Meanwhile, she had lectures to give, postgraduate students to encourage or hector, depending on one's point of view. A full day, just how she liked them – and the prospect of an evening of potential sleuthing. Dr Margaret Murray rubbed her hands together and prepared to meet Friday head on.

Thirty-One Cavendish Street was no less dusty and spider-haunted for the extraordinary meeting than it had been when Margaret had called there on spec the day before. She suspected that Mrs Dunwoody did have help in the house, because there was a shadowy presence in the room at the end of the long, dingy corridor that led from the front door, though in a Spiritualist's house, how could anyone be sure? In the meeting room, there was a tray with some smudged glasses and a half-empty bottle of Amontillado of the cheapest kind, already being addressed by a large woman with a commanding bust. Margaret Murray, of diminutive stature and neat figure herself, often wondered how such women managed their avoirdupois. Did it all leap out of the fetters of corsets at the end of the day, rejoicing in its freedom? Or did it sag, depressed and beaten into submission, and have to be loaded into the kinder but no less confining contours of a nightgown to await imprisonment in the morning? She had never felt close enough to a woman of larger proportions to ask and, somehow, she didn't think this person would become a friend near enough to enquire about bosom management. Creating a bright smile, she put out a friendly hand.

'Good evening,' she said, brightly. 'I am Henrietta Plinlimmon.'

The large woman looked down a substantial nose, over the crest of her bust, and took in the archaeologist with an uninterested glare. 'Are you?' she said, then cocked her head, listening. She nodded once or twice, then smiled so briefly it was like a flash of cold lightning. 'Ojigkwanong bids you welcome,' she said.

'Morning Star,' Margaret said, bowing. 'Your spirit guide, I assume?'

The woman's bust almost took on a life of its own. 'Are you trying to be *clever*, Miss Plinlimmon?' she hissed. 'Are you trying to be *sarcastic*?'

Margaret took a step backwards, to avoid the heaving whalebone and the flying Amontillado. 'Not at all,' she said, hurriedly. 'A . . . friend of mine . . . studied the Algonquin and I remember him mentioning the name once . . . umm, at dinner. Yes.' She smiled and the woman's frown became less ferocious. There was no need to tell her at this juncture that there was a small room along the corridor from hers in University College inhabited by a small, intense man whose lifelong study was how names rose above the strictures of language and could be considered universal. Nothing he had written or divulged in his rather rambling lectures proved his point but, somehow, by being cheap to employ and generous with cigars, he had managed to keep his toehold. Sitting next to him at dinner was torture, both because of the boredom and the smell of old tobacco, but one did pick up some unconsidered trifles nonetheless. She certainly wouldn't be telling this person that her pronunciation left rather a lot to be desired. Presumably, Morning Star was not picky.

The enormous woman took in a deep breath and Margaret feared she would actually levitate, presumably something relatively normal in this setting, but finally, she let her bust down and smiled again. 'Fascinating. When Ojigkwanong has more time, I am sure he would love to chat. However, for now, my name is Mrs Olivia Bentwood. Pleased to meet you.'

'Charmed, Mrs Brentwood.' Margaret Murray was not normally

hard of hearing, but there was some commotion behind her before
the door swung in and a group of three motley characters walked
in. One of them, a man in a blazer and a loud tie, clapped her
on the back and nearly sent her flying.

'Get it right, get it right,' he yelled. 'It's Bentwood, like the
chair. Ain't it, Ollie?'

Mrs Bentwood breathed in again, this time with much quivering
of the nostril. 'Indeed, Mortimer. Thank you for the correction,'
and, refilling her glass to the brim, she moved off to the far side
of the table and subsided into one of the more substantial chairs.

Margaret turned completely to face the new three people. The
man who had slapped her on the back stepped forward and thrust
out a hand, palm down, thumb out, making it almost impossible
to shake. In her life as a woman in a man's world, Margaret
Murray had not a moment's hesitation in labelling the man a
misogynist and all-round pain in the derrière. His voice, though
masked by the clearest case of mock-Cockney she had ever heard,
had nevertheless been honed on the playing fields of Eton, or
she was a Dutchman.

'Mortimer, that's me name,' he crowed. 'Ask me what me
surname is, go on. Yer know yer want to.'

'Henrietta Plinlimmon,' Margaret murmured. 'And I know who
you are, Mr Mortimer. I believe you were at Eton with my brother,
Henry Plinlimmon.'

The man's hand dropped and he peered at her closely. 'Knew
I knew yer from somewhere,' he snarled. 'Got his nose, aintchya,
poor cah.' Taking one of Mrs Dunwoody's best sherry glasses,
he gave it a quick polish on his tie and filled it from a flask he
took from an inside pocket.

Margaret took a deep, relieved breath. She hadn't lost her touch
when it came to dealing with the Mortimer Mortimers of this world,
she was pleased to see. The next person through the door was more
acceptable in any shipwreck than his ghastly predecessor. He
couldn't have been more than twenty-five, which surprised Margaret,
because she had always read that Spiritualism was a dying art, as
everyone grew older and no new blood joined. His face was that
of a Botticelli angel and his voice was low and gentle.

'Please forgive Mortimer, Miss Plinlimmon,' he said, shaking
her hand lightly before stepping back to a respectful distance.

'He means well and of course he is a very cherished member of
our group, being so adept. My word,' he turned his eyes up in
the accepted manner, 'we have had such messages from the
beyond whenever Mortimer is present. He is a *conduit*, you see,
Miss Plinlimmon, a *facilitator* for the spirits. My own dear mama
will descend through no other instrument.'

Margaret smiled encouragingly. She had thought for a moment
that she might have a kindred spirit here, but clearly not.

'I am Robert Grimes, Miss Plinlimmon. Welcome to our little
Circle.' With an almost imperceptible squeeze of her hand, he
moved off down the room and took a chair next to Olivia
Bentwood. Mortimer Mortimer, glowering balefully, sat one seat
removed from him on his left.

That left the third member of the little group and Margaret
Murray gave a gasp as she saw the woman, who could have
been her double. She was small and slight, with hair on the
very edge of being out of control of its pins. The only real
difference was that this woman was dressed at the very height
of fashion, with a short tailored jacket and a skirt just reaching
the floor, allowing the toes of some gleaming patent leather
pumps to just peep out. Margaret pulled ineffectually at the
back of her short alpaca coat, knowing it to be at least five
seasons out of date. She never bothered as a rule, but something
about this veritable fashion plate made it seem important for
the first time.

The woman stepped forward and grasped one of Margaret's
hands in both of her own. 'My goodness!' she breathed. 'We
could be twins! Did I hear your name was Plinlimmon? I'm
trying to remember if dear Papa ever mentioned the name as
being a Connection. Perhaps we could ask him tonight. He usually
comes through, though he doesn't always have a lot to say. Which
is a shame, because he just knew *so* much, dear Papa.'

Margaret had a sudden horrible, sinking feeling. If dear Papa
had been an academic, if she had ever met him, his family . . .
'Yes, that's right,' she broke in. 'Henrietta Plinlimmon. And you
are . . .?'

'Oh, goodness, so silly. I'll forget my head next.' Something
about talk of heads made the woman put a hand up to her hair
and push a recalcitrant pin into place under her small, fascinating

hat. 'Christina Plunkett. Of the Somerset Plunketts, you know. *Are* we related? It seems extraordinary if not.'

Margaret Murray took a leap of faith, her faith being in the fact that this woman was not half as bright as dear Papa. 'I believe my great-great-grandmother was a Plunkett,' she hazarded.

'Well, there now,' the woman said, smiling at Margaret Murray as if she had brought a rabbit out from a hat. 'I *knew* we had to be Connected. I will look it up in Papa's books when I get home, always assuming he can't help us tonight. What was your great-great-grandmother's other name?'

Margaret Murray thought fast, something she was very good at. She lowered her head and her voice. 'There was a Rift,' she said, darkly. She looked from left to right, suspiciously. 'I believe it involved . . . the Gardener. Or Gamekeeper, recollections vary.'

Christina Plunkett jumped as though shot. 'My poor dear,' she carolled. 'How very, very unfortunate! Perhaps we won't ask Papa. He can be very prudish, even still. With the Company he must be keeping, it must be hard to keep up Standards.'

Margaret Murray made a note to herself to try not to catch this woman's habit of speaking in Capitals. She had a strong feeling that it was not a habit that would go down well with Flinders Petrie, somehow.

She heard voices in the corridor outside again and the doorway filled with tweed. Two men stood there, dressed in one case for the grouse moor, in the other for a hard day sending miscreants to prison from the Bench. Behind them, Mrs Dunwoody was trying to make herself heard and finally she managed to muscle her way to the front and, with various twitterings, implied that everyone should sit.

Alexander Dunwoody's chair was empty at the top of the table and Margaret wondered briefly how that worked when they tried to contact the great beyond. Did the members of the Circle on either side have to stretch across, or did they make the assumption that the hon. sec.'s shade filled the gap?

In fact, it was much more prosaic. Once everyone was in place and a short silence had been held for Muriel Fazakerley, Mortimer and Grimes popped out of their seats and removed the chair back to the fireside. Then everyone shuffled round and looked expectantly at Mrs Dunwoody, who coughed deprecatingly and took a strengthening swig of Amontillado.

'Thank you all for coming at such short notice,' she said. 'Before we begin, I would like to introduce to you all Miss Henrietta Plinlimmon, who has taken the place of poor dear Muriel. I think you have all introduced yourselves except, perhaps . . .' she gestured to the grouse moor tweeds to her left, 'Colonel Carruthers.'

Margaret Murray could hardly suppress a laugh. He was so stereotypically a Colonel Carruthers, he might as well have been on stage in a West End farce. At least he wasn't wearing mess dress.

On cue, he turned a worrying shade of puce and barked. ''Tmeetchya,' which was presumably meant kindly.

'And General Boothby.'

The Bench tweeds were worn by someone a little less crippled with shyness than the grouse moor ones. Their wearer was younger and actually quite good looking, once it was possible to overlook the walrus moustache which perched incongruously below a rather well-shaped nose. The grey eyes which looked into Margaret's were frank and honest – possibly a rarer commodity than was a good idea in a magistrate's court.

'Good evening, my dear,' he said. 'Plinlimmon. That's an unusual name.'

'Yes,' Margaret said, hurriedly. She had had enough genealogy for one evening. 'Dies out with me, sadly. My brother is a monk.'

Everyone round the table looked a little disconcerted. But if nothing else, the newcomer was a little more interesting than Muriel Fazakerley and, General Boothby stroked his moustache reflectively, a damn sight easier on the eye.

'So,' Mrs Dunwoody rapped the table smartly with a small gavel, causing Margaret to have to bite the inside of her cheek to stop a laugh escaping, 'to business. Shall we go round the table?'

She looked to her left and Colonel Carruthers, if possible, became a shade deeper purple and shook his head, holding his breath from anxiety. Margaret found herself hoping he had never found himself in combat – surely, it could not have ended well for any troops under his command.

'Christina?'

'Thank you, Agatha, I don't think I have anything to bring up this evening,' the woman said in cultured tones. 'Except, of course, to express my sorrow and regret that Muriel passed to another plane so suddenly and before her time.'

'It's hardly your place to say whether it was before her time or not, is it?' Olivia Bentwood's bust glared at the woman.

'Now, now, Olivia,' twittered Mrs Dunwoody. 'You will have your turn. Remember our Circle rules.'

Margaret had spent enough hours – more than enough, some would say – in meetings, and this one was just like all the others. Points of order. Rules of engagement. Far from being a dangerous job that Andrew Crawford had given her, she feared that if she did die, it would be from excessive boredom.

Mrs Bentwood subsided, muttering, and it was Robert Grimes's turn. He looked up the table to Agatha Dunwoody and smiled his entrancing, Renaissance smile at her. 'No, Agatha,' he said. 'Nothing for me, thank you. Except to join Christina, of course.' He looked at his left-hand neighbour, willing her to cut in, but Olivia Bentwood was biding her time.

Reluctantly, and speaking as quietly as possible, the honorary hon. sec., said, 'Olivia? Anything from you?'

The woman's head came up and Margaret Murray was reminded of a trip to Madrid, when she had been persuaded to go to a bullfight. Once all the pomp and circumstance was over, when the matador, glorious in his suit of lights, had retired to await his re-entry, the bull had been revealed behind massive oaken gates. His head was down and he pawed the ground, slowly raising his massive horns and showing his red-rimmed, furious eyes to the crowd. Olivia Bentwood was that bull, to the life. Her pause was masterly in her judgement of its length. The room held its breath and Agatha Dunwoody had even opened her mouth to pass on to Mortimer Mortimer when, in a low rumble, the woman spoke.

'Yes,' she said. 'Yes, there is something from me. As you know, I was never very taken with Muriel Fazakerley. I am, I hope you all agree, not an unkind woman.'

The room was beyond silent. Margaret Murray had heard that crushing lack of sound only once before, when the tumbling blocks of a wall sectioning off a pharaoh's tomb had fallen for the first time since they were placed there millennia before stopped crumbling, and the dead spoke with silent lips.

'Muriel Fazakerley was Not Like Us.'

Mortimer Mortimer snorted.

'I don't include your faux persona in my assumptions, Mr Mortimer,' Olivia Bentwood said smoothly, 'so please, do not bother to interject. It was nothing to do with class, as it happens. It is to do with behaviour. Muriel Fazakerley, or Madame Ankhara as she liked to be known, was nothing but a fraud and a fake.' She ignored the indrawn breaths; she was getting into her stride. 'She used what tiny skill she may once have had to make money, to defraud the gullible, to demean our beliefs.'

At the top of the table, Agatha Dunwoody twittered on behalf of everyone. 'One must live, Olivia,' she said. 'Muriel had to eat, to have shelter.'

'Then she could have gone into service,' the woman snapped. 'Become a dressmaker. A milliner, even, though heaven knows she didn't have the first clue how to dress. A cook. But what she should not have become was a common fortune teller. She might just as well have been with a travelling circus.'

'That's a bit harsh.' General Boothby broke in and, this time, Agatha Dunwoody did not stop him. 'Poor old Mu did her best.'

'Poor old Mu?' Mortimer was on it like a dog with a bone. 'Poor old *Mu*? Sounds as if you were rather more than Circle members, General.'

The general puffed out his moustache and smiled. 'We did have a few . . . intimate moments, you might say,' he agreed. 'Though some time ago and . . .' he harrumphed in a way that reminded Margaret that he was indeed a military gent, 'strictly on a . . . currency footing.'

There was a sound from the direction of Colonel Carruthers that made everyone want to duck for cover. Some prehistoric memory in the hindbrain had them hardwired to recognize the sound of an erupting volcano and get out while the going was good.

Eventually, the generic noise became words. 'D'ya mean you *paid* the woman? Paid her to . . .' the old soldier was lost for words. 'Paid her to . . .'

Christina Plunkett patted his hand and tried to calm him down.

'Come now, Colonel. I'm sure the general didn't mean to cause offence. He was probably just helping her out, over a sticky patch, something like that. Eh, General?'

Boothby laughed and crinkled the edges of his eyes. Margaret Murray realized that he was not the bluff, straightforward, veering-towards-handsome soldier he at first appeared, but an out-and-out rotter, in everything for the main chance. Things were getting rather more interesting.

'Not really, Christina, but if that's what the colonel would prefer, then that is indeed it. I gave poor old Mu some money, to tide her over. And in return, she . . .'

'*General Boothby*!' Olivia Bentwood's voice made the windows rattle. 'I was *speaking*! It was still my turn. And frankly, we don't need to know the sordid details of your life outside this room. I think I speak for everyone?'

Around the table, heads nodded and the general leaned back, grinning under his moustache.

'So, to conclude,' Mrs Bentwood said, 'I think what I want to say is this. We know nothing about Miss Plinlimmon, but I want her to know that I am watching her. If there is the slightest, the smallest hint of anything untoward in her behaviour, she will be removed from this Circle. With prejudice.'

'I've often wondered what that means,' Christina Plunkett mused.

'You don't need to know,' Margaret said across the table. 'Because Mrs Bentwood will not be removing me, with or without it. Because there is nothing about me to find out. I am certainly the most boring woman in this room.' She chuckled. 'If not in the world.' She crossed her fingers in her lap as she spoke and looked up startled to find General Boothby watching her hands like a hawk. A small shiver went through her, but she smiled up at him as innocent as a newborn baby.

After that, the meeting was as boring as expected. Even Mortimer Mortimer had nothing to say and, after some biscuits as dry as the dust that lay on every level surface, the meeting broke up. Margaret scurried away and was soon ahead of the others, but even so, she listened for following feet. She made a mental note to ensure that someone met her in future. Andrew Crawford might cause talk. But Thomas, now . . . that would work.

*   *   *

The fire crackled in the grate. Everyone around the table knew that it was too late for fires, the evening too warm. But everyone knew that the spirits liked it, the spitting of the logs, the settling of the coal and, above all, the glow that filled the otherwise darkened room. The curtains were drawn and the shutters closed behind them. For minutes now, the only sound in that drawing room was the soft rise and fall of people breathing, people waiting for the moment, hoping for the impossible.

Evadne Principal knew how to control a room like this; she'd been doing it for years. As a precursor to her arrival, she had insisted on the total absence of servants. There must be no dogs; preferably, no animals at all, although she always made allowances for goldfish. After all, whatever happened in their little bowls, stayed in their little bowls. The fire was de rigueur. So was the locked door and the key was in her pocket. She wore a veil, black of course, the colour of mourning, the colour of death. She nodded to each of the Circle in turn, but she did not shake their hands. And they could not touch her before the séance began.

She sat with her back to the fire so that her face was in darkness and everyone else's was lit. When, after everyone was settled, she judged the moment to be right, she stretched out her pale hands, paler still against the black of her sleeves. Other hands reached out, male and female alternately around the table. Nine, the perfect number. Evadne looked at them all from behind her veil. And they didn't even know she was looking. How often had she seen them all before, these predictable idiots so ready to part with their money. She had not asked their names, their backgrounds – all that was the stuff of fairground tricksters. Evadne was above all that, above them all.

There sat the newly widowed, still in weeds, in shock, trying to come to terms with her loss. The newly departed may have had his hand in the till at the bank or his hand up the skirt of the downstairs maid; that made no difference to the widow, saturated in grief as she was. Nobody was more ready for a voice from beyond; nobody was more gullible. Beside her was the professional gentleman, possibly in insurance, precise, pedantic, pathetic. Evadne would have him for breakfast. Next to him the perpetual daughter, plain, buxom, the sort who had devoted her life to Mama because no man was interested in her. All her sad little life she had been at some ghastly harridan's beck and call; and now she was still waiting for her in the Great Beyond. What a waste; but it put bread and gentleman's relish on Evadne's table.

Next to her was a gentleman whom Evadne could indeed relish, were they to have met in different circumstances. He was tall, perhaps forty, with a military bearing. Had he served on the Veldt? Had he stood on the rolling deck of one of His Majesty's ships of the line? Did he dread nought? Evadne had to admit she couldn't quite pin him down to a particular type of sitter; he'd bear watching. At his elbow was the resident religious maniac – every Spiritualist Circle had one. She was a member of the local Spiritualist church, but it was not enough for her. What she wanted was not God's peace but a full-blown manifestation, an apport floating ethereally before her very eyes. Evadne had toyed with that tonight, but it carried its own risks and this niggardly lot simply wasn't paying her enough.

The others fell into place easily enough: the widower, completely at sea without the woman who used to run his life; the young thing whose fiancé had succumbed to that ghastly fog at the start of the year. The last one mystified her – a tall, angular woman with large shoulders and a knowing smile. There was something of the night about her, but it was indefinable, like a shadow.

Well, there'd be no shadows tonight. There wasn't time and there wasn't space. First, the mood, then the voices; that would have to be enough. Evadne squeezed the fingers of the men on each side of her, arching her back and shuddering. The newly widowed let out a gasp, but that was all. She noticed their heads moving, their eyes swivelling.

'Let us focus,' she said, so softly some of them had to bend closer. 'Think,' she said, louder. 'Think of those who have gone.'

She lowered her head and relaxed her fingers, sliding them back until only the tips touched. 'John,' she said, sharply and suddenly.

'Oh!' It was the newly widowed, right on cue.

Evadne allowed herself a little smile. Had she chosen Algernon, there would have been no response at all. 'He is here,' she said. 'Keep the circle tight. Let him come in.'

'Ah!' The newly widowed was better than any stooge. Evadne

had had several of those in her time, but they were unreliable and prone to using blackmail.

'Are you there, John?' Evadne asked.

The logs shifted in the grate and the medium answered her own question with a non-committal grunt.

'It's him! It's him!' The widow's hands flew to her mouth.

'Keep the circle!' Evadne hissed, and the woman's hands flew back to join the others. 'John,' she said, 'do you have a message for anyone here?'

She lowered her head.

'He's near,' she muttered, over and over again, swaying in front of the fire, the light on her hair making it seem to move, curling and twisting like the Medusa's snakes.

'My wife!' A thunderous voice came from nowhere, echoing around the room. It had taken Evadne Principal years to perfect that, just the right blend of breath control and larynx-work.

'John!' The widow was crying with delight. 'It's Alice. I'm here, my darling, I'm here.' The tears trickled unchecked down her cheeks and Evadne gave silent thanks for the name – they always did it and didn't even know they had given the information out loud.

'Alice?' The voice was still harsh and rasping, but softer now. 'Is it you?'

'Yes, yes, my love.'

'All is well,' the voice said. 'You must not worry. We will meet again . . .' The voice trailed away.

'He's going,' Evadne said, her back arched again, her eyes closed. 'I can't . . . John . . .' And she sank into her chair. 'Wait!' This was a second voice, deeper than the first, more commanding and with a hint of an unfamiliar accent. Evadne's head had dropped again and she took the opportunity to flick the veil into place with her tongue, so no one could see her mouth moving. Everybody obliged, not daring to breathe. Alice had been reunited with her love tonight; who knew what was next?

'What is it?' Evadne asked in her own voice. 'Wovoka, ghost-dancer, who is it that you seek?'

She dipped her head. There was a long pause. Then, 'One who is not who they seem,' Wovoka grated. 'An unbeliever in our midst.'

Neither man on either side of Evadne felt her fingers slip away. Neither felt them replaced by the wax replicas she carried in the folds of her skirts. No one saw her hurl the sprinkling of powder behind her into the fire. All they saw was the flash of sulphur, the shower of stars. All they heard was the loud bang as the ghost-dancer left their presence.

'Lights!' somebody shouted. It was Evadne herself but no one knew it.

The host broke the circle and Evadne's hands were back at the table as if they had never left. First one gaslight, then another, broke the moment, and the harsh light of the twentieth century filled the room.

The medium sat slumped at her place, her eyes closed, her lips drawn tightly.

'Miss Principal.' Someone shook her gently, as though she would dissolve and crumble to the floor with the dust of ages.

Her eyes flickered open and she took in the sea of anxious faces around her. 'What happened?' she asked. And of the eight other people in that sitting room, not one of them could give her an answer.

Evadne Principal was tired. There *were* more arduous ways of making a living, although few people not on the London stage could truly appreciate the strain a nightly performance entailed. She checked the clock in her hallway. It was nearly midnight and she had an early morning the next day. She had a sitting at Cliveden, and *this* was all bells and whistles, smoke and mirrors. What the Cliveden set wanted was a manifestation, no less, Wovoka himself, the ghost-dancer in all his buckskinned finery. Damn Buffalo Bill Cody! Why had his Wild West show been so popular? Why did *everyone* now think they knew what a Red Indian looked like?

There was a soft tap on the door, more the kind of noise she specialized in during her more intimate sittings than a proper knock. She sighed and considered ignoring it, but it came again, soft but insistent, and she opened the door just a crack.

'Yes?'

'Miss Principal,' the visitor said, 'I am *so* sorry to bother you again tonight.'

Evadne popped her pince-nez into place. The light was not good on her doorstep. 'Ah,' she said, stepping back and opening the door wider. 'You were at the sitting.'

It was the large woman with the shoulders and the enigmatic persona.

'I was, and may I say how captivated I was by your performance?'

'Performance?' Evadne's reaction was acid. 'Is that what you believe it was?'

'Well, of course,' the woman said. 'Superbly done. And I was wondering if I could trouble you for a private sitting? Just the two of us?'

'I don't do that,' Evadne told her. 'The presence is unbalanced with two. It doesn't work.'

The visitor fumbled in her handbag. 'Couldn't I persuade you?' She held up several pound notes.

'No, really, I . . .'

But the woman was already across the threshold. 'I'm sorry,' she said. 'I'm afraid I must insist.'

It was a different voice entirely.

FOUR

'**M**orning, Nacker. They don't let you out often.' Andrew Crawford had just alighted from his cab.

The man who seemed to have been born at the front desk at Scotland Yard grunted something incomprehensible and stepped aside to let the detective sergeant in. Crawford took in the place. Genteel and expensively done out. Very much what you'd expect of a well-to-do residence just off the Tottenham Court Road.

'Maid's in the kitchen,' Nacker said. 'The body in question is here.' He led the way into a comfortable sitting room, with dark Baroque furniture lining the walls. A woman sat on a chair at the circular table in the centre, face down and fully clothed. Crawford felt for a pulse. One of the first things he had learned as a police constable is that you don't take anything for granted, not even when a coroner or pathologist tells you something.

'Cold as a witch's tit,' Nacker confirmed, presumably from his comprehensive knowledge of the world of the occult.

'How long, do you think?'

Nacker was used to plainclothesmen asking his opinion. He'd been around the Aldwych a few times and there wasn't much among London's lowlife that missed his eagle eye. 'Midnight, give or take,' he said. 'Maybe a little after.'

Crawford raised the dead woman's head as gently as he could. Her hair was jet black and would have been her glory in life. Now it was matted with dark brown blood that had sprayed across her neck and shoulders and had soaked into the pink tablecloth. Her eyes were closed and there were red marks around her lips. Crawford breathed in.

'Almonds,' he said. 'Cyanide.'

'Or she was fond of nuts.' Nacker played devil's advocate to perfection.

'Who was she?'

'According to the maid,' the uniformed man flicked out his notebook, 'she was Evadne Principal, medium.'

'Was she now?' Crawford was intrigued.

'Is that ringing bells, Detective Sergeant?'

'Oranges and lemons,' Crawford confirmed. 'Next of kin?'

'We've not got much on that yet. There was a husband – Perceval Principal – but apparently, he buggered off some time ago. According to the maid, he didn't approve of her carryings on.'

'Carryings on?'

'In the Spiritual sense. She was the first choice of anyone wanting a better class of séance but he didn't want to know. The maid didn't remember him at all – before her time – but she knew from the late Evadne what his take on it all was.'

Crawford squatted and looked under the tablecloth. The woman's skirts were to the ground and there was no sign of any interference. 'Is the maid live-in?' he asked Nacker.

'No, and that's the problem. She found the body when she got here this morning; apparently, when she came in to lay the table for breakfast while the kettle boiled.'

'What time was this?'

'Seven this morning.'

Crawford looked around the room. 'Nothing disturbed, by the look of it. How many lads have you got with you?'

'Six, sir.'

'Right. Put three of them on door-to-door up and down the street. Did she hold séances here? Any visitors? That sort of thing. The other three; I want this place combed from top to bottom. Anything out of the ordinary, anything amiss, I want to know about it. Has Stockley Collins been informed?'

'I've got a bloke on it,' Nacker said. 'And he's bringing a photographer.'

'Good man.' Crawford tapped the man's shoulder and looked again at the dead woman. 'Another medium, eh? Now the guv'nor will *have* to listen.'

Andrew Crawford had questioned maids before. They came in all shapes and sizes, from raddled old matrons who could give fully grown dragons a run for their money, to doe-eyed little tweenies still in their teens who sometimes wore their virtue on their sleeves. Annie Stock was somewhere in between. Despite her red, puffy eyes and quivering lip, she was a beautiful girl, immaculately turned out in starched apron and cap. She sat in the kitchen at Number Thirty-Eight, hands clasped around a cup of tea.

'Oh, sir,' she said to Crawford once he had introduced himself. 'Can I make you one?'

'No, thank you, Annie.' He sat down in front of her. 'Now, I know the big sergeant has already asked you this, but can you tell me what happened this morning, when you arrived for work?'

She sniffed and took a deep breath. 'I got here just before seven o'clock,' she said. 'The Tottenham omnibus Number Eleven, like I always do.'

'Do you have a key?'

'Yes, sir.' She pushed a bunch of keys towards him across the table.

'And you let yourself in.'

'That's right.'

'Tell me, Annie, does anybody else have access to those keys?'

'No, sir!' The maid was horrified. 'I never let 'em out of my sight. Even at night, they're on my bedside table at home. My mum can vouch for that.'

'I'm sure she can,' Crawford smiled. 'What happened then?'

'Well . . .' Annie scrubbed at her eyes with a damp handkerchief. She was having difficulty with all this, more and more as she got nearer to the moment when she had opened the door into the sitting room.

'Take your time,' he said.

'The missus isn't usually up at that time and my first job is to get her tea for the morning. I knew she had an early start today – it's written on her calendar – so I lit the fire over there to get the kettle going before I went up to wake her. It saves time when she . . .' She scrubbed with the hankie again and Crawford waited patiently. 'Well, I was heading for the stairs, when I saw it.'

'What, Annie? What did you see?'

'The lamp was burning in the sitting room. It's usually in darkness. So I went in to turn it off and . . . and . . .'

She was trembling now, the cup rattling in the saucer as she tried to pick it up to take a sip.

'And you found the missus?' Crawford finished the sentence for her. Annie nodded, suddenly unable to look the man in the face.

'Tell me, Annie, was there anything wrong with the missus? Before, I mean. Did she say anything to you, about . . . oh, I don't know . . . somebody bothering her?'

'No, sir.' Annie shook her head.

'Can you think of anyone who would want to hurt her?' he asked.

Annie's face darkened. ''T'ain't for me to say, sir,' she said.

'Oh, but I'm afraid it is, Annie,' the sergeant corrected her. 'You see, the missus can't speak for herself now, can she? You'll have to do it for her.'

Annie blinked and gnawed her lip. 'Well, in the missus's calling, sir, there's any number of peculiar people.'

'Did you ever meet any of them?'

'Not to say meet,' Annie said. 'I opened the door to some of them, passed the time of day.'

Crawford leaned back, defusing the moment. 'I'll take that

cup of tea now, Annie,' he said, 'and you can tell me all about them.'

Stockley Collins had people for the heavy lifting. On that particular Monday it was Constable Leyton, a fully paid-up member of the Islington Photographic Club. The lad was staggering into Evadne Principal's crime scene, armed with a tripod, two cameras, lenses and rolls of black cloth. They had been taking photographs in situ since at least 1888, the year of the Ripper, and in mortuaries various for years before that. Men like Leyton were a new breed, however, more photographer than copper, more artist than beat-pounder, and he was very good at what he did.

Collins was carrying paraphernalia too, but all of it could be fitted into a Gladstone bag which he called his little bag of tricks, partly to impress colleagues with his technical wizardry and partly because, as a true-blue Conservative, he could not condone carrying luggage named after the leader of the Opposition. He hovered over the dead woman like a ghoul, flicking the tablecloth and chair backs with his little badger-hair brush and sprinkling everything with powder.

Leyton arranged his tripod and blacked out the windows once the inspector had finished. He fixed the camera and fiddled with the lenses, not once or twice but a total of fifteen times. He knew perfectly well that the late Mrs Principal didn't have a good side any more, but he was not creating poses for the National Gallery. These were photographs for a courtroom, a stark black-and-white record of what a room looked like after a murder had been committed. Colleagues would see his work, so would legal counsel, judges and possibly jurors, if the corpse was not too upsetting. Perhaps – just perhaps – some of them might end up in the Police Museum, and Nathaniel Leyton's name would live on, long after he himself had hung up his wet-collodion process; old school, was Nathaniel Leyton.

'Got what you need, Leyton?' Collins was at the photographer's elbow. 'We need to get this unfortunate lady to the mortuary. I can take her dabs there.'

Margaret Murray had set the day aside to check the proofs of her *Grammar* and mark some essays. This particular cohort contained no great intellects, she, usually the most generous of women, had to admit, but it contained no out-and-out duffers, either. The temptation was always there, when she looked at the teetering pile of foolscap, to just toss the whole lot into the air and mark them out of a hundred in descending order depending on how they fell. Jack Brooks was of a similar opinion and often shared it with her. She was very fond of Jack, in the same way that one can become fond of a dog which, though smelly and inclined to fleas, is fun to take for a walk and has an endearing look in its eye. Not that Jack Brooks was smelly, far from it; if anything, he was a little dapper for Margaret's taste. But he was easy to have around and she would miss his random witterings when the time finally came for him to be awarded his further degree. If that time indeed should ever come. He was wittering now.

'So, Miss Plinlimmon,' he said. 'And how is Tuesday treating you?'

'The same as any Tuesday, Mr Brooks,' she said, without rancour. 'I am pleased to note that you know what day it is, though. I seem to remember you sometimes have difficulty after a long weekend.' She looked at him over her pince-nez, donned ready for wielding her red pen on the essays.

'Ah. I did mention, didn't I, that I was going home for the weekend?'

'Of course. To most people, Mr Brooks, a weekend consists of Saturday and Sunday, possibly with the addition of Friday evening. Not Friday afternoon through to Tuesday mid-morning.'

'It was a special occasion, though,' he said, smiling. He could tell she wasn't really cross. He had experienced that often enough to be able to recognize it coming from a mile away.

'The special occasion being . . .?'

'The parents' anniversary. Thirty-five years, the pater has been under the yoke. Seems well on it, though.' He looked thoughtful. 'I wouldn't mind finding a girl like the mater. She was quite a looker in her day. Not so bad now, to tell the truth.'

Margaret Murray had met Lady Sylvia from time to time, at meetings of the WSPU, although she had never been convinced of her commitment to the cause. Her son was quite right; she was still very attractive, if one's tastes ran to statuesque.

'I was telling her about the Bermondsey Spiritualist Circle . . .'

'Mr *Brooks*! That was supposed to be secret, and anyway, how did you find out about that?'

He looked a little shame-faced, but only a little. 'You did have a note addressed to Miss Henrietta Plinlimmon in an envelope with their address on the flap,' he pointed out. 'It didn't really seem that secret, to me.'

Margaret Murray climbed down from her high horse. 'I do apologize, Mr Brooks. I had forgotten that the hon. sec. didn't get the memo. But I would be appreciative if, apart from your dear mama, you could keep it to yourself.'

'Well . . . I may have mentioned it . . . generally over the weekend. Long story cut short . . .'

'If you would.' Margaret patted the pile of essays.

'Mama would love it if you and the Circle could perhaps do a sitting when she's in town next.'

Margaret looked at her protégé. She wanted to say a definite no, but had learned over the years to keep things up her sleeve to see how the future worked out. And a place to hold a sitting, a neutral place, might not be a bad thing to tuck up her cuff.

'Well,' she said, finally, 'since it's you, Jack, and since it is for your dear mama, then let's say "perhaps", shall we?'

'Mama will be as pleased as Punch,' Jack Brooks beamed.

'No need to rush off and tell her, though,' Margaret Murray pointed out. 'From now on, shall we say mum's the word.'

Jack laughed and bent to his translation. 'Mama, please!'

'As you wish. Now, hush. I must mark these.'

For a while, the only sound was that of Margaret Murray's pen scratching and Jack Brooks's occasional frustrated sigh, as yet again a hieroglyph refused to cooperate. It was a companionable semi-silence and one in which Mrs Plinlimmon shared happily. The kettle clicked as it cooled, the hum of the university below their feet inconsequential in this fastness under the eaves.

There was a tap at the door and Margaret Murray looked up to meet Jack Brooks's eyes. They both put a finger to their lips and mimed a silent 'shush'. Experience had told them that, after a minute or two to catch their breath after all the stairs, most visitors just went away.

The tap came again. Margaret Murray tried to identify it. It wasn't William Flinders Petrie, who hadn't knocked on a door for the last thirty years – in his world, doors were to stop draughts entering, not him. It couldn't be the cleaner – she only came at dusk at this time of the year and it wasn't that by a long chalk. It could be one of any number of students, there to apologize for a late delivery of an essay or, unable to bear the suspense, find out ahead of the game what mark she had given. But something told her it was not a student. The knock, though not strident, wasn't apologetic enough. Just as she had decided to ride it out and find out later from the porter who had been to visit, the door opened a crack and Detective Sergeant Andrew Crawford's handsome face peered in.

'Do you have a moment, Dr Murray?' he asked politely.

Without being asked, Jack Brooks gathered up his papers and, with a nod at Crawford, took himself off to the library.

Margaret watched him go. 'He is a dear,' she murmured as the door closed behind him. 'I shall miss him when I have to award his PhD.'

'Have to?' Crawford was puzzled.

'Yes. He actually earned it before Christmas, but he's just so restful to have around, so I keep hanging on. But I will have to bite that bullet some time, I expect. However, Andrew, I don't expect you're here to arrest me for not awarding PhDs on time.' Fond though she was of the detective sergeant, she had got into something of a rhythm with her marking and hoped he didn't plan to stay too long.

'Indeed not. Although I am sure that carries serious time. I don't suppose you have seen the stop press today.'

'I haven't seen a newspaper. Mr Brooks omitted to bring his with him this morning.'

'There has been another murder. Tottenham Court Road this time, or as near as makes no difference. A medium. A Miss Evadne Principal. I just thought I would check with you whether she was at the meeting of the Bermondsey Circle on Friday or whether she was mentioned.'

'How did you know there was a meeting of the Bermondsey Circle on Friday?' Margaret Murray was a little surprised.

He looked at her, mildly perplexed. 'I am a policeman,' he said at last. 'You'd be surprised what I know.'

She chuckled and motioned him to a seat by the unlit hearth. 'True. I forget. No, she wasn't there, nor was she mentioned. It was not much of a meeting, as it happened. It was called to make sure everyone knew about poor Muriel – Ankhara.'

'Didn't they all know?' Crawford said, with a smile.

'That's an old joke, Andrew,' she said. 'Can we take it as read?'

He nodded solemnly.

'They were what I would have to call a mixed bunch,' she said. 'Apart from my good self, I would say that there was perhaps one other person there who could pass for normal in polite society. There was some antagonism towards the dead woman from one member, a rather surprising revelation from another and, to be honest, nothing much worth reporting from the rest. I have jotted it down.' She reached over and extracted a sheet of paper from under the pile of essays and handed it across.

Detective Sergeant Crawford glanced at it and folded it away in an inside pocket of his jacket. 'Succinct and perfect as always. Thank you for that. So, Miss Principal wasn't mentioned at all?'

'No. I don't think I have ever heard the name. Is it her real one?'

'Yes. I don't get the impression she was one for much prevarication, not like Muriel Fazakerley. She used her own name and seemed to specialize in sessions in other people's houses, though she sometimes used her own. She was due at Cliveden today, for example. The maid described a few visitors, but of course they don't always use their real names, so it was of dubious help. The uniformed men who attended went around the houses and took statements from the neighbours, but as this all happened in the middle of the night, so the people who might have seen something are . . . well, they may not be all that reliable.'

'I see what you mean,' Margaret said, understanding immediately. 'Depending on the actual address, not everyone is totally respectable in that area. Isn't there a brothel around there somewhere?'

Andrew Crawford's eyes opened wide. Even after all these years, he had to concede that Dr Murray could still blindside him.

'Don't look so amazed, Andrew,' she admonished him. 'I like

to think I know London quite well. The only place I know better, I would venture to suggest, is Karnak. Middle Kingdom, that is, not now, of course.' She also knew where the brothel was in Ephesus, but that was another story.

'Of course. But . . . um, you are quite right. There is a brothel at the end of Miss Principal's street, on the corner on the other side of the road. So the bedrooms on the one side have a good view of her front door. One of the girls was having a breather, as you might say, and glanced out at about half one and saw a man leaving. She gave quite a good description as a matter of fact, and we have her down at the Yard now, looking through the pictures of known miscreants.'

'Is that likely to be of much use?' Margaret Murray asked mildly.

'Not really,' Crawford sighed. 'But we have to start somewhere. And Stockley Collins does have a very comprehensive library now, filed by all kinds of physical parameters. Height, build, colour of hair where present, eyes, scars . . . you name it, it's there.'

'So . . . what did the man look like?' Margaret asked. 'From the girl's description, I mean.'

'That's the problem,' Crawford said. 'It could be almost anyone. A man, obviously. Average height. Average to portly build. She did give a little more detail there, but I won't bother you with it.'

'From that distance?' Margaret Murray was impressed.

'I know,' Crawford said, rolling his eyes. 'I said that, but apparently it's all in the walk.'

'And it was . . .?'

'Average.'

'Ah. Hair colour?'

'Now, that was a little more helpful. The hair was receding but not thin and was pepper and salt, heavy on the salt. He wore glasses and peered through them as he walked, so she thought he was really quite short-sighted. She said he sort of looked down his nose, with his head tilted back.'

'An observant young lady.'

'The uniformed chap was most impressed, though whether it was strictly speaking because of her recall and skills of observation or otherwise, it's hard to say. She seemed pleasant enough and didn't mind coming round to the Yard, though she must be tired, having been up all night, as it were.'

Margaret raised an eyebrow. 'I'm sure even ladies of her calling get rests every now and then, Andrew. They are not machines. And they ought by now, of course, to have a trades union.'

Crawford forbore to answer. He suspected on this occasion he knew more than even the esteemed Dr Murray.

'He wasn't a client of hers, I assume.' It was obvious, but needed saying.

'The uniform did ask that. Sometimes these girls have a bit of an axe to grind. Mean tipper, that kind of thing. But she seemed quite genuine when she said she didn't know him. And if it was a grudge, she'd give clearer indications, wouldn't she, rather than leave it to chance?'

'True. May I ask the cause of death?'

'Cyanide. Or at least, that's what I think. We'll need to know what they find in the morgue. Whoever it was wasn't leaving anything to chance. She was also bashed over the head.'

'It is rather worrying, Andrew, isn't it? I know every man's death diminishes every one of us, but these women seem so vulnerable. They invite strangers into their homes and are often alone with them, in the dark, no proper names being given – is there a way of warning them?'

'It's in the papers. I don't think we can do more, to be honest.'

'I suppose not. But are your superiors doing more this time? Does Inspector Kane think this may be part of a pattern?'

'I hope so. But who knows, with the powers that be. Do you happen to know whether Inspector Reid is in town at the moment?'

'Good heavens, Andrew. This medium thing must be catching. He was certainly here at the end of last week. He lives full time in Hampton-on-Sea now, you know. A delightful little house, with a view over the water.'

'So you've stayed in touch. That's nice.' Andrew Crawford was never sure about Margaret Murray. In some ways she was very proper, but he wouldn't put it past her to go and stay with a widowed gentleman living alone by the sea, just because she could.

'Off and on,' she said, enigmatically. 'Off and on. He popped in to see me last week. About Muriel Fazakerley, as it happens. He had seen it in the paper and . . . well, it had piqued his interest. As it did yours, in fact.'

'I might pop in and see *him*,' Crawford mused. 'Where does he stay in Town?'

'He's at the Tambour House Hotel. He always stays there. I have the telephone number somewhere. Now . . . where did I write it down? It's on my desk.'

They both looked hopelessly at the welter of paper on the top of what may have been an item of furniture; it was hard to tell.

'Don't worry,' Crawford said, getting up. 'I need to go via the Yard anyway, to see if Daisy Lorne has made an identification yet.'

'Daisy Lawn? How is she spelling that?' Margaret was amused.

'L-o-r-n-e, I think. There may be no e.'

'I think,' Margaret Murray said, 'that that girl will go far. Let's hope she has identified the right man. It would be so wonderful to find and arrest him before more lives are lost.'

Detective Sergeant Crawford looked at her solemnly. 'It sounds as if you don't hold out much hope of that,' he said.

'There's always hope, Andrew,' she said. 'There's always hope. It's just that sometimes, there isn't all that much.' She sat down behind her desk again and pulled another essay towards her. 'Do keep me informed. There is another meeting of the Bermondsey Circle this Friday, and I need to know everything before I attend. If you have indeed caught the miscreant, I don't even need to go.' The booming drone of Mrs Bentwood filled her head briefly. 'And that is an outcome devoutly to be wished. As you go out, can you turn the notice on the door to "Do not disturb", there's a good policeman?'

And before he was even out of the door, she was tutting and striking through inanities on the great god Osiris as if he had never been there.

At Scotland Yard, things were in a bit of a flutter. Ladies of the night were hardly a new occurrence there – the queue waiting for processing often wound down the corridor and out into the street – but there were several unusual factors in this case which made the appearance of Daisy Lorne, with or without an 'e', rather refreshing. For a start, she hadn't been hauled in by a disillusioned and exhausted constable on night duty, fed up to the back teeth with complaints from respectable neighbours about what they almost always referred to as 'goings on' in the alley adjacent to their houses. Nine nights out of ten, the constable would reason with the householders and then go and shout a general warning up the alley in the hope of quietening things down. But sometimes, enough was enough and an arrest would be made; the lady in question would end up simmering nicely and adding up all her lost half-crowns and factoring in the fine. And every red-blooded policeman in the building had to admit – Daisy was a looker! She had one up on her lower-caste sisters in that she had been able to get out of a nice bed and primp and prepare in a bathroom shared by only three other girls. Mrs Mountfitchett kept a high-quality house and didn't stint when it came to keeping her girls in comfort.

Like many other ladies of the night, Daisy Lorne was a once-respectable girl who had fallen on hard times. She had an elementary school education and had even won a certificate for good attendance. As to her chosen profession now, they didn't give awards for that, unless, of course, you were born to polite society and knew the king personally. Daisy had never met him as such, but knew some girls who had and she lived in hope.

To be perfectly honest – and Daisy wasn't that often – she felt a little uncomfortable helping the police with their enquiries. Where she hung out her shingle, you didn't bend over backwards to help the esclops, no matter how much they were prepared to pay. And anyway, in Mrs Mountfitchett's establishment, most of the more exotic positions were left to Milly Molly, who had run away from the circus.

Inspector Stockley Collins fascinated her. She had never seen a man with a bigger moustache or a more pronounced quiff, but then, she wasn't all that used to men in the vertical position. Alongside him in the Anthropomorphic Department, a sketch artist was hard at work. Everybody may have expected too much of Constable Bob Velasquez, but he was giving it his best shot.

'No,' Daisy yawned, looking at the doodles. 'Too much hair. I saw the geezer from above, remember, so his hair was something I particularly noticed. Except for the bit covered by his hat, of course.'

It was Inspector Collins's turn to yawn. 'You didn't mention a hat earlier, Daisy.'

'Didn't I?' She sat upright, treating the policemen to a flash of her ample cleavage. 'Well, he had one.'

Stockley Collins was a man on a mission. For the best part of four years now, his mind had been filled with those mesmerizing little whorls and ridges on the end of everybody's fingers. In the filing cabinets around him were thousands of drawings, of noses, ears, eyebrows, lips and other parts that made up the human condition. He even had the prehensile lower mandible of Charlie Peace the burglar somewhere, the one he used to change the shape of his face. But all that had been swept away by finger-prints. He'd always secretly doubted that habitual homicides had long earlobes, that conmen had wide nostrils and that cat burglars had six toes, but he hadn't liked to rock Signor Lombroso's boat.

Constable Velasquez made a final flourish with his pencil and swivelled the sketch to face the girl. 'There,' he said. 'How's that?'

'That's *him*!' Daisy shrieked. 'That's the bloke I saw, to a tee!'

The bloke Daisy Lorne saw to a tee sat nervously in the Jeremy Bentham that Tuesday afternoon. Under the table, his knees were shaking. Above it, he was chewing his nails. Thomas the propri-etor knew all the signs. He brought the tea and sat next to the man, slipping something stronger into the Darjeeling.

'What's the matter, Adi, you old Norwegian?'

Adi looked at his old friend through narrowed eyes. 'My old trouble,' he said.

Thomas looked astonished. 'Never!' he said, so loudly that other customers noticed. One of them was Margaret Murray, but she was not one to judge. If Thomas spoke more loudly than was strictly acceptable in the Jeremy Bentham, there had to be a good reason.

'The word's on the street,' Adi said, 'that some tart has identi-fied me as a man seen leaving the premises of a murdered woman.'

'Where was this?' Thomas was all ears.

'Off the Tottenham Court Road,' Adi told him.

'What? Round the corner from the nick? Are you mad?'

Adi's mouth hung open. 'But it wasn't me, Tom,' he said. 'It never is.'

The door crashed open and three very large constables marched in.

'Can I help you, gentlemen?' Thomas was on his feet in seconds, trying to shield the quivering man at the table. 'Tea for three? We have an irresistible offer on French fancies at the moment.'

'We're not that interested in your private life, sir.' One of the constables moved the proprietor to one side. 'Hello. What have we here?' He was grinning at the man at the table.

'I was just leaving,' Adi said, throwing his napkin on to the table and pushing back his chair.

'Indeed you are,' another constable said. 'With us.'

'Adolf Beck,' the third constable stood in front of him. 'Also known as Lord Willoughby. Also known as John Smith. I am arresting you in connection with the murder of Miss Evadne Principal of Thirty-Eight Arundel Street on or about the fifteenth of May last. In other words, yesterday. You are not obliged to say anything, but if I was you, I'd sing like a canary, save us all a lot of trouble.'

They bundled Beck towards the door.

'Remember, Adi,' Tom called. 'No comment's the word!'

One of the policemen rounded on him. 'I don't think the accused needs that kind of unsolicited advice,' he said. 'Unless, of course, you know something we don't.'

There was a tap on the man's shoulder and a little woman stood there, looking up at him. 'I should think that the proprietor of the Jeremy Bentham tea rooms knows a great deal that you don't, Constable.' She pointedly took out a notebook and carefully jotted down the man's collar numbers. 'As I think my good friend Inspector Kane of Scotland Yard would agree.'

The constable glowered at her. 'And you are . . .?'

'The small voice of justice and humanity in a vicious world of police brutality,' she said.

'Yes, well . . .' The constable was lost for words and followed the others out to the waiting Maria, felons for the use of.

Thomas reached out and grasped the little lady's hand. 'I don't normally do this to my guests, Prof,' he said and he kissed her on the cheek, 'but you've just made my day.'

'That man,' Margaret said. 'The one they arrested – who is he?'

'Adolf Beck.' John Kane leaned back in his chair at the Yard. 'The year before you joined the Force, I think, Crawford. It was quite a cause célèbre. Some people have "victim" written all over them.'

'What happened, guv?'

'Beck is of the Norwegian persuasion, which of course makes him guilty before he ever saw the Old Bailey.'

'What did he do?' Crawford asked, 'apart from be foreign, that is.'

'A number of women accused him of defrauding them of not inconsiderable sums. None of them knew him as Beck, of course. To some, he was Lord Willoughby. To others, John Smith.'

'John Smith?' Crawford laughed. 'Oh.' The look on John Kane's face told him that this was no laughing matter.

'The victims were adamant that Beck was the man. Identified him and swore under oath. But one little mistake counted in his favour.'

'Oh?'

'As part of the – shall we say, defrauding process? – Lord Willoughby exposed himself to at least two of the ladies.'

'And?'

'They were both very graphic in their descriptions of the event. Lord Willoughby was circumcised. Adolf Beck wasn't.'

'Ah.'

'I pointed this out to the powers that be, but by that time, poor old Beck had done the best part of two years in the Scrubs . . .'

'. . . which is where I met him.' Thomas was whispering in Margaret's ear. 'Well, obviously, Prof, we were all innocent in there, weren't we? But Adi really was. As soon as I heard his story, I knew it. That bit about his wossname clinched it, although of course, it didn't come out in court; I mean, there are proprieties.'

'Indeed there are,' Margaret nodded.

'There was a bit of unpleasantness when some old duchess or other wanted to have another look, just to be sure, but they managed to get away without another identity parade. Luckily for Adi, he had a friend on the outside, one from the most unlikely of places . . .'

'. . . and that was me.' Kane lit his pipe. 'John Smith, as you noticed at once, wasn't really the man's name. He was Wilhelm Meyer, an Austrian, so he sounded a bit like Beck to the untutored ear. He had had a good education but had fallen on hard times. And he *did* look like Beck. Quite extraordinarily like him, in fact. Did you see that photo in the paper the other day? The Prince of Wales and his cousin, Tsar of All the Russias?'

'I did, as a matter of fact,' Crawford said.

'Uncanny, wasn't it?' Kane said. 'Especially as they'd swapped uniforms. Well, it was as uncanny as that, Smith and Beck. They say we all have a double somewhere in the world.'

'So you got things moving,' Crawford said, 'in the interests of justice . . .'

'. . . He's a rare copper, that John Kane,' Thomas said. 'Who'd have thought that justice and the law sometimes go hand in hand, eh? So, poor old Adi was released, only to be re-arrested again some months later.'

'No!' Margaret was horrified.

'Really?' Crawford couldn't believe it.

'So, this time, I went in person to the Home Office,' Kane said. 'I've never seen a Home Secretary do an about-face so quickly. I just mentioned that the *Daily Mail* might want a word. It never fails.'

'Yes,' Thomas was getting into his stride. 'They say Kane had a right go at the Home Secretary. Blackened his eye and all sorts. There's talk of false teeth being broken in half in some quarters. He was off work for weeks. I've got nothing against police brutality if it's in a good cause.'

'So what will happen to Mr Beck now?'

'Oh, don't you worry, Prof. They had to pay him a packet for all the confusion before, they won't be keen to do that again, you can be sure of that. Kane'll have him out of there before you can say "Another French fancy, please, Thomas!"'

All in all, it wasn't a bad Margaret Murray impression.

FIVE

Margaret Murray saw him before he saw her, something which happens when one is a little below other people's eyeline. 'Oh, Lord!' was her immediate reaction, although of course, she had been far too well brought up to say it out loud. Her ayah would have been horrified. Instead, she smiled. 'Mr Merrington, good morning.'

The artist was dressed as his calling demanded these days, with a down-swept wideawake hat and a scarf that almost reached the ground. He wasn't even following the convention of leaving his bottom waistcoat button undone, *à la* the king, but had it fastidiously fastened. He stood in the atrium of the Petrie Museum with eyes wide, mouth hanging open.

'Oh, Dr Murray,' he said, almost as an afterthought. 'I'm so sorry.' He kissed her hand. 'But I have never been here before. The sense of the ages . . . it's . . . it's . . . overwhelming.' And he had to sit down. 'Wait a moment.' Suddenly, he was on his feet again. 'Is that Anubis?' He was pointing to a statuette in a glass case.

'It is,' she smiled. 'Handsome, isn't he?'

'Exquisite,' the artist cooed. 'Did you find him? On a recent dig, perhaps?'

Margaret laughed. 'Professor Petrie allows me more freedom on digs than most of us ladies in the field,' she said, 'but there *are* limits. The most I can claim is that I cleaned him thoroughly, drew him and made notes.'

'You must show me your drawings,' he said.

She laughed again. 'As Mr Quaritch reminded me, only too forcefully,' she said, 'there is a world of difference between archaeological accuracy and the kind of art that sells books. That's where you come in, Mr Merrington.'

'Indeed.' He hauled up a leather portfolio, 'and I hope, after an unfortunate beginning, that I have made amends. May I show you?'

'Let's go to my office,' she said. 'We won't be disturbed there.'

She was already having to shout over the excited hubbub of a score of schoolgirls, all of whom seemed very impressed with various aspects of scantily clad pharaohs in bas-relief. Margaret was secretly glad that the *really* Rabelaisian stuff was kept locked away in an inner sanctum.

Merrington followed the archaeologist through passageways without number, every bit as labyrinthine as anything beneath the sands of time in the Valley of the Kings.

'Here we are.'

The artist took in the jumbled artefacts on the shelves and across the desk. A Black Forest inkwell held pens and pencils in a cluster and a whole range of magnifying glasses cluttered the chair. One particular item caught Merrington's attention.

'Is that a stuffed owl?' he asked. Among the stone, basalt, marble and papyrus, it seemed curiously out of place.

'That is Mrs Plinlimmon,' Margaret said. 'The wise owl of Athena. Normally I keep her in my room at the college, but occasionally I let her flex her wings a bit and fly her here.'

'Plinlimmon,' Merrington mused. 'I've heard that name somewhere. It's very unusual.'

'Not if you live near Cullercoats on the north-east coast,' Margaret said with a smile. 'Round there, you can't throw a brick without hitting a Plinlimmon. Now . . . the drawings?'

'Yes. Yes, of course. The drawings.' He unlaced the folder and produced three superb examples of his work.

'Oh, I say,' she said, using not one, but two magnifying glasses, one for each eye. 'These are excellent, Mr Merrington. Truly excellent. I'm sure Mr Quaritch will be delighted.'

He looked at her sternly. 'You, Dr Murray, are the arbiter. I don't want to sound rude, but I regard publishers much in the same way that the very late Lord Byron did; they are tradesmen. Quaritch wouldn't know a scarab from his left elbow. But you . . . if someone of your professional standing finds my work acceptable, then that is praise enough, believe me.'

'Well, well.' Margaret always thought herself immune to

flattery, but she was only human, after all. 'But there are only three . . .'

'Indeed,' Merrington said. 'I wasn't sure you'd like them, so I held back at that point. I would be more than happy to finish the job, but now . . . well, now, I have a favour to ask you.'

'Oh?'

'Having glimpsed the wonders of the museum, I wonder if I might work here? My medium is pen and ink, so there's very little mess. If I might sketch some artefacts in the cases and find a corner to work them up to the finished article . . . would that be too much of an imposition?'

'No, not at all,' she said. 'Sketch away. And I'm sure we could find you such a corner . . .'

'Oh, Margaret, I . . . oh, I'm sorry. I didn't realize you had company.'

Andrew Crawford's head prepared to disappear around the door as suddenly as it had arrived.

'Andrew . . . No, not at all. Come in. Kirk Merrington, this is Andrew Crawford. Andrew; Kirk Merrington.'

The men shook hands.

'Are you an archaeologist too, Mr Crawford?' the artist asked.

'Er . . . of sorts,' Crawford said. 'Strictly amateur.'

'Andrew does his detection work in a rather newer purlieu than I do,' Margaret said.

'I am a detective sergeant,' Crawford explained. 'Scotland Yard.'

'Oh, dear . . .'

Crawford was used to that reaction. 'But I was a student of Dr Murray's a couple of years ago. Hence my visit.'

'Well, then.' Merrington collected his portfolio. 'I'll take my leave. Would it be too soon to start sketching right away, Dr Murray? I can find my own way. I have asked Courtney to bring me an easel, if that won't be too much of an imposition.'

'Not at all,' she said. 'Sketch away. If any of those brattish girls downstairs give you any trouble, talk to Kirby, the doorman. He'll see them on their way.'

'Thank you again, dear lady,' and he kissed her hand. 'Mr Crawford.'

When he had gone, the detective sat down. 'What was that?' he muttered.

'Now, Andrew, don't be such a policeman. Mr Merrington is working on the art for my latest book – and I have to say, his preliminary drawings are rather good after an unfortunate start.' She waved an arm over the sketches and the amateur archaeologist in Crawford had to agree – they were. 'Now,' she said, sitting opposite him at her desk, 'what news?'

'I just thought I would tell you that Kane is now in charge of the medium killings.'

'You must be relieved.'

'I know it may sound silly, but I just didn't want a killer to wander from division to division, picking off innocent people, just because no one was looking.'

'Any feathers this time?' Margaret had mulled the feather over and over – it was too much of a coincidence to mean nothing. And besides, since when had feathers been an ingredient of mulligatawny soup?

'No,' Crawford told her. 'But there was . . . well, it's probably nothing.'

'It's the "nothings" of this world that solve problems, Andrew,' she said. 'So what is this nothing?'

'Well, it was a tarot card.'

'Not unusual in a medium's apartments, surely?'

'Ordinarily, no. But this one was crumpled up in her left hand.'

'Ah.'

'And there was no sign of the rest of the pack.'

'Does the left hand have any significance, over and above the classic "sinister" connotation?' Margaret Murray made a small bet with herself that Andrew Crawford was probably one of two policemen in London that morning who would understand that, the other being Edmund Reid.

'Not much. Except that, according to the maid, the late Mrs Principal was right-handed. Having said that, we found a pair of wax hands in her portmanteau – all part of the tools of her trade, of course.'

'The tarot card.' Margaret pursued it. 'What was it?'

'The hanged man,' Crawford said.

There was a sudden thud outside the office door, for all the world like a trapdoor crashing back and a felon at the rope's end hurtling through open space. Both of them jumped.

'Who's there?' Margaret called.

There was a knock on the door and a cleaning lady stood there, mop and bucket in hand, looking back over her shoulder. 'Sorry I'm so early, mum,' she bobbed. 'But I've finished upstairs and the professor told me to bugger off, 'cos he was busy. And I can't go next door until . . .'

Margaret tutted and rolled her eyes heavenward. 'Sorry about that, Gertie,' she said. 'You know what he's like. Come on in. Mr Crawford and I were just going.'

The lounge at the Tambour House Hotel was not exactly crawling with guests at that hour and at that time of year. It was ex-Detective Inspector Edmund Reid's favourite watering hole when he was up in Town. And he was up in Town because there was a murderer on the loose.

Andrew Crawford sat in the well-worn leather chair across the hearth from Reid, coppers of the old school and the new, enjoying the warm glow of the house brandy, both of them blowing rings of cigar smoke to the ceiling, already brown with the years of tobacco.

'It's good of you to see me, Mr Reid,' Crawford said.

'What else are old flatfeet for?' Reid chuckled. 'And that's Edmund, by the way.'

Sergeant Crawford's generation went in awe of coppers like Reid. The man was a legend, having cut his teeth in the slums of the East End, Whitechapel and Bethnal Green. The Irish gangs, the Jewish money-lenders, the Russian riff-raff; they had all found their way to the teetering rookeries of the Ghetto and men like Reid had been there to welcome them. Add to that the man's conjuring skills, his daredevil balloon ascents and his rich tenor voice and you had one of the greatest of the greatest city in the world. Pygmies like Crawford could only crawl along in their shadows.

'I wanted to pick your brains on the Muriel Fazakerley case,' the sergeant said.

'Even more so now that we have the Evadne Principal case.' Reid sipped his brandy.

'Ah, you picked that up,' Crawford nodded.

'I can hardly avoid it, dear boy. The papers are full of it.' Reid waved to the pile of them on a corner table. 'From *The Times* to the *East London Observer*, there's little else. Oh, apart from two other little items that are likely to cause you boys in blue a not-inconsiderable amount of trouble in the days ahead.'

'Such as?'

'Well, it's taken him a couple of weeks, but after the failure of the Woman's Suffrage Bill, an MP has come out with – and it was *so* looking for trouble, I can remember it verbatim – "Men and women differ in mental equipment with women having little sense of proportion".'

Crawford laughed. 'I hope my wife hasn't seen that,' he said.

'You can be sure Dr Murray has,' Reid nodded. 'At least from her, the most the suicidal MP can expect is a curt letter. Oh, it'll be withering and if I received it, I'd hang myself, but at least she's not likely to brain him with a brick in her handbag. Which is more than I can say for some of the suffrage sisterhood.'

'What was the other little thing?' Crawford asked.

'A new organization,' Reid told him. 'The Automobile Association. Among other things, they'll be warning motorists about the speed traps you boys are setting up. No more lurking in the shrubbery for you, my lad.' He winked.

'Twenty miles an hour is fast enough for anybody,' Crawford commented.

Reid roared with laughter. 'You old fuddy-duddy,' he said. 'That should be *me* talking, not you. But,' he took the decanter and freshened both their glasses, 'to the larger picture. What's Inspector Kane's take on the murders?'

Crawford shrugged. 'He's keeping an open mind,' he said. 'You never worked with him, did you?'

'After my time,' Reid said.

'Well, he keeps things close to his chest, does my guv'nor. For instance, it was six months before I realized he doesn't drink.'

Reid's face darkened. 'Oh, that's bad,' he said. 'You can't do a job like his stone-cold sober.'

The two men sat in silence for a while, staring into the pile of elegant logs that filled the fireplace now that spring was

officially here. Then, Reid said, 'Picking my brains might not
be all that useful, Andrew. A Division was always cutting edge
and you boys have all this new technology at your . . . excuse
the pun . . . fingertips.'

'Even so,' Crawford nodded. 'Policing is policing. Your
generation hunted the Ripper.'

'Yes,' Reid sighed. 'And we couldn't catch him, could we?
However,' he took a deep draw on the cigar, 'it's funny you
should mention that.'

'Why?'

'Back in 1888 to '89, we must have had well over two hundred
letters, all anonymous, addressed either to the Yard, cop-shops
various or the gentlemen of the press, purporting to come from
the Whitechapel murderer.'

'Yes,' Crawford said. 'I've read some of them in the Police
Museum.'

'The second one is the one everybody remembers,' Reid said,
leaning forward, 'the Dear Boss letter.'

'The one that gave the "Jack" monicker?'

'That's right. Now, you and I know that they were all hoaxes,
more than one written by journalists anxious to make hay with
the story. But there's one line in "Dear Boss" that's always stuck
in my mind – "I am down on whores and shan't quit ripping 'til
I do get buckled."'

'That's right.' Crawford remembered it too.

'Well, the writer may not have been Jack, but the motive was
right. So it is here – Fazakerley and Principal – sound like a firm
of quantity surveyors, don't they? Two mediums – or should that
be media? – murdered within a week or so of each other. I'll
wager you John Kane doesn't believe in coincidences, however
little he tells you about his methodology.'

'So we should be looking for somebody who has a hatred of
sensitives.' Crawford underlined it. 'But why?'

Reid sighed and from nowhere produced a pack of cards which
he passed to Crawford. 'Shuffle,' he said.

A little nonplussed, the sergeant did.

'Pick a card,' Reid said. 'Any card.'

Crawford did.

'Now, without letting me see it, stick it on my forehead.'

The sergeant looked around, wondering how the other couple of guests would take this bizarre experiment.

'All right,' Reid said. 'Now, again without letting me see it, put it back in the pack.'

Crawford did as he was told.

'Shuffle again,' Reid told him.

The sergeant obliged.

'Right.' Reid leaned back. 'Now, find me the card in question. It's the three of spades, by the way.'

Crawford stared at him, open-mouthed, and began to lay the cards down. It took a moment or two, but the sergeant eventually had to say, 'It isn't here.'

'No,' Reid smiled. 'It's here.' And he peeled it off Crawford's forehead, holding it up for the man to see.

'No,' Crawford muttered. 'No, that's not possible. How . . .?'

Reid laughed. 'Tricks of the trade, dear boy,' he said. 'I've got a million. Care to put some money on it and try again?'

'No.' The sergeant was adamant. 'Not on your life.'

'No.' Reid was grimly serious. 'Just on the lives of Muriel Fazakerley and Evadne Principal. The point I'm making, Andrew, is that mediums, sensitives, call them what you will, are conjurors. I hesitate to call them charlatans because I've made a bob or two out of card tricks myself. But mediums are like vampires; they prey on the newly dead, the recently departed. I lost my wife recently.'

'I'm sorry,' Crawford said.

'These things happen.' Reid had come to terms with it. 'But I'd have been less than pleased to find some ghoul hovering at my elbow claiming to be able to talk to her in the Great Beyond. *And* charging me a hefty fee into the bargain. Would you like to see a photo of my wife?'

'Er . . . yes,' Crawford said. He would much rather not go down a sad memory lane with this man, however much he admired him, but the sergeant was a kind man and didn't want to upset the old boy. 'Yes, of course.'

Reid ferreted in his wallet and pulled out a crumpled photograph. 'There she is, sitting on the left. What else do you see?'

'Er . . .'

'Come on, man.' Reid seemed to be enjoying this. 'You're a detective, trained to observe.'

'Umm . . . Mrs Reid. That's you, in the centre with the teapot. A third person, on the right.'

'The Reverend Philpot,' Reid confirmed. 'That's his garden. We're all having tea. I was mother that day. What else?'

'Er . . . table, cloth, china . . . are they cakes?'

'Look to the right, behind the vicar.'

Crawford did. 'Er . . . oh, it's a dog. It's . . . no, wait a minute. It's . . . disappearing.'

Reid laughed. 'Exactly,' he said. 'The ghost dog of Micheldever. Except that it's not.'

'I don't understand.'

Reid took the photograph back. 'If I were a medium, specializing in that sort of thing, I'd claim that that is a spirit photograph, a phantasm manifesting itself before our very eyes and caught on camera – the one witness that never lies.' He dropped the echoing, stage voice. 'In reality, it's Nanky Poo, the vicar's shih-tzu, relieving himself. The reason he's disappeared is all down to slow exposure time on camera.'

'Good God.'

'Which is why all the photographs of Uncle Ebenezer, Great Aunt Matilda and Catherine the Great floating in the ozone are just so much fakery. Did I ever tell you about Miss Goodrich-Freer?'

'I don't think so.'

Reid reached across and poured them both another stiff one. 'I don't know, Andrew, if you are of a nervous disposition, but you might want to fortify yourself for what you are about to hear.'

Crawford smiled. He had been brought up on *Varney the Vampire*; nothing that went bump in the night held any terrors for him.

'Miss Goodrich-Freer was a medium – perhaps still is, for all I know. She was called in to a haunted house. I know because I was there already, as a young copper investigating the disappearance of a little girl, Eliza Mumler, eight years old. She had last been seen in the orchard of her parents' house on the edge of Hampstead Heath one November morning . . . this would have been 1878. The parents called the police and we combed the place from top to bottom. We quizzed the family and the servants. We went house to house. We searched the Heath – and, believe me, it's bigger than you think. Nothing. But the girl's father was a member of a Spiritualist Circle and he called in Goodrich-Freer. She was an oddity and no mistake; one of her eyes didn't work properly, sort of drooped. Her very presence frightened the bejesus out of the Mumler's tweenie. Anyway, long story cut short, Goodrich-Freer said she heard knockings in little Eliza's nursery and felt cold spots along the landing. She organised a séance in the nursery itself. I sat in on that, although she wasn't very keen on the idea and I must admit, it was impressive.'

'What happened?'

'When we were all sitting comfortably, we heard a noise, a shuffling of feet, then a sob. Then we heard a little girl's voice, "Mama, Mama. It's dark. I'm cold. Where are you? Papa? Where are you?"'

'God!'

'It was Goodrich-Freer, of course, but the girl was talking through her and it was obvious she was dead.'

'An actual manifestation?' Crawford was indeed sipping his brandy.

'The next night, we all tried again, because Goodrich-Freer said she felt that poor Eliza was so close and that she wanted to come to us, to see her mama and papa again, because where she was, all was water, all was ice.'

'And?'

Reid leaned back in his chair, closing his eyes for a moment. 'I've never seen anything like it. Goodrich-Freer made contact with Eliza and, as we watched, sitting there, fingertip to fingertip in that pitch-black room, a dead girl appeared, shimmering in a green light, her eyes rolling white in her head, her long dark hair plastered to her forehead and dripping on to her shift. Her breasts—'

Crawford interrupted. 'Breasts?' he repeated. 'I thought you said she was only eight.'

Reid raised his head and the frozen look of horror on his face broadened to a grin. 'Ah, well spotted, Sergeant,' he said. 'We'll make a detective of you yet. I turned on the gaslight there and then because it occurred to me that the recently departed Eliza had aged at least eight years. There stood the phantasm, a dripping wet girl of sixteen who had been hired by Goodrich-Freer for the occasion. Turned out that the girl doubled for any female corpse from poor Eliza to Boadicea.'

'That's appalling,' Crawford said.

'That's a fraudulent medium,' Reid shrugged. 'I spent the rest of the evening trying to stop Mr and Mrs Mumler from strangling Goodrich-Freer and her stooge. I arrested the pair of them – the mediums, not the Mumlers – but they were only done for fraud and false pretences. I'd have thrown the book at them.'

'And Eliza herself?'

Reid shook his head. 'We never found her body.' He downed his drink. 'And that doesn't sit well with me, Andrew; not well at all. So, to get back to Fazakerley and Principal, that's what we're looking at, somebody like the Mumlers, who has reason to detest mediums. Somebody with the will and the ability to do something about it. Somebody who was not stopped by a nosy policeman in time.'

The two men looked at each other as the clock chimed the hour on the mantelpiece.

'Well, you're a nosy policeman, Andrew,' Reid said. 'Time you did something about it.'

'Thomas?'

There was a serious look on Margaret Murray's face. And to the proprietor of the Jeremy Bentham, a beckoning finger always provoked a response; it usually meant trouble.

'Anything amiss, Prof?' When you are the purveyor of delicacies to the great and good of Bloomsbury, it could be *anything*. Thomas had had to clear the dining room on the Wednesday of the previous week when a reader in Pure Mathematics and a professor in the new department of Quantum Physics had had a knock-down, drag-out fight over whether the sugar cube was or was not the perfect way to sweeten tea. So as he approached Margaret Murray's table, he had an open mind as to what might come next.

'No, no,' she assured him. 'But . . . have you a moment?'

Thomas looked around. The Girls Who Did were beavering away and the Linguistics Faculty from the college seemed immersed in whatever mumbo-jumbo only they understood, so he sat down.

'You know,' she said, 'that I occasionally get myself involved in what, for want of a better word, the world at large might call skulduggery?' It was not so much a question as a statement of fact.

'Hmm,' he said, non-committally.

'Well, you will also have noticed that I am barely five feet tall and my name is rarely mentioned in circles where self-defence is called for.'

'Hmm.' Thomas was still playing things carefully.

'I needs must talk to some people tonight, not far from here.'

'You want some company, Prof?' He was beginning to catch the archaeologist's drift.

'Not per se, no,' she said. 'Fond of you as I assuredly am. I wondered . . . can you be my shadow? Sort of hover, when I have left my rendezvous? I have a feeling that I am going to meet a murderer, if not tonight, then soon, and I would rather that didn't happen in a dark corner of Bermondsey.'

'Blimey, Prof,' Thomas frowned. 'Perhaps you shouldn't go . . .'

'Probably not,' Margaret said. 'But the alternative is to send Sergeant Crawford and I'm not sure a full-blown police enquiry will yield the kind of information I'm after.'

'Well, then, Prof,' Thomas smiled. 'Shadow it is.'

Olivia Bentwood was as waspish as ever. She didn't see why, she told the others at the Circle, that now that dear Muriel had joined the choir invisible, that she, Olivia, should not assume her mantle. Ojigkwanong was metaphorically champing at his rawhide bit to deliver snippets from the Great Beyond, not to mention Olivia's mother, a force to be reckoned with, if the rumours still whispered around Bermondsey were even half true. Olivia Bentwood drew herself up and her stays creaked a warning.

'After all,' she said, finishing the argument as far as she was concerned, 'I have a certain rapport with the Other Side.' She let her eyelids quiver briefly as her pupils rolled up into her head. 'And my dear mother, of course, is often in touch.'

'With respect, Olivia,' Agatha Dunwoody said, 'we need a professional. A known clairvoyant would lift all our spirits, if I may be light-hearted for a moment.'

'Agatha's right, Olivia,' Mortimer chimed in. 'Someone with a proven record. Someone on the world stage.'

'They're all dead,' George Boothby grunted. 'Or exposed as frauds, or both.'

'Those wretched people in the Society for Psychical Research,' Olivia fumed. 'Killjoys all.'

There were murmurs all round. It wasn't often that the Bermondsey Spiritualist Circle were in agreement, but this was one of those times.

'Christina.' Olivia rounded on the little woman. 'You're very quiet tonight. Have you no views?'

'I . . .'

'No, I thought not.'

'We mustn't be discouraged, everybody,' Robert Grimes chipped in. 'What happened to Muriel is unfortunate, but life and death have to go on.'

'What about Eusapia Palladino?' the crimson-faced colonel suggested.

'An Italian peasant?' Olivia bridled. 'I hardly think so.'

'Oh, don't be such a snob, Olivia,' Grimes chided.

'Eusapia Palladino is the last woman standing,' Mortimer pointed out. 'No one has ever caught her out in trickery. And, who knows, she may be able to shed some light on what happened to poor Muriel.'

'She drowned, Mortimer,' Olivia snapped. 'It could happen to any one of us.'

'Not in our mulligatawny soup, though, surely?' The colonel had been a stickler on the square and was a stickler still.

'Perhaps not in your imperialist circles,' Olivia came back at him. 'But this is Bermondsey, not some ghastly hill station in India. Anything is possible. All of us in this Circle should appreciate that. And anyway, you know how Muriel was, all that eye-rolling and holding her breath. She could have drowned in a cup of tea if she was taken like that at the wrong time.'

'I've known some delightful hill stations,' Margaret said, speaking for the first time, and Robert Grimes stifled a guffaw. 'But on a more serious note, I have it on good authority that Muriel was murdered.'

She looked around the room at the wide eyes and gaping mouths.

'What "good authority"?' General Boothby was the first to speak.

'Oh, I couldn't possibly divulge.'

'Henrietta,' Mortimer said quietly, 'you can't possibly drop a bombshell like that and then say nothing.'

'Let's just say,' Margaret said, 'that I am talking about Scotland Yard.'

'You clearly have hidden depths, Miss Plinlimmon,' Olivia Bentwood bridled. After that, the silence in the room was deafening.

'Tell me, Henrietta,' Boothby leaned closer to her. 'Do your good authorities have a name? What do the police say? Someone in the frame?'

Margaret kept them all guessing, the ticking of the grandmother sounding like the Approach of Menace. 'As a matter of fact, they do,' she said, smiling at them all.

Olivia was about to savage the little archaeologist, when Agatha Dunwoody suddenly changed the subject altogether. 'We need to stick to the purpose of our Circle. We owe it to poor Muriel, however she left this vale of tears. We should have a vote. This Circle proposes that we contact Miss Palladino and invite her to attend a séance at her earliest convenience.'

'Seconded,' Mortimer chimed in.

'May I make a second proposal?' Margaret asked. 'Since I do happen to know both Oliver Lodge and Arthur Conan Doyle, might I write to Miss Palladino?'

'Seconded,' Mortimer said.

'You can't "second" more than once in one evening, Mortimer!' Olivia snapped.

'I think that would be excellent, Henrietta,' Agatha smiled. 'Thank you so much.'

When all votes were taken, all hands except Olivia's reached skywards.

'That's it, then.' General Boothby said, but Margaret couldn't help but notice that he patted her thigh rather than his own and she moved subtly away.

The nearest port in a potential storm for Margaret was Robert Grimes. He stood furthest away from the general, which was a good start, and he had less of the old lecher about him. Conversations were breaking out in the sitting room as Agatha Dunwoody was handing out the pastries. She may have just dropped a mortar, but Margaret didn't want to be the first to leave.

'Mr Grimes,' she smiled up at him. 'I've been meaning to ask how you came to join the Circle.'

'My local, I suppose,' he said. 'I used to attend Finsbury Park, but it all got a bit tame.'

'Excitement?' She took up the theme. 'Is that what attracted you to Spiritualism?'

'I suppose so, yes. It all goes back to when I was a lad.'

Margaret suppressed a laugh. Robert Grimes was still a lad, not that much older than her students at college. 'Tell me about it,' she said, keeping a weather eye open for a general with wandering hands.

'Oh.' They sat on the sofa, side by side. 'I'd have been about twelve, I suppose. A relative took me. He said – and I've never forgotten it – "Do you want to see a ghost, Robbie?"'

'And did you?'

'Did I want to? Or did I see one?'

'Either,' Margaret chuckled.

'I wanted to, yes. I was brought up on Dickens – Marley, Christmas Past, all that sort of thing. So we went along.'

'Was it usual for one so young to attend a séance?'

'I suppose not,' he laughed. 'But the Grimeses are an unusual family. It was raining, I remember. And it was a Friday.'

'Where was this?'

'Walthamstow – don't ask me why. We all sat round an oval table and it was dark. The curtains were thick and closed. There was no fire, even though it was winter and I remember shivering. I'd never seen a glass moving before, but it did that night. We all placed a finger on the upturned stem and when the medium – a terrifying old bag . . . er . . . lady as it seems to me now –

asked the time-honoured question "Is anybody there?" the thing
slid to "Yes".'

Margaret winked at him. 'It would have put you all in a pickle
had it said "No", wouldn't it?'

Grimes laughed. 'I wasn't as cynical then, Henrietta,' he said.
'In fact, I believed that everything I heard and saw that night
was real.'

'And what did you hear?' she asked. 'What did you see?'

'Whatever it was moving that glass had a message from
beyond,' he told her. 'A message that seemed directed at me.'

'At you?' Margaret frowned.

'The glass spelled out "Boy".'

'And what did the message say?'

'Nothing. Not at first. The glass began to spell out a word,
but it didn't make sense. Then, the thing went berserk. It scraped
across that table with a screech that froze my blood. It was
moving so fast. And then, it shattered.'

'Of its own volition?' Margaret was sceptical.

'Yes. No one was touching it at that stage and it just
fragmented, then and there.'

'What happened next?'

'Somebody screamed; I don't know who. That's when it
started.' Suddenly, the carefree young man with the debonair
approach to life became still, his face a mask of memory.

'What, Mr Grimes?' Margaret asked. 'What started?'

He was staring into the middle distance. Wherever he was
at that moment, it was not in Agatha Dunwoody's parlour at
Thirty-One Cavendish Street. 'The voice,' he said softly. 'I'll
never forget the voice. I couldn't tell where it was coming from
either. It seemed to echo around the room as if its owner were
moving about, moving among us.'

'What did it say?'

'"No. No. No." Over and over again. And then, there was a
choking sound and a laugh.' Grimes shuddered. 'I'm sorry,
Henrietta,' he said, back from wherever he had been. 'That laugh
was how I imagine the devil to sound, mocking us all the way
from hell.'

'You had quite an imagination,' she said softly, 'for a twelve
year old. Alexander the Great was twelve, allegedly, when he

first rode Bucephalus and his father told him to find a kingdom big enough for him because Macedonia was too small. He went on to conquer a third of the known world.'

'I'm not sure,' Grimes was smiling again, 'that the Stock Exchange can quite compare with that.'

'Was there anything else that night?' Margaret asked.

'An intense cold,' Grimes remembered. 'I told you the room was cold anyway, but we could suddenly see our breath, as though we were outside on a frozen winter's night. And there were the words.'

'The words?'

'I can only describe it as a miasma, a glowing light or series of lights, hovering over our heads. It moved to the far wall and stayed there, curling like mist over a river. Then it vanished.'

'And the words?' Margaret was none the wiser.

'Well, the session ended there. There were protests, but the hostess whose house it was, was thoroughly rattled by these goings-on and lit the lamps. There, on the wall where the mist had hovered were the words "Look at me".'

Margaret frowned. 'Do you remember, Mr Grimes, if this was in handwriting? A scrawl?'

'Yes, very untidy,' he nodded.

'As if someone had done it in a hurry before the lamps were lit?'

Grimes laughed. 'I know, I know,' he said. 'In the years since then, I've tried to rationalize the whole thing. I've been to séances without number trying to recreate the setting, to witness the same thing. I never have.'

Margaret smiled. 'Could it be,' she asked him, 'that it was just part of your childhood that you never fully understood? A memory that has grown out of all proportion, like Alice when she was ten feet tall?'

'Yes,' Grimes said, wistfully. 'Yes, I suppose it was something like that.'

SIX

I t was more like an echo than anything else, no more than a whisper on the wet pavements. It had been raining while the Bermondsey Circle had been holding forth and, at this hour, the hansoms were getting to be few and far between, and so although the night was now fine and Margaret was a walker of some repute, over hill, dale and Egyptian sand, she suddenly felt safer in the leather-scented interior of a cab than in the open. She knew that when she reached the end of Gower Street, somewhere in the Bloomsbury darkness, Thomas had promised that he would be her shadow. He had wanted to be waiting outside the Dunwoody residence, but for now, Margaret didn't want to tip her hand too obviously. So she had promised him she would hail a cab as soon as possible and that she would alight precisely at the corner of Gower Street and Torrington Place, near enough to home to make it convenient if no attack took place, far enough away to give any would-be assailant time to make their move. Thomas was unhappy about the whole shenanigans, as he told her, but what the Prof wanted, the Prof got and so he waited in a doorway with his eyes peeled in the gloom.

The black bulk of University College loomed over Gower Street along with the outlines of the other buildings Margaret knew so well. The lamplighter had been and gone and the streets glistened with the memory of the spring rain which had left the air smelling sweetly of distant countryside. It was the merest glimmer, but something pale suddenly flashed over her left shoulder.

'Miss Plinlimmon . . .' was all she heard before there was a crunch and a squawk. She spun round to see Thomas holding a man up against a wall, the man's arm wrenched painfully behind his back, his face in much closer proximity to the grimy London brick than was strictly comfortable.

'I'll Miss Plinlimmon you, sunshine!' Thomas growled. He lashed out with his left boot and the man crumpled to the pavement. 'Oops,' he said. 'How careless of me.' And he rested the same boot on the man's head.

'Well, well, Mr Mortimer,' Margaret said. 'I must admit, I wasn't expecting you. Now, Thomas, don't hurt him. Is there somewhere we can talk?'

'The Jeremy B's quiet this time of night,' the proprietor said, hauling Mortimer upright, 'seeing as how it's well past ten o'clock and I've got the only key. But don't you want this piece of wossname round the police station?'

'Possibly,' Margaret said. 'But I'd like some answers first.'

'You have absolutely no right to do this!' Mortimer snapped.

'Citizen's arrest, mate,' Thomas said, clicking closed the Hiatt handcuffs to the leg of Mortimer's chair. 'Just don't ask where I got these.'

The three of them were sitting in the Jeremy Bentham. The shutters were closed and a solitary candle burned on the table.

'Why did you follow me?' Margaret asked the handcuffed man.

'Because I believed you are not quite what you seem,' he told her.

'Are any of us?' she asked. 'You, for instance, are not called Mortimer, are you?'

'No,' he admitted, and the faux-Cockney had gone. 'I am Archie Flambard. May I reach into my pocket?'

'Slowly and carefully,' Thomas said.

'My card.' Flambard flourished it and Margaret read it.

'The Society for Psychical Research,' she said. 'You're a ghost hunter.'

'We in the Society prefer the term occult investigator,' he said.

'A rose by any other name, Mr Flambard,' she said, leaning back. 'You are in the Bermondsey Circle to expose frauds.'

'They're all frauds.' He leaned back too, as far as the handcuffs would let him. 'Delusional people obsessed with nonsense. Trust me, there are no such things as spirits.'

Margaret smiled. 'You have not stood in a pharaoh's tomb in the Valley of the Kings,' she said.

'Granted,' Flambard agreed, 'but these people are obsessed.

I have no problem with that. My quarrel is with those charlatans who make money out of others' gullibility.'

'Muriel Fazakerley,' Margaret said.

'I was on to her and was about to expose her when she died. And you don't know what a relief it is to use that word instead of the silly euphemisms of the Circle – passed over, crossed the Great Divide, et cetera, et cetera.'

'It is the *manner* of her passing that concerns us, Mr Flambard.'

'Clearly,' he nodded, 'but one correct name deserves another. I took you for another occult investigator, but clearly you are something more.'

'I am Margaret Murray,' she said, 'lecturer in Archaeology at University College around the corner. This is Thomas.'

Flambard nodded at the man who had manhandled him; introductions were all well and good, but the two would never be friends.

'When did you see Muriel last?' Margaret asked.

'The day she died,' Flambard said. 'And I realize that that fact alone darkens my reputation. I needed to find out *exactly* what her modus operandi was. I visited her home, took the opportunity to find the usual apparatus. Without wishing to speak *too* ill of the dead, Muriel Fazakerley was not exactly top-notch. Eusapia Palladino, now – that's a different matter. That's why I pushed for the Circle to invite her. She won't come cheap, of course, but it would be a huge feather in my cap to catch her in flagrante, as it were.'

'What time did you leave Muriel?' Margaret asked.

'Ooh, let me see, it would be about eight o'clock. I felt I had enough information to put before the Circle at the next meeting and she had a private sitting.'

'A sitting?' Margaret echoed. 'Did she say who?'

'No.' Flambard tried to put his hand to his forehead to aid his memory but was cut off short as the handcuffs did their work. 'But it was someone she didn't like.'

'From the Circle?' Margaret checked.

Flambard shrugged. 'Who knows? I *do* know that they all had private, one-to-one sittings from time to time. General Boothby in particular.'

He raised his handcuffed arm again, rubbing at the wrist with his free hand. 'Look, could we do something about this? It's deuced uncomfortable.'

'That's the idea,' Thomas said. 'Prof?'

'Unshackle him, Thomas,' Margaret said. 'We probably owe Mr Flambard the benefit of the doubt.'

Thomas did the honours with a flick of his key.

'You were about to tell us about General Boothby.'

'Look him up in the *Gazette*,' Flambard shrugged, 'and that will tell you very little. Commissioned in the Artillery, made his name in the Second Afghan War. The rest of his career was all about contacts, as these things usually are. It's what the *Gazette* doesn't say that's interesting.'

Margaret and Thomas leaned in closer, their faces lit eerily from below by the candlelight.

'Rather like poor mediums,' Flambard said, 'the general has wandering hands.'

'Is there a Mrs Boothby?' Margaret asked.

'There was, but she left him back in '93. It was all hushed up, of course. Only the *Manchester Guardian* tried to run an exposé but, as you know, no one takes any notice of provincial newspapers.' Flambard lowered his voice. 'There was talk of dalliance with the Duchess of Buccleuch.'

Margaret and Thomas looked at each other.

'More,' Flambard was in his element, 'there was talk of dalliance with the duchess and a stable-boy – I am assuming on the same occasion or occasions, but I have not been able to find out his name or the precise details. However, Lady Boothby filed for divorce at once and polite society turned its back. Oh, there'd be no more promotions for him, of course, but he'd more or less retired anyway. And the pension of a brigadier is hardly to be sneezed at. The exit of Lady Boothby merely gave the man carte blanche to let his hands wander further.'

'How far?' Thomas felt it was his place to ask, rather than embarrass the professor.

'Most of the way up Duke Street, at least. He joined three Spiritualist Circles before Bermondsey in the hope of getting lucky.'

'And you believe he "got lucky" with Muriel Fazakerley?'

'I believe he wanted to,' Flambard said. 'As far as I could tell, he had no affinity with the Other Side at all. He just enjoyed pressing himself between two women; the traditional seating arrangement of a séance was perfect for him.'

'So he may have been Muriel's visitor?' Margaret persisted.

'He may. Then again, it could have been Olivia Bentwood.'

'Ah,' Margaret nodded. 'Almost literally the elephant in the room.'

'You will have noticed, Margaret, that Olivia Bentwood is a most objectionable woman.'

'I don't judge,' the archaeologist said, primly, at which Thomas snorted and quickly turned it into a cough.

'She is not only terminally bossy, but was jealous of Muriel. Saw herself as a conduit to the Hereafter.'

'Wouldn't Muriel have been suspicious of both of them?' Margaret asked. 'Boothby and Bentwood?'

'Quite possibly,' Flambard nodded, 'but never underestimate the arrogance of a medium, Dr Murray, even an average one like Madame Ankhara. She would have assumed, even against all common sense as we would see it, that Mrs Bentwood had come to hear her spout her rubbish for the good of her soul, or whatever. And of course, General Boothby admitted in front of all of us that he had often paid poor Muriel for her favours.' He glanced at Margaret Murray to see if she were offended, not realizing that offending her was next to impossible.

'And how do you explain the feather?' Margaret looked at the man.

'The what?'

'A black feather found in the poor woman's mouth,' she told him. 'Placed there, I have no doubt, by the murderer.'

'Olivia Bentwood's spirit guide!' Flambard clicked his fingers. 'Ojigkwanong wears feathers.'

'You've seen him?' Thomas sat open-mouthed.

'Of course not. He's a figment of Olivia's warped imagination. She's suitably vague in her description of him, of course. He's anything from a Seminole from the swamps of Florida to a Yankton Sioux from the great plains. Recollections vary.'

'Indeed they do,' Margaret sighed. 'But even if Ojigkwanong is a genuine manifestation, I doubt he is able to leave mementoes at scenes of crime.'

'I'm glad we agree on that,' Flambard said.

'Thomas.' The archaeologist smiled at her right-hand man. 'Could you rustle us up a pot of tea and perhaps a rudimentary breakfast? I would very much like Mr Flambard to tell us about the rest of the Bermondsey Circle and I fear it may be rather a long night.'

The rain of earlier had passed but in Jamaica Road, Bermondsey, under the trees which overhung the road from the park, the pavements were still damp. The patrolling policeman, making his way at a stately two and a half miles an hour and looking forward more and more with every step to his midnight cup of tea, was therefore somewhat surprised to see a heap of bundled clothing against the railings separating the road from the shrubs which marked the edge of King's Stairs Gardens. Vagrants were nothing new. Working girls were ten a penny – he thought back to his youth when that was almost literally true with some regret. But neither would choose to lie out on a pavement, albeit poorly lit, in such a damp spot. The gardens and the park further down the road both had benches and dry spaces under the packed rhododendrons where a relatively pleasant night's sleep was to be had. He slowed his pace a little as he got closer, then put out a tentative toe.

Constable Arnold Boggs had not come to the end of a long if not very exciting career by meeting trouble halfway. If this pile of jumbled fabric covered something dead, he would walk on and leave it for someone else to discover. After all, a stiff wasn't going to get that much stiffer if it had to wait a while. If it covered something alive, the decision was even simpler. And he tried that from the outset.

'Move along, there,' he said, making the nudge more of a kick. 'Move along, there, missus. This is no place to take a nap.'

Arnold Boggs was a man of few ideas, but they were firmly entrenched in his head and he shared them wholeheartedly with his wife of many years whom he referred to at all times and often to her face as Mrs Boggs. They believed that the country was Going To The Dogs. That in general terms, most people were No Better Than They Should Be. The streets were full of garbage both animate and inanimate. The policeman shook his head and almost spoke aloud as if Mrs Boggs was standing at his elbow. Here was an Unfortunate who had taken a drop too much. He and Mrs Boggs had a nice bottle of sherry in every year for Christmas, but other than that, they abstained. Unlike this one here. He prodded her again with his toe and was just deciding that he could walk on under the 'stiff not getting appreciably stiffer' rule, when the pile of clothing gave a groan and turned over, her face fitfully illuminated by the policeman's bullseye lantern.

He bent down. His worst nightmare lay at his feet. Not a drunk. Not a corpse. A woman who seemed to be quite seriously injured, but still alive. Muttering imprecations, he fished out his whistle, disillusioned police constables for the use of, and sent its sharp blasts echoing across the empty park and into the teeming streets at his back.

The woman, dimly aware that help was at hand, let her head flop back and darkness overtake her. She wasn't quite sure what had happened, but it was all going to be all right now. The golden clouds which had parted above her head to reveal her parents, brother and sister and – for some unfathomable reason – next door's late dog, closed up again, the heavenly choirs became quieter and soon, if she could currently hear anything at all, Christina Plunkett was rocked on the waves of running feet, shouts and bells that betokened that London's finest were on their way.

'So,' Margaret put her feet up on the sofa now that she, Flambard and Thomas had retired to the softer seats reserved for the very few, 'Colonel Carruthers.'

'Eddie Carruthers is a slave to the bottle,' Flambard told her, helping himself to another round of Thomas's toast.

'No!' Margaret feigned horror and surprise, though she had noticed in the first few minutes of being in the man's company that it would be unwise to go near him with a naked flame.

'He didn't get that high colour by serving in India. In fact, as far as my researches have gone, the furthest east he has been is Colchester.'

'Did he see Muriel privately?'

'I get the impression not, though I could be wrong.'

'I had him down as a rather shy, sweet man, a bit of a simple soul,' Margaret said. 'I was quietly astonished that he'd reached the rank he has. I always assume colonels had to have a certain steel about them.'

'Pay Corps,' Flambard said in a hail of crumbs. 'Man's a glorified accountant.'

'The demon drink, though,' Margaret said. 'We all know how it can change a man.'

'It can,' Thomas chimed in. 'I remember a vicar back when I was first . . .' he glanced under his eyelashes at Margaret. His past wasn't all something he would wish to share. 'First in service.' That would do. 'And he used to hit the old communion wine something chronic. In the end, he saw things crawling up the vestry walls and they had to put him away. Took four of them in the end, just to hold him down.' He sighed, far away and long ago. 'The good old days.'

'Agatha Dunwoody.' Margaret moved the conversation on.

'Sweet enough old girl now,' Flambard said, 'but in her youth, a little light of finger.'

'Oh?'

'She married well – Alexander Dunwoody, of Dunwoody, Dunwoody, Pettigrew and Dunwoody – but after the birth of her first child, she became unhinged. Some women do, apparently. It's all part of the human condition. She was caught shop-lifting in Harrods.'

'No rubbish, then,' Thomas commented.

'Again, as with Boothby, it was kept out of the papers, even when she did it several times more – Liberty's, I believe.'

'Tut, tut,' Thomas shook his head. 'Her standards were slipping. Much more of this and it'll be Isaac's Old Clo' Emporium in the Balls Pond Road.'

The others ignored him.

'Dunwoody stepped in, as only lawyers can, and made it all go away.'

'That's a far cry from murder, though, isn't it?'

'It is,' Flambard agreed, 'but you must remember, Dr Murray, that my brief, as given to me by the Society for Psychical Research, is to expose fraud, not find murderers.' He smiled wryly. 'I leave that to finer minds.'

'Robert Grimes.' Margaret was stirring her second cup of tea.

'Ah,' Flambard sat up. 'Now, this one is interesting. What do you make of him?'

'I was a little surprised to see him there,' Margaret said. 'He's by far the youngest of the Circle and rather flippant, I'd say.'

'So would I,' Flambard agreed, 'To the extent that I wondered whether he might not be another occult investigator – strictly amateur, of course.'

'Of course.'

'He seems to be something in the City – and not short of a bob or two. As for his interest in the Other Side, I have no idea. I came to the conclusion that he was in it for the laughs. There is one thing that's slightly odd.'

'Say on.'

'Well, an archaeologist like you must spend many a happy hour rummaging about in the Record Office, public museums and the like.'

'I do,' Margaret agreed.

'Well, I don't. I find family trees utterly bewildering. So, it took me several weeks to track down young Grimes's antecedents.'

'And?'

'Well, I don't know how much this sort of thing runs in families,' Flambard said, 'but Grimes had an uncle who was hanged for murder.'

'The hanged man.' Margaret remembered the tarot card at the murder scene of Evadne Principal.

'The same,' Flambard said. 'Now, don't tell me you read the cards, Dr Murray.' He was chuckling.

'As the Bard reminds us, Mr Flambard,' she said, 'there are more things in heaven and earth . . .'

'Yes, well,' Flambard scowled. 'William Shakespeare would never have been allowed into the Society for Psychical Research, I can tell you – far too gullible. Ghosts and ghoulies, floating daggers and lions whelping in the streets – what a load of rubbish!'

'Do you have the details of the Grimes murder?' Margaret asked.

'Of course,' Flambard bridled. 'I may not *enjoy* archives, Dr Murray, but I *do* get results. Gregory Grimes was a confidence trickster, helping himself to other people's money. He was too cocky by half and one of his victims threatened to expose him. Her name, if memory serves, was Rachael Cadman – the

Worcestershire Cadmen, several times removed. She had it out with him, and he killed her.'

'Do we know how?' Margaret asked.

'Stoved in her head with a blunt object they never found.'

'Where and when was this?'

'The papers were full of the war at the time. Mafeking was on every page. The Grimes case was consigned to the small print. The Billingtons made a killing, of course, as always.'

'Goes with the territory,' Thomas growled. Some of his closest friends had had narrow misses with the Billington family.

'As to where,' Flambard went on, 'I believe it was Sydenham. Specifically in Miss Cadman's front parlour.'

A silence descended.

'And last,' Margaret broke it, 'and perhaps least of the Bermondsey Circle, Christina Plunkett.'

It was just a short drive in the ambulance to Guy's Hospital from Christina Plunkett's temporary resting place in Jamaica Road. A constable ran into the hallway in advance of the stretcher, calling for help, and soon the nurses and one rather disgruntled doctor surrounded the little woman, who was by now deeply unconscious. The doctor didn't bother even to remove his coat, but looked down from the lofty height of one who knew that his station in life did not require him to deal with drunken prostitutes.

'Dead,' he barked. He jabbed a thumb over his shoulder. 'Mortuary.'

The police constable at the head end of the stretcher looked furtive. He wasn't a doctor, he would be the first to admit, but he had been a stretcher bearer in Africa in the late, Great War and knew a dead person from a live one and this woman was definitely alive. She was actually moving, something which he had always considered to be something of a decider in such matters. His oppo at the feet end hefted the weight of the woman and set off in the direction of the mortuary, as designated by the signs on the wall and the black arrows on the floor.

'No, Jim,' the ex-stretcher bearer said. 'She's not dead.'

The other constable looked over his shoulder. 'Doc says she is,' and set off again, almost dragging his colleague along behind in his zeal to get rid of this job and go on to something more congenial, known colloquially as Mrs Maw, the landlady of the Havelock Arms just across the railway line from where he was standing, if he popped out the back way, through the mortuary exit. He tugged at the stretcher again. He could almost feel the compliant weight of Mrs Maw wrapped around him and he was in a hurry.

'But she *isn't!*' Constable Michael Crawford had not reached the exalted heights of his cousin Andrew, nor had he made an advantageous marriage. He didn't have his cousin's brains, or his looks. In fact, the family always went a little misty eyed when comparing the two, taking into account Michael's unfortunate squint and his habit of passing wind when stressed, but they all had to agree that they had one thing in common. Once they had decided on something, they were like the proverbial ox in the furrow. Constable Crawford had decided that this woman was not going to the mortuary and he spread his feet and hung back accordingly.

A nurse hurrying past with a bedpan stopped by the bickering pair. 'Is there a problem?' she asked, in the tones of someone who doesn't want to get involved any more than she had to be.

'No,' the foot-end policeman said, tugging.

'Yes,' Crawford said. 'This woman isn't dead.'

The nurse glanced down. 'No,' she said, crisply. 'Of course she isn't. Why are you arguing? She has her eyes open, for heaven's sake.'

The foot-end constable was dubious. He had seen more corpses than many people had had hot dinners and as many of them had had their eyes open as shut. 'Means nothing,' he said.

'It does when she's blinking,' the nurse said, passing the bedpan to a passing porter. 'Get her on to a bed, quickly.' She looked around and saw a vacant one in a corner. 'Look, over there.' She bent to the woman who was starting to look rather frantic, the smell of carbolic and the random screams of the hospital's night-time denizens beginning to pierce the mist of her injuries.

Constable Crawford, suddenly the important one with the head end, led the way, and Christina Plunkett was placed carefully on the bed where she relaxed, closing her eyes again with a sigh. There was something about the four-square cast iron of the frame and the flock of the mattress that made her feel that perhaps, after all, she wouldn't be passing over any time soon.

The nurse bustled in between the constables and the bed, shooing them away as only a nurse can. Constable Crawford turned to the woman for one last look. It wasn't every day you could tell yourself you had prevented someone making a trip to the morgue. He took in the diminutive stature, the wildish hair, the kindly face and he froze. He tapped the nurse on the arm.

'Yes?' She was now in charge and wanted him to know it.

'Is there a bag or anything under the blanket?' He knew he was a policeman, but even so, rummaging in a lady's doings seemed a little too familiar.

The nurse looked and shook her head. She hated these cases. She had seen too many women come in with no name and no home and sadly, all too often, nothing to put on their grave.

Constable Michael Crawford felt his heart beating in his throat. He had been at his cousin's wedding and, although it was a few years ago now, he thought he knew this woman, one of the honoured guests. This was Dr Margaret Murray, or he was a Dutchman.

Archie Flambard had not been able to find out anything to Christina Plunkett's detriment, much to his annoyance. He liked to describe himself as someone who spoke as he found, called a spade a spade and similar clichés, but the truth was sometimes almost too boring for words. Her parents and a couple of siblings were dead, something that she had in common with a large majority. She had a small but adequate income from canny invest-ments by a grandfather, so she lived comfortably enough, though not in splendour. Her maid, who came in daily, either knew nothing bad about her or was above reproach when it came to taking bribes. In short, Christina Plunkett might very well have been the only member of the Bermondsey Spiritualist Circle who had a spotless record. Archie Flambard chewed a nail and hunched forward over the table, annoyed at his failure.

'Some people are just . . . good people,' Thomas said, though in his life he could think of few to whom that would apply and one of them was sitting right there.

'He's quite right, Mr Flambard,' Margaret added. 'It is bad research to look for something until you find it. You must approach this kind of thing with an open mind and no end in view for it to be relevant.'

Flambard looked unimpressed. That didn't sound like much fun to him.

'When I met Miss Plunkett, I must say I immediately felt she was a very nice woman. She shone as the best of the whole Circle. Friendly. Open.' She shrugged and turned to Thomas with a grin. 'And, following the principle of *similia similibus curentur*, you would agree that she has to be very pleasant, as she and I could be sisters.'

Thomas nodded wisely, as he often did when in Margaret Murray's company. He had learned a lot that way.

Archie Flambard agreed. 'You certainly do have more than a passing resemblance,' he said. He lifted the lid of the teapot and peered in. 'I could squeeze another cup out of this, Thomas,' he said, 'but . . .'

'I'll go and make some fresh.' Hospitality had not always been Thomas's strong suit, but he found it suited him these days and it was good to him. 'Anyone got any room for more toast? A muffin?'

His guests both shook their heads.

'I've got gentleman's relish.'

'Oh, go on, then,' Margaret said, turning to Flambard. 'He makes his own, you know. Pounds the anchovies and everything, from scratch. He's such a stickler.'

They sat in silence for a while. Margaret was not impressed with Archie Flambard, either as a researcher or a person. He had lied to her, which she found somewhat unappealing, conveniently forgetting that she had done just the same. But his research – woeful. Wrong technique and dubious results. But at least she could cross him off the list of suspects. Possibly.

There had been quite a lot of discussion in the Crawford household about the telephone. Of course, they had to have one, Angela knew that. Although Andrew was currently only a sergeant, she knew he was destined for greater things. But she thought it was rather common to have it anywhere other than in the study, where men spent their time, at least in the world in which she had grown up. He, quite sensibly as far as he could tell, pointed out that emergencies seldom happened when a gentleman was taking his ease with brandy and a cigar after dinner. They happened in the early hours, when he was just turning over and having a good scratch before getting up to face the day. They happened when everyone with any sense was fast asleep. So he wanted to have it by the bed. The children and the servants, after all, slept a whole floor above, so it wasn't as if the bell would disturb anyone but them. And if Angela found it disturbing, she could always wear earplugs. So, the bedroom it was.

Andrew Crawford was in the middle of a very complex dream when the bells started to ring. He couldn't work out why, in the middle of a swim in the Thames accompanied by several mermaids, some cows and a hippopotamus, there should be bells, but there were and very persistent ones too. Then, one of the mermaids poked him in the back and shouted at him, though he couldn't make out the words. It was probably because she was playing a tenor saxophone at the time. Then, suddenly, like an explosion, everything was clear and he was sitting up, the earpiece to his ear, the mouthpiece in the general position of his mouth.

'Hello?' He knew he should say his name, but couldn't quite call it to mind. 'Hello?'

'Andrew?' The voice was familiar but he couldn't place it. 'Andrew, it's me, Michael.' The caller waited for recognition but with a sigh realized there would be none. 'Michael. Michael Crawford. Your cousin. Michael.'

'Oh. Michael. Of course. Umm . . . how are you?' Crawford was looking around frantically for his pocket watch, for a candle, for anything to give him some kind of grounding. Just knowing what time it was would help enormously.

'Sorry to ring so late.'

Ah, that was something. At least they hadn't overslept.

'But I thought I should let you know, because she doesn't have any identification on her, so we don't know who to contact.'

No. This wasn't helping. They seemed to have gone back to square one. Should he know what this was all about? He hadn't seen his cousin since the wedding, but he knew that family feuds could rumble on unnoticed for years, so perhaps . . .

'Then I remembered you were on the phone.'

'Right. So you have rung me to say . . .'

'There's no easy way to tell you.'

'Michael.' Crawford had heard his cousin prevaricate for hours and decided it was time for some straight talking. 'Easy or hard, please tell me your news. If it's something to do with the family, tomorrow will do. If it's anything else, spit it out, man.' He was aware that Angela was growing somewhat restive and he could see a night or two in the dressing room in his immediate future.

'It's Miss Murray. From your wedding. She's in Guy's Hospital not expected to live through the night. I thought you'd want to know. Andrew? Andrew?' Michael Crawford looked at the earpiece of the phone he was using on the desk at the Walworth Police Station, as if it could tell him where his cousin had gone. But it was mute and, eventually, he hung it respectfully back on its hook. He wished he had been able to do more, but he had done his best and, as his and Andrew's old granny used to say, you can't do more than your best.

With a nod to the desk sergeant, Police Constable Crawford stepped out into the Bermondsey night, to patrol until dawn at the regulation two and a half miles an hour, to carry on doing his best.

SEVEN

As Andrew Crawford pulled on his clothes, he mulled over what to tell Angela. She was, after all, in a delicate condition and there was no need to upset her. On the other hand, she had known and loved Margaret Murray since before they even met, so she really should be told. As he knotted his tie, he came to a decision. If she was awake, he would tell her now. If she was asleep, then sufficient unto the day was the evil thereof. Booted and suited, he peeped round the bedroom door and listened. Angela's breathing came soft and regular, with the little snore every now and again that was endearing before midnight, hell after three. He decided to let sleeping dogs lie, with no offence intended to his beautiful wife; he had a full night ahead of him and, as he ran as lightly as he could down the stairs, he planned out his best itinerary. He should really go as soon as he could to Guy's, but in some ways he thought that was presumptuous. Although he and Margaret were friends, he knew she had people much more precious in her life and he wouldn't want to intrude on what may be a painful time. He could hardly knock up Flinders Petrie and, by definition, his wife. Scuttlebutt had it that Mrs Petrie was an understanding soul, but how understanding would any woman be if she were to be awoken in the middle of the night to be told that her husband's occasional bedfellow was lying fatally injured in hospital? Then there was the guilt aspect. It was clear that Margaret had been attacked after the meeting of the Bermondsey Spiritualist Circle and although he comforted himself with the knowledge that there would have been no stopping her and he had not coerced her in any way, it still felt as if it was his fault. That would be a hard one to live with. Standing irresolute on the pavement, a sudden idea came to Detective Sergeant Crawford – Thomas would know what to do. He had known Margaret Murray longer than anyone, and who knew what he had gleaned about her family and private life in their late-night musings over coffee after the Jeremy Bentham had closed? And in any event, she would be pleased to see him, should Michael's reading of the severity of her injuries be overblown. He dithered for another moment, between cab and running, and in the end settled down to a steady jog. Gower Street wasn't far and anyway, he couldn't whimper with fear and worry while running.

Archie Flambard sighed the sigh of a man as full as an egg. Margaret Murray was right – Thomas's gentleman's relish was food of the gods, with a little more bite than usual and something indefinable in its depths. He wiped the plate around with his finger so as not to waste a scrap. Margaret Murray watched him with the proud demeanour of a parent whose child has just completed a solo of unusual difficulty in the end-of-term concert. She looked at Thomas fondly.

'Thomas has a wonderful touch in the kitchen,' she said, smiling at him. 'He has found his niche.' The fact that Thomas had filled many niches in his time, not all as laudable as a perfect relish, she and he allowed to pass them all by.

'I ought to be going, Margaret,' Flambard said. 'I hope you have forgiven me for my little subterfuge.'

She hadn't, but as ever, she was polite. 'I too was not totally straightforward,' she said. 'So we can call it quits, perhaps.' She stood and held out her hand. 'I'll see you at the next meeting no doubt, Mr Mortimer.'

'Indeed you will, Miss Plinlimmon.' Flambard shrugged on his coat, momentarily a Cockney again. 'Perhaps we will have heard from Eusapia Palladino by then?'

'Perhaps.' Margaret Murray was non-committal.

Thomas opened the door into the lobby and ushered his guest out. He couldn't help smiling. Life with Margaret Murray in it was certainly never dull, you could say that for her. He pulled back the heavy bolts top and bottom and opened the door, only to have Andrew Crawford, covered in sweat and somewhat wild-eyed, almost fall into his arms.

'How . . .' he took a gulp of air into his burning lungs. He was getting out of shape, he needed to run more, to exercise more. He was supposed to be at the peak of fitness and here he was, fighting for breath. 'How . . . how did you know I was here?' he asked finally.

Thomas was confused. 'I didn't,' he said.

'But you opened the door, just as I was about to knock.' Crawford was standing bent over, his hands on his knees.

'Doors work both ways,' Thomas said, a trifle acerbically. He was a working man, after all, and really had better things to be doing than bandying rubbish on his doorstep with a policeman in the middle of the night. 'I was letting this gentleman out, as a matter of fact.'

Crawford gave Flambard a cursory glance and then grabbed Thomas by the lapels. 'You've got to come with me,' he said, shaking him. 'You've got to come with me now.'

Thomas pulled the man's hands from his clothing and held him off at arm's length. This was far from being the first time a policeman had demanded the pleasure of his company, but he knew in this case he had strong grounds for refusing. 'Sorry, Sergeant,' he said, pleasantly. 'I don't think I do have to come with you.'

Crawford, breathing painfully through his nose, nodded his

head. 'Yes,' he said, 'yes, you do. It's Margaret. She's in the hospital, not expected to last the night.'

'Goodness,' came a mild voice from the doorway. 'And here was me thinking I just had a touch of indigestion.' She raised a ladylike hand to stifle a burp. 'Too much toast late at night always affects me that way.'

Crawford looked around Thomas at the little woman lit from behind by the candlelight. He blinked but she was still there.

'I . . . I was told you were . . . Well, who's in Guy's, then?'

Margaret sighed. 'I would need to make sure, but I think I know. It's Miss Christina Plunkett, of the Bermondsey Spiritualist Circle. We are . . . well, let's say that she is Adolf Beck to my Wilhelm Meyer. They say everyone has a double somewhere in the world. Mine happens to live in Bermondsey.'

'I . . . Margaret, I . . . I really thought you were as good as dead.' He looked at Flambard. 'Who's this?'

'It's a long story,' Margaret said, reaching for her coat which was hanging on a peg by the door. 'We'll tell you on the way to the hospital. Won't we, Mr Mortimer?'

After a long, long night, Detective Sergeant Andrew Crawford looked moderately smart and ready for anything as he waited in his guv'nor's office the next morning. He would need to bring Kane up to speed on the attack on Christina Plunkett, but as Michael's miserable prognostications had not borne fruit, the lady in question now sitting up if not exactly taking notice, he thought there would be time enough for that. He and Margaret had left Mortimer Mortimer sitting by her bedside for when she woke up properly. Allowing for a substantial bandage around the woman's head and one arm in a sling and a leg in a thigh-high plaster cast, the resemblance between her and Margaret Murray was uncanny – and close enough to fatal as made no difference. But that would all have to wait. For now, looking into the murder of Evadne Principal was the order of the day.

'Divide and conquer, then, Andrew.' John Kane was sifting the papers on his desk at the Yard.

'Who do you want, guv?' the sergeant asked.

'Well,' Kane was smiling. 'It's not often enough that a copper gets an opportunity like this, but I'm going to start with Richard Grosvenor. Or, to be more accurate, Mr Justice Grosvenor.'

'That old shit from the Western Circuit?'

'That's the one. Retired now, of course, but I've had my knuckles rapped by that out-of-touch irrelevance once too often. And if I can pin the murder of Evadne Principal on him in the process, so much the better.'

Both men laughed. Both men knew that was not John Kane's way. He'd get his man, all right, but it would be the right one.

'I'm going for the female persuasion first,' Crawford said. 'Lucinda Twelvetrees.'

'Anything known?'

'Just an address in Tooting.'

'Ah,' Kane smiled. 'That's punishment enough.'

'I don't have all day, Inspector.' Mr Justice Grosvenor didn't like policemen. He'd come across too many of them in his day job and they were, to a man, morons. He vaguely remembered this one, but they did, in the end, all look alike. The judge was standing at the end of a long library in his town house, adopting peculiar postures while swinging a Number Two iron. There was no golf ball, for which John Kane, in particular, was grateful. The ricochet effect off bookcases didn't bear thinking about.

'Then I'll come straight to the point, sir,' Kane said. 'Evadne Principal.'

The judge paused in mid-swing. 'Who?' he asked.

'The medium whose séance you attended on Monday night.'

'You are very well informed,' Grosvenor scrutinized the man more closely.

'I am a detective, sir,' Kane said.

Grosvenor looked the man up and down. From his shabby suit to his co-respondent shoes, that much was evident. He resumed his tee practice. 'Well, what of her?' he asked.

'You may have missed it in the press, sir,' Kane said, 'but she was found dead the morning after the séance of which I spoke. Murdered.'

This time, Grosvenor's swing didn't miss a beat. 'I can't say I am surprised,' he said, 'although I confess I missed it in *Tatler*.'

'You're not surprised?' Kane took it up. 'Why?'

Grosvenor sighed and put the club down. 'Look, the sun's over the yardarm somewhere in the world, officer. Would you like a tincture? I find these days I concentrate more with the warm glow of a brandy or three inside me.'

'Not for me, sir, thank you. Duty and all that.'

'Yes,' Grosvenor sneered. He rang a little silver bell on a side table and a flunkey appeared with a tray in his hand. 'Tincture, Hackett,' he said. 'Better pour two in case the inspector changes his mind.'

Hackett obliged.

Grosvenor sat down and waited until he had gone. 'I attend séances for the thrill of it all,' he said. 'I must admit I miss my days on the Bench – the adversarial clash of counsel, the pomp and ceremony. And there's something exquisite about having a black cap on your head as you hold the power of some wretch's life in your hands. Contacting the Other Side is a bit like that – the frisson of the unknown, the unknowable. What, for example, goes on in the mind of a man who bludgeons his wife to death; a lunatic who stabs a bishop in the street? We of the normal persuasion can't understand that, any more than we can fathom what lies Beyond.'

He sipped his brandy.

'The problem is that most mediums are charlatans, confidence men and women who can perform almost anything for the right amount of what I believe the criminal classes call "readies". *That's* why I'm not surprised that the Principal woman was murdered. It's a kind of justice.'

'And you were not its instrument?'

Grosvenor sat open-mouthed. 'Are you seriously accusing me of murdering the ghastly woman?'

Kane smiled. 'Oh, no, sir,' he said. 'Be assured that when I do, I will have a considerable body of factual evidence to make my case.'

'Miss Lucinda Twelvetrees?' Andrew Crawford touched his hat. He couldn't see much more than an eye peering through the crack of the door.

'Yes.' The voice was soft, muted, almost girl-like.

'I am Detective Sergeant Crawford of A Division, Metropolitan Police.' He flashed his warrant card. 'May I have a word?'

'Yes.'

Nothing happened.

'May I come in?' Crawford asked.

'Oh, no,' she said. 'I couldn't possibly be in the same room as a strange man. It wouldn't be seemly.'

'But I am a policeman, madam,' he said. 'And this *is* 1905.'

'I am aware of both of those things,' Lucinda Twelvetrees said, 'but it doesn't change the situation. I have never failed to return a library book in my life.'

This was more difficult than Crawford had expected. He wished now that he had opted for the High Court judge. 'I'm not here about a library book, Miss Twelvetrees,' he said. 'I'm here about a murder.'

There was a screech and the door slammed shut.

Crawford knocked again. 'Miss Twelvetrees. Open the door, please. It's vital that I talk to you.'

'You're wasting your time there, mate.' The voice seemed to be coming from the hedge that separated the Twelvetrees house from the one next door. 'Poor old Lucinda's away with the fairies.'

Crawford peered through the privet and saw a gardener, complete with smock and gaiters, clipping the foliage. 'You are . . .?' he asked.

'Looking forward to the day when the Hedgeclippers' and Borderkeepers' Union of Great Britain gets its voice heard in Parliament.'

'Absolutely,' Crawford said, wondering whether this entire street in Tooting wasn't one large lunatic asylum. 'In the meantime, I am from Scotland Yard investigating a murder.'

'Blimey!' The gardener stopped clipping. 'That's exciting, ain't it? I shouldn't think poor old Lucinda's got anything to do with it, but you might try four doors down. Veronica Makepeace. She's poor old Lucinda's minder. And don't say you haven't been warned.'

A policeman's lot is not always a happy one and it's not always very productive either. When John Kane got back to the Yard to put his feet up and down a cuppa, he flicked through his notebook.

After a little verbal sparring, during which the judge had told Kane just what he thought of policemen, the inspector had left the vast town house, realizing, not for the first time, that he had chosen the wrong arm of the law as his career.

Then, he had caught a cab to Fleet Street, much against his better judgement, to talk to Alfred d'Abo of the *Daily Mail*. Perhaps the single line he had written in his notebook – 'foul-mouthed arsehole' – was not one he could repeat in court, but it summed up Mr d'Abo perfectly. He got an unsolicited lecture on the sanctity of the fourth estate and had never heard the word 'alleged' so often in one conversation in his life. Yes, Mr d'Abo had attended Evadne Principal's last séance, in his capacity of scientific correspondent for his newspaper. Yes, he remembered exactly who was there, but he couldn't divulge that information without a court order. No, he was not impressed by the sleight of hand of Miss Principal, who, at best, was merely an average ventriloquist. As to who might have killed her, had the inspector considered any number of other mediums driven to murder because Miss Principal was giving them all a bad name by the unconvincing show she had put on?

Kane, at the Yard now, shook his head. The next two on his list of séance attendees were no-shows. Henry Angel was a dealer in ladies' fol-de-rols currently exhibiting his wares somewhere in Hartlepool. Auguste St-Remy was a sculptor who flitted from séance to séance in search of his Muse. Unfortunately, as his landlady told Kane, the Muse was hovering over Paris's Left Bank at that moment and that was where the inspector could find him. That left Hilda Ransom.

This time, Andrew Crawford got more than an eye peeping out. He got a stately woman the wrong side of forty who seemed to be wearing surprisingly little for that time in the afternoon, in an out-of-the-way street in Tooting.

'Veronica Makepeace?' The sergeant tipped his hat.

'Charmed.' She held out a hand, intending him to kiss it, but Crawford was a policeman and a married policeman at that. He shook it instead.

'I am from Scotland Yard.'

'Are you?' she purred. 'How delectable. Come in.'

There was something of the spider and the fly about the pair of them in that passage and Crawford was shown, appropriately enough, into a parlour. When he was a very young copper, the sergeant had seen places like this, bordellos, which hid behind the respectable façade of suburbia.

'Sherry?' she asked him. 'Or something a little stronger?'

'Information,' he said. 'I tried to talk to Lucinda Twelvetrees.'

'Ah, poor old Lucinda,' the woman said. 'Never the same since her mother passed. She virtually lives in séance-rooms.'

'I understand you look after her,' Crawford said.

'Ah, you'll have heard that from the gardener,' she smiled.

Crawford sat down, careful to keep a distance between them. 'Do I understand that you accompanied her to the séance at which Evadne Principal was the medium?'

'Indeed I did.' Veronica poured a very large sherry. 'I quite enjoy them, actually. A chance to extend my own client base.'

Crawford ignored that. 'Did you notice anyone new, perhaps, someone not usually there?'

'No, I . . . oh, wait. Yes, there was one woman, tall, big shoulders. Heavy on the mascara.'

'Did you catch her name?'

'I did, as a matter of fact, because it was rather unusual. It was Exeter. Valerie Exeter.'

'I take it that you and Miss Twelvetrees were regulars?'

'We were. Are. I shan't stop taking Lucinda to the sessions. She derives a great deal of spiritual comfort from them. I'm sorry I can't be of more help.' He suddenly found her sitting beside him on the settee, fondling his leg. 'Or perhaps I can be?'

He looked into her deep, dark eyes and took a deep breath. 'Thank you, Miss Makepeace.' He stood up suddenly. 'If I need you, I'll be sure to call.'

She stood up with him. 'Be sure you do, you naughty man.' She flicked her feather boa, the one that was doing its best to cover her breasts, across his face. 'Friday nights are best for me. The queue isn't so long.'

'You know her?' John Kane sensed a breakthrough. 'Personally, I mean?'

Hilda Ransom took the pins out of her mouth and shook the yards of taffeta free of her lap. 'Yes, I did. I won't pretend I wasn't shocked by Evadne's passing, Inspector, but I am content in the knowledge that she is safe on the Other Side and will, no doubt, be coming through early next week.'

'Can you think of anyone who would wish her harm?' Kane asked.

'Ah, you must ask the spirit world,' Hilda said, fiddling with the bobbin of her Singer sewing machine. 'Most of those we talk to are benign souls, wandering in the Void and wanting to reconnect with loved ones. *Some*, however,' she looked around her, furtively, 'are malevolent. The Tudors knew them as Kit-in-the-Canstick, Puck and Boneless, and that silly man Shakespeare turned most of them into elves and faeries. In fact, they are unhappy ghosts, demons of the night.'

She saw the scepticism in his eyes.

'You must understand, Inspector, that the Evadne Principals of this world go boldly into the next. They cross the Great Divide with almost nothing to protect them. The spirits don't like that. They whisper. They plot.'

'But do they murder?' Kane asked.

'Oh, indubitably they do. Evadne merely annoyed the wrong one.'

'I was thinking of a more . . . earthly . . . explanation,' the inspector said. 'Someone who perhaps had a grudge against Evadne.'

'No, I'm sure I . . . oh, but wasn't there another sensitive who came to a sticky end a week or so ago?'

'There was,' Kane nodded. 'Muriel Fazakerley.'

'Well, there you have it,' Hilda said, poising her foot to begin treadling again. 'If you won't accept what is staring you in the face, Inspector – that the spirit world is behind all this – then you must needs look to another obvious source. Mean, disbelieving people seeking vengeance on the medium world. And you could start with those obnoxious bastards in the Society for Psychical Research.' She bent to her task and sewed a fine seam, biting off the thread at the end. 'Pardon my French.'

Kirk Merrington bored easily, as he had admitted to Margaret Murray some time ago. He had finished fifteen of the thirty drawings for her book and was beginning to dread the sight of *another* mummified corpse.

'Isn't it funny,' the umpteenth visitor to the Petrie Museum would say, 'how all these pharaohs had red hair.'

'It's the acidity in the soil of Egypt,' he told more than one of them, yawning as he did so. Instinctively, they had moved away.

'Hey, fella,' one brash American of the Vanderbilt persuasion hailed him. 'Those sketches are pretty good. Maybe one day you'll be as famous as Meikle Angelo.'

That was when Kirk Merrington moved away, taking his pencils and pads with him. And he all but collided with Margaret Murray.

Both of them screamed.

'Oh, Mr Merrington,' she laughed, clutching her choker. 'I'm *so* sorry. Are you all right? You look as though you've seen a ghost.'

The artist chuckled too. 'Dr Murray, I *do* apologize. Not looking where I was going, I'm afraid.' Since the archaeologist barely reached to the man's chest, he thought he ought to check on her general well-being. 'Are you all right? I could have sent you flying.'

'Of course,' she said. 'I'm fine. Now, do you have anything for me?'

'Indeed I do,' and they scuttled down the passageway to Margaret's inner sanctum.

It was the end of another long day at the Petrie. Margaret Murray was putting on her hat ready to go home. Jack Brooks was sitting at a desk, sorting papers.

'Shall I drop these round to Quaritch's now, Dr Murray?' he asked. 'The Merrington drawings.'

'Thank you, dear boy. That would be kind. I doubt at this hour that Bernard Q himself will be there, but I expect he has an army of underlings slaving away until the last moment.'

As one of those underlings himself, Brooks knew that feeling all too well. 'May I be permitted to make an observation?' he asked.

'Please,' she said, brushing a speck of dust off Mrs Plinlimmon, currently residing on her desk.

'Well, the drawings are excellent, but the pharaoh's faces – they're all the same.'

Margaret chuckled. 'It's Mr Merrington's way of portraying family likenesses,' she said. 'And we none of us knows exactly what they looked like, do we? Good night, Jack.'

She hummed a tune as she scuttled down the stairs, smiling at the cat god Bast as she usually did. Whoever had carved that basalt beauty in the days of the Middle Kingdom clearly had had a wicked sense of humour. Bast was smiling and licking her lips as the last of the cream went down.

'Good night, Kirby,' she called to the uniformed man on the door.

'Good night, Dr Murray – oh, there's something for you.'

He rummaged in his little booth and passed her an envelope. It had a Royal Artillery crest on the corner and a small red seal on the flap. She opened it.

'Well, well,' she said, and smiled at Kirby again. The doorman was a prey to gossip, especially concerning the staff of the museum, and he would have given Nefertiti's right arm to know what the letter said. Margaret knew that perfectly well. She tapped her nose with the envelope, stuffed it into her handbag and marched out into Bloomsbury, a skip in her step and a possible solution to one of life's little mysteries in her heart.

Members called it The Rag. To the outside world, it was the Army and Navy Club, a solid, square building along Pall Mall. Margaret had never crossed its portals before and she had no idea what to expect. What she had *not* expected, was a dinner invitation from a man she hardly knew, who, as far as she was concerned, knew her as Henrietta Plinlimmon. It was *very* intriguing and that was why she had accepted. There had been no time for a formal acceptance, but it was clear from the speed of the whole thing that her host was in something of a hurry. Margaret had no Thomas to watch over her, but then again, she *was* forearmed; would, at all times, be in the company of officers and gentlemen; and the murderous hat-pin that lay in her clutch bag was a deterrent made of the best Sheffield steel.

She showed her invitation to the flunkey on the door and he

in turn took her through winding corridors where scarlet-faced soldiers of the late queen stared down at her from their canvases. At the last corner, the huge white marble nose of the Duke of Wellington shone like a beacon. The flunkey knocked on a side door and opened it.

'Ah, dear lady.' General George Boothby was tucked into his mess dress, all scarlet and gold lace. He took Margaret's hand and kissed it. 'So glad you could join me.' He shot a glance at the flunkey that said, 'Put this on my slate and keep your mouth shut' and the man departed.

'Can I offer you a sherry?' Boothby ushered Margaret to a chaise longue, not the safest item of furniture to find in the private apartments of a man with wandering hands.

'You can offer me an explanation,' she said, sitting demurely, with her clutch bag firmly on her lap.

'Ah, yes.' Boothby poured for them both and she couldn't help noticing that her glass was filled considerably fuller than his. In fact – she tipped her head and closed one eye – yes, she was right. The cunning old general was using a toasting glass, with a thick bottom; for every one glass he drank, she would be getting the equivalent of three. 'I suppose you mean, how did I have my dinner invitation delivered to Dr Margaret Murray, when you are actually Henrietta Plinlimmon?'

'Something like that,' she said.

Boothby sat beside her, but at a gentlemanly distance. 'Do you, by any chance, play poker, Dr Murray?'

'I'm more of a bridge woman myself,' she told him, 'but I have been known to dabble.'

'I thought so,' he smiled. 'I know a poker face when I see one. Someone who has the inner steel to meet trouble head on and yet come out smiling. Well, I have that ability too. As soon as you were introduced to us all at the Circle, I knew who you were.'

'Really? How, pray?'

'That old rogue Flinders Petrie. I met him in Egypt . . . ooh, now, let me see, six . . . no, seven years ago. I was advising the Khedive on how to bolster his southern defences and Flinders was rummaging up to his neck in sand. We became as thick as thieves. And he spoke of you constantly.'

'He did?'

Boothby nodded. 'If I remember rightly, you were the new girl at the school then, weren't you?'

'My first year as junior lecturer at University College, yes.'

'Yes, well.' Boothby sampled his sherry. 'Saving your blushes, you came across as something rather more than that. Something a little more . . . extra-curricular, shall we say?'

'I don't think I care for the sound of that, General,' she said, her drink untouched.

'Forgive me, dear lady,' he gushed. 'I mean no offence. But Flinders was clearly smitten. And I, I must admit, was intrigued. When I finished my tour of duty and came home, I followed his exploits in the papers and, sure enough, there you were, photograph and all – a year or two ago, in the Valley of the Kings.'

'Well, I'm flattered, of course,' Margaret said, although that wasn't exactly how she felt.

'So, imagine my surprise when you turned up at Aggie Dunwoody's out of the blue, posing as somebody else entirely.'

'I had my reasons,' she said.

'I'm sure you did,' Boothby nodded. 'And I'd be delighted to share.'

'Since you were kind enough to invite me to dinner, General,' she said, 'I'd be delighted to share a meal with you. More than that would be a step too far.'

Boothby drained his glass and went for a refill, regretting his choice of vessel. 'That Scotland Yard business was intriguing,' he said, watching the candlelight twinkle on the amber liquid. 'It was a ploy, of course.'

'Yes,' she said, looking him in the eye. 'And it was true.'

'Was it?' He sat down again, closer this time. 'I know for a fact that despite the protestations of the ghastly Women's Social and Political Union, there is no such thing as a female policeman. So I was wondering in what capacity you can be so well informed.'

He was leaning over her now, relatively easy at six foot, and his left hand was resting on his knee, perilously close to hers.

'The murder of Muriel Fazakerley has become something of an interest of mine.'

'An obsession, even?' A vein throbbed in his temple.

'No,' she said quietly. 'I wouldn't put it as strongly as that.'

'But you think it was one of us? One of the Circle?'

'That is possible,' she said. 'Perhaps you can help me in that respect.'

'Oh, Dr Murray . . . Margaret . . . I can help you in a number of respects.'

She felt his sherry breath on her cheek and saw his hand hover inches above her skirts but a knock on the door shattered the moment. Another flunkey stood there, as ex-soldierly as the first, but with the uniform of a mess waiter and a trolley covered with gleaming silver-topped dishes.

'Dinner, sir,' the man announced with a hint of the obvious.

'Not now, Private!' Boothby hissed, but Margaret was already on her feet.

'When you invited me to dinner, General Boothby,' she said, 'especially at the Army and Navy Club, I assumed that it would be Ladies' Night, at long regimental tables with toasts, claret and convivial company. I had no idea that I was to be lured into a cul-de-sac and propositioned by a man old enough to be my father.'

'Cul-de-sac?' Boothby was on his feet too. 'Propositioned? My good lady, this is 1905!'

She rounded on him, standing on tiptoe. 'I am well aware of the date, sir,' she said. 'But if the twentieth century has no more to offer than the ineffectual fumblings of an ageing roué, I'm heartily glad that I spend most of my time in the Egyptian Middle Kingdom, when women were treated with respect.'

Margaret knew that that last bit wasn't true, but she was confident that Boothby didn't and it was a good exit line. She spun on her heel, then lifted one of the tureen lids. Damn! Devilled kidneys. And they looked and smelled delicious.

'Devilled kidneys,' she bridled. 'How revolting! Waiter, could you see me to the door?'

EIGHT

Andrew Crawford had never been keen on visiting the sick. He remembered toe-curlingly embarrassing Sunday afternoons when the family visited his maternal grandmother, traipsing around her little village with her special nourishing soup, a concoction he knew for sure would be down the privy before their shoes hit the pavement. Now, his visiting was usually to people *in extremis*, who had been beaten, often to the point of death, and it was no easier. The nurses seemed to be a special breed, not very big some of them, but with the temperament of a bear with a sore head. One such met him at the door of Christina Plunkett's ward.

'Can I help you, young man?'

Sergeant Crawford looked down to meet the implacable gaze of a little turkey-like woman. There was so much starch in her clothing that everything would have stood there, whether or not she was inside. She positively crackled, with both attitude and laundering.

'I'm here to see Miss Plunkett, if she is well enough,' he said, politely. 'I am a detective sergeant with the Metropolitan Police.'

Her lip curled with derision. 'A po*lice*man, are you? Well, you and your colleagues were doing an excellent job when Miss Plunkett was attacked, weren't you?'

'We can't be everywhere . . .' Crawford looked for clues on the woman's uniform. There were no badges to denote rank, but the blue was quite deep in colour, something he had noticed before often meant someone a little superior to the usual, so he tried a leap of faith. 'Sister.'

The woman smiled frostily and he sighed with relief. There was nothing worse than under-ranking a nurse.

'My colleague did find her very soon after the attack and got her to the hospital with some despatch, as I understand it.'

There was no arguing with that and the sister was not immune to a pretty face, so she begrudgingly stood aside and half-opened the door, before stopping Crawford with a firm hand. 'Please don't expect too much from Miss Plunkett,' she said in almost human tones. 'She's had a severe shock, let alone the physical injuries, which are not inconsequential. Like many women of her class, she had thought herself invulnerable from attack, so to be taken for a common street walker . . .'

'Is that what happened?' Crawford was surprised. He hadn't heard that detail.

'Well, surely?' The nurse was now also confused. 'There's no other reason, is there, for her to be so savagely beaten? We had all assumed that a man . . .' she managed to invest that single syllable with all the venom at her disposal '. . . had made an assumption and, on being rebuffed, had taken his revenge.'

Crawford felt he had to stand up for mankind in general. 'I have certainly seen women beaten for that reason,' he said, 'but generally it is just a single blow, often just an open-handed slap.' He realized what he had said as soon as the words were out of his mouth. 'I don't mean "just" as in not important, but merely to . . .' He was hopelessly mired in what had once been a sentence and he dithered to a stop.

'I know what you mean, Detective Sergeant,' the sister said, with a slight twitch of the lips. Sometimes men were so easy to tease it was a sin.

Crawford got himself in hand. 'Men who attack women for that reason usually do it out of frustration, if you will excuse my use of the word, and the only thing on their mind is to get on with business with someone else. Miss Plunkett was not interfered with.' He made it into a question, although he knew the answer and the nurse shook her head. 'So why did he linger to beat her so severely? I think there is a personal reason. I need to speak to her to see what it might be.'

The sister pushed the door open more fully and pointed. 'Down there, on the right. Behind the screen.'

Crawford wasn't quite sure on the details of screen etiquette. Did one call softly, tap a shoe on the floor lacking a door to knock on – what? He settled for a quiet 'Miss Plunkett? May I come in?'

'Who is it?' The voice was soft and held more than a little sound of strain.

'Detective Sergeant Crawford.'

'The police?' The voice became more anxious. 'Have you caught him?'

Crawford risked putting his head around the curtain and she bridled a little but gestured for him to come in. A hard chair was pulled up next to the bed and he sat down, decently on the edge, not looking as though he meant to stay long.

'I'm afraid not, Miss Plunkett. We don't have a description, so we need your help, if that's possible.'

She closed her eyes, still black and puffy. The dressing around her head was smaller than when he had seen her just after the attack, but was still substantial, looking like an outdated and slightly lopsided toque. Her leg was in a plaster, suspended by ropes and pulleys from the ceiling, and her left arm was in a sling, deposed on a pillow across her lap. All in all, Miss Plunkett had received a beating which would have killed many a lesser woman. Crawford thought that it was not just in outward appearance that she resembled Margaret Murray, although he suspected that the little archaeologist would probably have given her attacker a few mementoes to take away. Perhaps this woman had too.

'For instance, did you manage to scratch the man, perhaps?' He waited patiently for her answer.

Tears pooled under the swollen lids and she shook her head carefully, wincing.

'Punch or slap?'

'No, officer, I'm sorry,' she said. 'I was walking home. I had a lot on my mind. The meeting had been rather . . . well, not very peaceful. I used to like the meetings, they were calming and pleasant. But since poor Muriel, things have become rather more confrontational and I was considering resigning my membership. There are always others wanting to join, so my chair wouldn't be empty for long.' She stopped and cleared her throat, pointing at a glass of rather dusty-looking water on the table at the side of the bed. Crawford passed it to her and she sipped, swallowing with some effort. 'I think because of my being in somewhat of a brown study,' she went on, 'I didn't hear the man come up behind me. I was aware of nothing before a savage blow to my head which knocked me into the railings. Then – nothing until the policeman who came to my aid.'

Crawford didn't disabuse her. He knew the 'stiff not getting stiffer' rule and knew how lucky she had been.

'The nurses tell me I was kicked violently in my back and sides. Even my . . .' she blushed and looked away, '. . . personal parts are bruised. My leg and arm were broken by blows from a heavy object.' She now began to cry in earnest. 'I don't know what I could have done to deserve such cruelty.'

Crawford could reconstruct the attack in his head without needing to ask more questions. Whoever it was had hoped that the blow to the head would be the *coup de grâce*, but when it failed to finish her off, had kicked her, hard and repeatedly, in the hope that shock would do its work. And if PC Boggs had not come along when he did, then it would probably have been a hope which would come true.

'I don't think you have done anything, Miss Plunkett,' he said kindly, putting a hand over hers as it lay, trembling slightly, by her side. The slight flinch she gave made him sad for all small, frightened things. 'Do you know a Miss Plinlimmon? From the Circle?'

The woman nodded and smiled a little. 'She seems very nice,' she said. 'She . . .' Her eyes opened as wide as they could. 'She looks a lot like me, doesn't she? Do you mean that someone mistook me for her?'

'We think that that is possible,' Crawford said and felt her hand clench.

'Whatever has she done? What could make anyone hate another person so much?'

'It's not hate,' Crawford said, half to himself. 'It's fear.'

Late May evenings were not the Spiritualist's friend. There was something about the light as the year raced towards the longest day that made it hard to create the right ambience. Thick curtains helped, of course, keeping the room dark, but the sheer exuberance of spring outside could not be completely kept at bay. The birds sang late into the night and a blackbird was singing his heart out in the nearby branches of a plane tree outside. Florence Rook lit a lamp in the corner and shaded it with a crimson shawl thrown over a couple of carefully placed statuettes of dancing nymphs. The room was suitably dark and just the tiniest bit stuffy.

When Florence had been learning her trade as a girl, Spiritualism was still very much the thing, mediums were in great demand at country house parties and suburban homes alike. There was a good living to be made, as long as you could avoid the attentions of those intent on upsetting the apple cart, such as the dreaded Society for Psychical Research – charlatans all – and Florence could hardly forbear to spit as they crossed her mind. Busybodies and killjoys every one of them. Florence's mentor, the wonderful and talented Mrs Cook, on whom she modelled herself, had been ruined by them. Florence stood quietly for a moment, eyes closed and arms extended to the Great Beyond, centring herself and re-establishing her link to her spirit guide, the great and powerful Osthryth, a queen of Mercia when England had been not one kingdom but seven. Friends in the business tried to get her to contact a Plains Indian chief – they were, apparently, the coming thing – but Osthryth, though somewhat of a challenge to anyone with a denture, had done her proud over the twenty years she had been bringing the bereaved into contact with their loved ones, and Florence was sticking with what she knew.

The glory days were gone, she knew that, but there were still enough enlightened people, in London especially, who knew that Death was simply a Veil. Her sitting tonight was very exclusive. She had been approached after a séance with a group in Hammersmith by an extremely *soignée* woman in a veiled hat who had asked for a private consultation. She had lost a very dear friend just a few days before, another medium, and she just knew, she had said, that her friend was desperate to reach through the Veil.

Florence was flattered and also rather touched. She had heard of the death of two mediums in the last few weeks – who hadn't, in her line of work? – and was thrilled to think she might be the one to not only talk to a recently departed who knew how many beans made five, but also that she might be able to crack the case. Imagine the publicity. Newspapers. Periodicals. She closed her eyes but this time with the excitement of it all. Talking to a proper Spirit – imagine it. She clapped her hands in ecstasy. It was the culmination of her career – if this was her last séance, she would die happy!

*   *   *

The cats'-meat man's day was already over and it was barely
nine o'clock in the morning. Say this about the denizens of Rose
and Crown Yard, Westminster, they were cat-lovers all and nothing
was spared in providing the very best horsemeat for their furry
friends.

Bill Molton was wheeling his empty cart towards the Mall
and his attention was taken momentarily by a troop of the Life
Guards clattering towards Horse Guards Parade, the morning sun
flashing on their helmets and breastplates.

'One of them would fetch in the crowds to your cart, Bill.'

Harry was a regular. He and Bill went back, seeing as how
they serviced the same locale. Bill brought the cats' meat; Harry
cleaned the windows. 'What d'ya reckon?' Harry went on, hauling
his buckets on to his shoulder. 'Sixteen hands of thoroughbred'd
keep a whole herd of cats going indefinitely, wouldn't it?'

'Not the greedy bastards I deal with,' Bill grunted. 'And that's
a gluttony, by the way.'

'What is?'

'Cats. It's not a herd of cats; it's a gluttony of cats.'

'As you wish,' Harry laughed and turned towards his next
house.

Bill Molton had just stashed all his sacks away and was rinsing
his bloody fingers at the stand-pipe when he heard a most
un-window-cleanerly shriek coming from his old oppo behind
him. He spun round, assuming that Harry had fallen off his ladder.
In fact, he was still four rungs up, his right arm pointing rigidly
ahead through the window.

The cats'-meat man was at the ladder's foot in seconds.

'What's up, Bill?' He'd never seen the man look so pale.

'It's the missus,' Harry gasped, his voice barely a whisper.

'*Your* missus?' Bill was confused.

'No,' Harry snapped. 'Not *my* missus. The missus what lives
here. I think she's dead.'

Technically, it was M Division's patch, but Superintendent Mason
of that august group of gentlemen was all too happy to pass the
buck to headquarters. That was the problem with his Division's
boundaries – he had to know what was going on *both* sides of
the river.

So it was that Detective Sergeant Crawford, from A Division, was the second policeman on the scene that morning; the first being Constable Mather.

Crawford had met Mather before; the man had never met a cliché he didn't like. 'Who found the body?' the sergeant asked.

'Him, over there. Harry Cheviot. Salt of the earth is Harry. Honest as the day is long.'

'Quite.'

'There was another bloke, too. Cats'-meat man, name of Molton, but he had to bugger off. I've got his address, though.'

'Good. Plant your size elevens on that doorstep, Constable. Once I'm inside, nobody comes in.'

'Got it, sir,' Mather said. 'If the commissioner himself were to arrive, I'd have to exercise my constabulary duty nonetheless. There's no such thing as one law for us and another for them.'

Crawford clapped the man on the shoulder and crossed the road to where the window cleaner sat disconsolately on the kerb, his ladders against the wall, his buckets neatly stacked. 'Detective Sergeant Crawford,' he said. 'Are you Harry Cheviot?'

'To tell you the truth, sir, after what I just seen, I don't rightly know.'

'Yes,' Crawford nodded, sitting beside the man on the kerbstone. He winced; London pavements were like iron. 'Distressing. Did you know the deceased?'

'Only to get money orff of her – in the line of duty, you understand.'

'Do you know what she did for a living?'

'More of a dying,' Harry said, 'if you'll excuse the pun at a time like this. She was a medium, was Mrs Rook, clairvoyant, teller of fortunes. Funny what fortune had in store for her, wasn't it?'

'How often did you clean her windows?'

'Once a month, guv. Back and front. Outside only, of course. No hanky-panky with Mrs Rook. Proper, she was.'

'Hanky-panky?' Crawford raised an eyebrow.

Harry looked from right to left. 'In my calling,' he said, under his breath, 'you get to see things. Well, it goes with the territory, really. There's some women get pretty bored. Well, you know how it is, hubby's away at the office. They've got no kids and they can't vote, 'cept in local councils and how much fun is that? None, is how much. So, some of 'em . . . well, a handsome young window cleaner comes along and he's a breath of fresh air, ain't he? A bit of what the doctor ordered.'

'But Mrs Rook didn't require your services . . . doctor?' Crawford checked.

Harry nudged him in the ribs and immediately regretted his forwardness. 'No, no. No how's your father at all. Unlike Mrs Hipcress at Number Sixty-Three. There was one time . . .' but something in Crawford's face made the window cleaner's happy memories fade away. 'Poor Mrs Rook, though, eh? What a bugger.'

'What time did you start work?' the sergeant asked.

'Half past six – usual,' Harry said. 'I start at the top and work down.'

'Did you see anybody in the yard during that time?'

'Only old Bill Molton, the cats'-meat man, and some blokes from the Life Guards.'

'We may need to talk to you again,' Crawford said, and crossed to the threshold of the murder scene. The last he saw of the outside world was Constable Mather folding his arms and blocking the front door like a juggernaut at rest.

There was blood in the passageway and Crawford was careful to step around it. He squatted over one particularly large blob, but there were no footprints or anything helpful like that. He checked the kitchen to his right. All was in order, with no sign of disturbance. There were two bedrooms on the first floor, both containing double beds, both made up. On the second floor was a boxroom under the eaves that had been converted recently into a bathroom. There was dry soap on the washbasin and dry towels on their rail.

Crawford went back downstairs. To his immediate right, a sitting room lay in semi-darkness. He hitched up the blinds which gave him a view of the tiny garden and, beyond the angles of various buildings, a distant and disappointing view of Horse Guards Parade.

He took a deep breath and entered the crime scene itself. Florence Rook, the medium, sat at her table, shattered glass over the purple velvet cloth and the swirling patterns of the carpeted floor. Her hands were stretched out in front of her and her head, what was left of it, was face down on the table. Crawford knew he should have waited for Stockley Collins and his photographer, and he also guessed that Constable Mather had already traipsed over the place in his size elevens. Still, he sensed that time was of the essence. This was the third medium to die in as many weeks and, judging by the devastation to the back of the head, the level of violence was escalating. Gingerly, he lifted the woman's head and looked at her deathly white face. Her eyes were closed, puffy and purple with bruising, and several of her teeth lay on the tablecloth where they had been smashed from her mouth. Dark brown blood ran in rivulets down her forehead, skirting her nostrils and accentuating the lines around her mouth and chin. Crawford carefully placed the head back as it was and checked the woman's clothing. Buttons were in place and fastened. Nothing had been tampered with.

He paced the room with a grim sense of déjà vu. The scrying ball had been shattered and may have been used to demolish the woman's skull. On the sideboard lay a planchette, one of those gadgets used in spirit writing and, alongside it, the newfangled Ouija board, made in Berlin. Briefly, he looked through cupboards and drawers, looking for any sign of disturbance and found none. Everything was meticulously clean and neat. Except for the woman who had been the cause of it all. And whatever story she had to tell, she wasn't talking.

NINE

John Kane had not been convinced when the first medium died but he needed no convincing now. He had seen the crime-scene sketches and could see at a glance that here was someone who needed stopping and the sooner the better. But the world of the medium was a shadowy one. In some ways, they trod a line which was often on the wrong side of the law and there was a thickish file among the shoeboxes in the basement which contained the names and details of mediums who had had complaints made against them and – perhaps more importantly at this stage – those who had made the complaints. If one name cropped up more than once, it would give them somewhere to start from because, at the moment, they couldn't find one single set of facts which tied the women together.

Kane sighed and leaned back in his chair, running his hands through his hair and ending by rubbing his eyes. 'I don't mind telling you, Sergeant,' he said, keeping it formal, 'that I am at my wits' end with this one. If I have one more raddled old constable taking me aside in the canteen and telling me that it's the Ripper all over again, I swear to you I will swing for the old bastard.'

Crawford was young enough to be indulgent. 'It was their most exciting time,' he said. 'My grandfather-in-law is the same about the Wairau Affray.'

Kane dropped his hands to the desk and cocked his head interrogatively. 'The do what now?'

'Exactly. He was sent to New Zealand when they were having trouble with the Maoris. He didn't see any other action and when he came home, he resigned his commission and went into the family business.'

Kane remembered. 'Scouring powder.'

'The same. But you can see how fighting some largely invisible and scary warriors in a foreign country trumps selling scouring powder any day. We refight the arrests of Te Rauparaha and Te Rangihaeata every Christmas, without fail. I've only seen it done using mustard pots and the remains of a goose, but it was apparently very exciting. It's the same with these old constables. They've beaten the same bounds for decades – they don't want to waste a moment if it comes to telling a whippersnapper where he's going wrong.'

Kane chuckled. 'I don't feel much of a whippersnapper most mornings when I first think of getting out of bed,' he said, 'but you make a good point. It doesn't help up with this case, though, does it? He's ramping up the violence and I don't know where it's going to end.'

'It will end with him being caught,' Crawford said, decisively.

'It must be a him, mustn't it?' Kane said. 'I thought at first

. . . poison, you know. Woman's weapon and all that. But this.' He glanced at the sketches again. 'Surely, no woman is capable of such violence?'

'In the normal run, I would say no,' Crawford agreed. 'But there seems to be a vein of what we have to call madness running through it all. The feather in Muriel Fazakerley's mouth, the tarot card in Evadne Principal's hand.'

'And in this case?'

'Nothing yet. But Florence Rook isn't even on the slab yet. Something may turn up.'

Kane furrowed his brow. 'Florence Rook? That rings a bell, doesn't it?'

'Almost,' Crawford agreed. 'Florence Cook was a famous medium. She was unmasked by the Society for Psychical Research back in the Sixties, I think it was. The victim had a picture of Cook's spirit guide on her wall.'

'A picture of a spirit guide? Bit tricky to have one of those, isn't it? Aren't they . . . well, aren't they invisible?'

'You'd think so, wouldn't you?' Crawford agreed. 'But Florence Cook's spirit was a girl called Katie King and she would appear almost every time she gave a sitting.'

'Coo.' Kane liked a bit of spooky as well as the next policeman.

'Except, of course, Katie was Florence dressed up and when she was unmasked, the whole thing came crashing down. It did a lot of damage to the medium business and lots of women making good money had to turn their hands to something else.'

Kane raised an eyebrow.

'Wriggling into and out of small spaces had made most of them very limber, if you get my drift,' Crawford said. 'And they had a lot of contacts, so they did all right.'

'How do you know so much?' Kane said, shuffling his papers, his usual precursor to getting his subordinates out of his office and on to the street.

'I've been reading up on it,' Crawford admitted. 'Also, Angela's mother is a bit of a follower, on the quiet. Angela's father thinks it's a load of old tosh.'

'I should think scouring powder keeps a person's credulity levels set rather high,' Kane said, then paused. 'Or do I mean low?'

'He's a hard man to fool, that's true. But I don't think this has anything to do with any supernatural element, no matter what the murderer is trying to make us believe. I think this has a very prosaic explanation, if we could only find it.'

'I understand a woman from a Spiritualist Circle was injured the other night – how is she and is it connected?'

'She seems to be coming out of the woods but has been left very nervy. I think it is connected.' Crawford made an instant decision to leave Margaret Murray out of it. 'But I don't know how.'

'Well,' Kane said, getting up and ushering Crawford out. 'I think we need to go back to basics. Go and visit the sister – I think Muriel Fazakerley had a sister, am I right?'

Crawford nodded.

'And see where we go from there. Let me know how you get on.'

And without any obvious effort, Detective Sergeant Andrew Crawford found himself outside on the landing.

Maud Whitehouse was giving her front step a darned good larruping with a stone and some soapy water when Detective Sergeant Andrew Crawford arrived. Alone of the women of her street, Mrs Whitehouse kept her step in an almost constant state of perfection and so this was the second scrubbing it had had that morning, her husband having committed the almost mortal sin of stepping on it on his way out to work. She looked over her shoulder at Crawford and glared balefully.

'Mrs Whitehouse?' Crawford asked politely, touching the brim of his hat in the official Metropolitan Police manner.

'Who's asking?' she said, giving the step, which was beginning to take on quite a dip in the middle with all the scrubbing, one last wipe. She struggled to her feet and turned to look him up and down. 'If it wasn't for the suit, I'd say you're a copper.'

Crawford looked down. He and Angela had chosen the suit with care. He had told the tailor to make it look like a suit off the peg and the man had almost passed out with the shock. But he had done his best, using slightly less than top-quality cloth and skimping on the lining. But even so, it looked a cut above the usual blue serge. 'Yes, Mrs Whitehouse. I am a policeman. Can I come in?'

She stepped ostentatiously over her threshold on to the spotless lino within. 'As long as you don't mess up my step. And bring the bucket, would you?' She set off down the dark hall, made more gloomy by brown-painted anaglypta. 'And don't forget the stone and the cloth,' she said, without turning round.

Crawford picked up her impedimenta and followed her, careful to avoid the gleaming step. He could sense rather than see the curtains twitch up and down the road. 'That Maud Whitehouse,' the twitches seemed to say, 'no better than she should be with young men in the house at all hours.' The fact that the only young man in Maud Whitehouse's abode on any given day was her son Alfred made no difference to the gossips – you had to find your own amusement in Needlemans Street, Rotherhithe.

'So.' Maud Whitehouse stood in her scullery, her back to the chipped sink, a mother tiger at bay. 'So, who's done what? My Matilda is a good girl, she is, for all she's a milliner. And as for Nathaniel, well, it was all a misunderstanding—'

Crawford was quick to interrupt. 'It's about your sister, Mrs Whitehouse. Muriel.'

'Muriel? She's dead, you know.'

'Yes. Precisely. That's why I'm here. Has no one told you we believe now that she was murdered?'

The woman narrowed her eyes. 'Murdered? But the inquest . . .'

'Yes. But that was all before the other murders . . .' He stopped. 'Do you take a daily newspaper, Mrs Whitehouse?'

'A newspaper?' she echoed, incredulous. 'Do I look like some-body who has time and money to waste on newspapers? I pick a few out of the ash-heap sometimes to put down to keep the floors clean, but that's it. What's been in the newspapers?'

Crawford explained about the two dead mediums but could see that the woman was not interested. Her world was small, her husband, her children and, until she died, her sister. She didn't regret the past or look forward into the future. Yes, she had been upset when Muriel died. It is never nice to be the last man standing and mortality tapped her on the shoulder that day. But her sister's death had been out of the ordinary and Maud Whitehouse only did ordinary, at best. But she accepted that this young man was nicely dressed, nicely spoken and no doubt meant well, so she edged past him and led the way into the parlour.

The parlour was clean, if anything cleaner than the hall and kitchen. No speck of dust was allowed to stay for long on its treasured surfaces. There were piecrust tables, delicate-looking chairs, antimacassars to protect the antimacassar which lay beneath. Crawford had never seen so much crochet and tatting in one place in his whole life.

Maud Whitehouse looked around proudly. 'All this furniture is from my eldest, Bobby,' she said, 'no offence. He has his own business, you know.' She folded her hands in her lap and looked at Crawford complacently. The look told him that he didn't have his own business, never would, so there was no need to feel superior. Looking closer, Crawford could see that every piece was mended, sometimes with the simple expedient of a piece of wood tied on with string. He also knew Robert Whitehouse, Totter, Prop. Est. 1902; he had missed incarceration by a whisker several times. But there was no need to remind his mother of that.

'So, Mrs Whitehouse,' Crawford got out his notebook and pencil. 'What can you tell me about your sister?'

'Muriel was always the pretty one,' she said, patting her hair and inviting Crawford to argue, which he did through various nods and winks. 'Her looks were going, but she could still look good in a weak light.' She leaned in and dropped her voice. 'It was no secret that she sometimes made a little bit on the side. There was some bloke from that Circle, some soldier as she told it, who would come round sometimes.'

Crawford nodded and pretended to make a note, though he had had that from Margaret Murray already.

'She claimed to be a sensitive, but she wasn't really.' Maud Whitehouse gave a laugh which turned into a cough. 'Well, she wouldn't have drowned in her soup if she could see the future, would she?'

'I suppose not. Did she have any enemies?'

Maud Whitehouse snorted. 'Enemies? Who has enemies? Only policemen ask that sort of stupid question. I've got people who don't like me. *You've* got people who don't like you – more than I've got, I shouldn't wonder. But enemies? That's not for the likes of us.'

Crawford was a patient man, and just as well. 'Did your sister have anyone who didn't like her?'

'Of course,' the woman said, promptly. 'Me, for one, a lot of the time. My husband when she came round here, whining about people at that Circle. They didn't like her doing sittings. Said it gave Spiritualism a bad name. But you've got to live, haven't you? They didn't put bread in her mouth. Even that general, he hadn't been round as much lately. And when he did, he didn't pay her much. Told her that she should be grateful for his attentions.' She shuddered. 'That moustache would put me off, let alone some of his ways.' She stared at Crawford defiantly. 'Let me tell you, Mr Policeman, if my Tom tried any of that, he'd get the keys to the street. Filth. That's all it was. Filth. Poor Muriel was quite upset sometimes. She'd say to me, Maudie, she'd say—'

'Indeed. But did she ever say she was scared of anyone, worried at all?'

Maud Whitehouse looked up to the ceiling and did some ostentatious thinking. She even tapped her chin once or twice with a water-bleached finger. 'No.' After all that thought, it was a simple enough answer and Crawford knew he would get no more.

'Do you have a picture of her I can borrow?'

Maud Whitehouse looked around vaguely. 'I've got one some-where. I'm not a great one for pictures, to be honest. Have a look in the drawer, there.' She pointed to a sideboard rammed into the corner, hedged by small chairs and a lopsided bamboo whatnot. 'That's where I keep pictures, if I keep them at all.'

Crawford picked his way carefully across the floor, avoiding toppling anything over by just the merest chance. He pulled the drawer open and suppressed a sigh. It was rammed full with photographs, some on thick cardboard and clearly an expensive studio offering. Others were on flimsy paper, curling and already fading as someone's amateur effort at developing proved to be, in the end, ineffective.

'She did do a cabinet photo a couple of years ago. And to be fair to her, she kept her hair. She didn't have no greys in it, being mousey.' Even in death, Maud Whitehouse wasn't going to call her sister attractive – it wasn't what they did in their family. Call a spade a spade, that's what the Fazakerleys had always done, always would do.

'Is this her?' Crawford held up a picture of a woman staring out challengingly at the camera, arms folded decidedly under a bust like a roll-top desk.

Maud Whitehouse squinted at it short-sightedly. 'No. That's Auntie Gert.'

'Right.' Crawford continued to rummage and held up another. 'This?'

Maud Whitehouse got up to lean nearer. 'No. That's my second . . . no, third daughter, Maisie. But you're getting closer. They don't look unalike.'

Crawford looked into the face of Maisie. He saw even features, clear blue eyes and an uncertain smile. The hair was indeed mousey and done up in a Gibson style, or as near as she could get to it with what nature had given her. He returned to his search and almost immediately found another picture, which could be the girl's older sister. 'This?' He held it up.

This time, Mrs Whitehouse got up and walked over, taking the picture from him and holding it to the light seeping unwillingly through the draped window. 'Yes. Yes, that's Muriel. See – it says "With best wishes from Madame Ankhara" printed across the bottom. She had some done for clients and this was spare. My Tom didn't like it at all. Thought it was fast.'

The picture showed a woman in her late thirties or could be early forties. She did look very like her niece, though her hair was rather less bouffant and her eyes a little more tired. Her smile was welcoming though, and Detective Sergeant Crawford could see that, had he been in need of comfort from beyond the veil – or indeed, on a more earthly plane – this woman would have been an easy choice. 'May I borrow it, please?'

Maud Whitehouse flapped a hand, something Crawford would never have risked in that crowded room. 'Keep it,' she said. 'Like I told you, I've no time for pictures. Only gather dust. I don't know what you think you're going to find out, but good luck to you at any rate.'

With a skill that John Kane would envy, she had somehow guided Crawford to the door and he found himself on the pavement, the gleaming step nudging at his heels. Inside, Maud Whitehouse leaned on the inside of the door, tilted her chin and let the tears run down her cheeks, soaking into the collar of her

workworn dress. Tears for Muriel and also, though she would
have denied it vehemently, for herself. She sighed, sniffed and
wiped her face with the back of her hand and plodded back to
the kitchen. That policeman might have been nice and polite, but
he would have trodden on her step, as sure as God made little
apples.

Dr Wilfred Henderson never knew quite how he had ended up
where he did. Nothing wrong with Westminster, of course, right
at the beating heart of empire as it was. No, what surprised him
whenever he took stock of his life was that he had become a
police surgeon. When he wasn't patching up bloodied coppers
and attending to living victims of street violence, he was
crouching over corpses, in alleyways, parlours, in one instance
on the upper deck of a bus. And all too often, it ended up here
in the Westminster Mortuary in Horseferry Road, with bodies
lying on burnished steel, nearly as white and dead as the walls
around them. Was he still making a difference, he asked himself
every time his scalpel opened a thoracic cavity? He had to tell
himself that he was.

'Well-nourished woman, John,' he muttered, making his way
around Florence Rook. 'Mid- to late forties. No obvious signs
of having done manual work. Not a virgin, but never gave birth.'
He glanced up at the inspector lolling against the far wall. It was
John Kane's birthday, but nobody at his place of work knew that,
or, if they did, they were woefully short on greetings. 'But I
don't suppose you want to know any of that, do you?'

'I've got a maniac on the loose, Wilf,' Kane said flatly. 'Not
that I'd put it quite like that to the gentlemen of the Press.'

'So you need to know how she died and when.'

'Preferably,' Kane said.

'She was beaten to death hours ago, give or take. What we in
the medical profession call repeated blows to the cranium with
a blunt object.'

'Solid glass ball, perhaps?' Kane had read Crawford's report
and had been to the crime scene itself.

'That would do it, yes. I presume you have such an object in
mind.'

'I do.' Kane came forward for a closer look at the late

Mrs Rook. 'It's currently in pieces in a shoebox at the Yard, crime-scene evidence, for the use of.'

'Well, if your lads can stick it together again, we'll have an approximate hand size of the killer.'

'That'll be music to Stockley Collins's ears,' Kane said, 'Although, in my experience, there isn't that much difference in hand size, at least between adult males.'

'You're looking for a man, then?'

Kane nodded. 'Women don't kill like this. Poison. Gun at a pinch. But bludgeoning? No, that's men's work. There *is* no poison, I assume?'

'No signs that I can see. As you know, I wasn't in on your first two mediums, so I can't vouch but there was poison there, wasn't there?'

'In Evadne Principal's case, cyanide. In Muriel Fazakerley's, God knows. Mistaken diagnosis, I'm afraid. Mulligatawny soup masks a multitude of sins.'

'I can believe that,' Henderson said. 'Florence here lost four teeth, all at the front. I'd need to see the tablecloth, but I'm prepared to bet she was hit from behind and above with her face pressed down on to it. After the first blow, it's unlikely she would have felt anything. Oh,' he wiped his hands and crossed the room to where a series of steel bowls held internal body parts. 'This might interest.'

'What is it?'

'Paper. I got my assistant to dry it out.'

'Dry it out?'

'It was in Florence's mouth. Covered in blood and saliva, of course, but still just about readable.'

Kane took the flimsy contents of the bowl to the high window, the one that let the street-level light into this chill basement. He squinted, angling the page this way and that.

'As dry leaves that before the wild hurricane fly, When they meet with an obstacle, mount to the sky, So up to the house-top the coursers they flew, With the sleigh full of toys, and St Nicholas too.'

'Does that mean anything to you?' Henderson asked.

'Yes and no,' Kane said cryptically. 'If memory serves it's from *The Night Before Christmas*. I'd have to look up who wrote it and when.'

'Christmas?' Henderson echoed. 'And here we are about to enter flaming June. Whenever I start to think how impossible my job is, John, I think of yours.'

'Thank you, Wilf,' Kane sighed. 'Much appreciated.'

'Are you any further forward, then?' the doctor asked him.

'Not really, but there *is* a kind of pattern here. Muriel Fazakerley had a feather in her mouth. Evadne Principal had a tarot card crushed into her hand – cadaveric spasm, or so I am reliably told. And now this, a fragment from a child's poem.'

'I'm glad,' Henderson said, 'that I opted for medicine all those years ago. It's bloody and it's depressing, but it's not impossibly cryptic, like your job.'

Kane picked up his hat from the bench where he had left it. 'Cryptic, definitely,' he said. 'But impossible? Not on my watch.' And he made for the door.

'Good luck, John,' Henderson called. 'Oh, and by the way – happy birthday!'

Andrew Crawford liked to walk around London, always had. Even his days as a constable, walking his beat back and forth at the regulation speed had not dimmed his enthusiasm. But Rotherhithe to Tottenham Court Road on a busy morning was a bit of a stretch so he treated himself to a cab. He reckoned that Friend's Scouring Powders could probably afford it. He hadn't married the lovely Angela Friend for the family money, but it certainly didn't hurt. He stopped his cabbie at the corner of Arundel Street and the main thoroughfare and paid him with a substantial tip. The cabbie drove off, calling, 'Good luck to ya, guv'nor!' and clicking his teeth suggestively. It was only when the man was out of sight that he realized he had got out more or less under the portico of Daisy Lorne's place of employment and he regretted the size of the tip. Some people had no sense of decorum!

Number Thirty-Eight was in some disarray, that much was clear from the corner. There was a ramshackle cart pulled up to the door and wooden crates spilling straw were stacked precariously on the pavement. Not only that, there was a lot of shouting – screaming, even – coming from inside and, as Crawford watched, a jug came out of an upstairs window and shattered in the middle of the road, making the nosy neighbours who were beginning to gather jump back into the safety of their doorways. Crawford broke into a run.

'Hello, hello, hello,' he yelled in the empty hall, having loped up the three low steps from the street. 'Police. Who's here?'

Three heads appeared over the rail at the top of the stairs, two women and a rather refined-looking man, with an eyeglass and hair slicked back from an intelligent forehead.

'Police?' the man said, looking to the women to his left and right. 'Who called the police?'

Both women shrugged and the man came down the stairs, carefully giving them a wide berth and watching them intently as he embarked on the journey down.

Standing in front of Crawford, he showed himself to be taller than his rather delicate features had suggested he would be. He held out a hand and Crawford shook it, almost recoiling from the damp, limp, fragile-feeling fingers.

'And you are?' Crawford said.

'Perceval Principal. This is . . . was . . . my wife's house.'

'I understood you and your wife were estranged, sir,' Crawford said, reasonably, resisting the urge to wipe his hand on his trousers.

Principal looked surprised. 'Whyever would you understand a thing like that, officer? It was scarcely something we broadcast from the rooftops.'

'I was told you didn't approve of her . . . Spiritualist leanings.'

The willowy man drew himself up, affronted. 'I had no problem at all with her leanings, officer,' he said. 'I had problems with never being able to call my soul my own, people in and out at all times – the oddest people you could imagine at that. Evadne would sometimes not return until dawn, having been table-turning all night, or at least, that was what she told me. Eventually, it all became too much and I went to my club and from there, to a little pied de terre belonging to a friend who is currently out of the country.'

'And yet you stayed in touch?' Crawford asked, innocently.

'Not really.'

'But you're here now, clearing out her house.' Crawford didn't like this man and was having difficulty keeping the information to himself.

'Exactly!' The voice from above could have etched glass. One of the women from the landing was making her way down the stairs, using a stick and a good deal of willpower. 'He just barged his way in, Constable . . .'

'Sergeant,' Crawford murmured, but was ignored.

'And started packing up Evadne's things.'

'She was my wife,' Principal pointed out.

'With the emphasis on *was*.' The woman turned to Crawford and grasped a lapel. 'He broke my daughter's heart, Constable,' she said, shaking him with every phrase. '*Broke* it, do you hear? All she did, poor darling, was to try to bring comfort to the bereaved and he treated her as though she was walking the streets. You *pig*!' she suddenly screamed at her erstwhile son-in-law. Then, in normal tones to Crawford, 'All men are beasts, I'm afraid, Constable.'

Crawford decided it was time he took control. He held the two protagonists out at arm's length and as far as possible from each other. 'Let us get a few things clear, sir, madam,' he said. 'Firstly, I am a detective sergeant, not a constable.' They both shrugged – it was of less than no interest to either of them. 'Secondly, I was unaware that this house had been handed back to the family by the police, as it is a crime scene until work on your wife's,' he turned his head, 'daughter's murder is complete.'

The woman huffed. 'There were a few padlocks,' she said, 'but I assumed this *pig* had fitted those.'

'No, madam. They would have been Metropolitan Police padlocks. I hope this isn't the case, but by doing what you have done here, you may have completely ruined any chance we had of catching Mrs Principal's killer.' He stopped to let it sink in, but if he was expecting remorse, he was doomed to disappointment.

With a sigh, Crawford resumed. 'So, what I would like to happen now is that everything currently on the pavement and on the cart is brought back into the house. And that one of you, I don't care which, finds me a picture of the late Mrs Principal, which I can take back to the station and use as part of my investigations.' He looked first at the husband, then at the mother and thought, not for the first time, how some people just seemed to draw the short straw when it came to family.

'Well,' Perceval Principal drew himself up again and tugged his jacket straight after it had been touched by constabulary fingers. 'I certainly don't intend to do any lifting of anything. And I don't have a photograph of my wife; I don't believe in images of people, it smacks of idolatry.'

'You must have been a lot of fun to live with,' Crawford remarked, surprised to hear the words coming out loud. 'I suggest in that case, you leave the building and, on your way out, tell your men to return the crates. And you, Mrs . . .?'

'Farquharson,' she told him, begrudgingly, as if each syllable cost money.

He didn't bother to repeat it back to her but carried on with his demands. 'You will also leave the building, but I am sure that as her mother, you have a photograph?'

She looked him up and down as if he smelled like the Thames with the tide out. 'No,' she said, 'indeed I do not. I warned her, I *warned* her not to marry that man and when she did, I removed all of her pictures and have never replaced them. Your superiors will hear of this,' she said, with a final nose-wrinkled glare, and swept out on the heels of her son-in-law, only to collide with a packing case carried by a burly carter.

'Sorry, m'um,' he muttered, touching the brim of his cap.

'*Pig!*' she screamed and was heard clattering down the steps and, he fervently hoped, out of Andrew Crawford's life for ever.

'I've got a picture, Mr Crawford.'

The soft voice at the sergeant's elbow made him jump and he looked down. 'Oh, hello, Annie,' he said to the maid. Crawford prided himself on remembering names and he could tell she was pleased as her face wreathed in a smile. 'I didn't recognize you up there on the landing.'

'You wouldn't have been expecting me, Mr Crawford, I don't expect,' she said. 'But Mrs Farquharson, she came round for the keys and I come round, to see what she was doing. You could have knocked me down with a feather when I saw as he was here. No right, neither of them.'

Crawford decided to play devil's advocate. 'I suppose, as next of kin . . .'

'So they might be,' Annie said. 'But Mrs P, she left all her things to me. Look.'

And she took a long, official-looking envelope out of her pocket and held it out.

Crawford glanced through it. It was a will, all properly witnessed, by a couple of girls from the brothel on the corner, judging from their names. It left all of which Mrs Evadne April Principal née Farquharson died possessed to her faithful maid, Ann Elizabeth Watkins. Short. And, for anyone who might be watching the faces of Perceval Principal and Mrs Farquharson when it was revealed, very sweet.

He smiled down at Annie. 'That was very kind of her,' he said.

'Well, she didn't think of herself as having no family,' Annie said, simply. 'And that lady being offed . . . I mean, passing Beyond the Veil . . . she wrote this out and got it witnessed as soon as she heard. She said you can't be too careful.'

'Indeed, you can't,' Crawford muttered. Was this another red herring dragged across his path, with another suspect in its wake, or . . . he looked at Annie, her face turned up to him full of trust. 'Look, Annie, if you need any help with you-know-who, just show this card to any policeman and they will let me know. And meanwhile . . . the picture?'

'Oh, yes.' She rummaged in another pocket. 'Here she is, poor lady. Looks different in this picture, don't she? Than when . . . well, you know.'

Crawford looked at the postcard he held between finger and thumb. Very different from the dead woman stretched out in her séance room. But very like Muriel Fazakerley. Very like indeed.

TEN

Like most people who had seen Florence Rook after she died, Crawford had tried to wipe it from his memory. And in any case, she was not looking her best. He made his way to Rose and Crown Yard to find a picture, but he knew already what he would find. That without the hair matted with blood and the missing teeth, the swelling and the trauma, Florence Rook would look very much like her two dead sisters. He knew that he would probably face some derision from his colleagues – after all, there was nothing to stand out about these women; theirs were faces which, with the occasional quirk and twitch, could be encountered on any street of any town in the land.

One person who could not be encountered in any street of any town was the moustachioed and quiffed figure of Stockley Collins. He and Constable Leyton were at work in the dead medium's house, clicking, dusting, adjusting as usual. The lad had felt a little queasy over this one, it was true, but he'd pulled himself together and had got on with the job.

'Hoping for a match, Stockley?' Crawford asked him.

'Expecting one rather than hoping,' the fingerprint man said. 'Ten to one the same incriminating dabs will be all over this place as they were over Evadne Principal's – and, had I been called in, Muriel Fazakerley's. Whether any of said dabs will match the collection at the Yard, however, is a different matter.'

'How many have you got now?' Crawford asked.

'Thirty-six,' Collins told him, 'and that includes the two Stratton brothers. I reckon by the time we've got a meaningful collection in the shoeboxes, it will be the year of our Lord 2022 or thereabouts.'

'Constable.' Crawford turned to the young man crouching under the black hood, rather like a wretch facing the Billingtons. 'This is what the late Mrs Rook used to look like.'

Leyton shook his head.

Collins looked at the photograph too. 'Arsonist,' he said, 'with a tendency to kleptomania and sadistic impulses.'

'Really?' Crawford was nonplussed.

'No, but pretty well everybody back at the Shop believes all that Lombrosian mumbo-jumbo. It'll take young Leyton and my good self years to show them the error of their ways. Don't . . . oh, bugger.' Collins nudged Crawford aside. 'I'd just dusted that and you've brushed your bum against it.'

He wondered, as he walked back to Scotland Yard, how seriously he would be taken when he pointed out the similarity to John

Kane. Kane was a reasonable man and probably gave Crawford more rope than almost any other inspector would give a lowly sergeant, but even so . . . he mulled as he walked, his mind elsewhere than on his direction, so it came as somewhat of a surprise to him to find, when he stubbed his toe on a low step, that it was the step up into the Petrie Museum, rather than his place of work.

He stood for a moment, looking up at the façade of the building in some confusion. It was true that he would probably get more sense out of Margaret Murray than anyone at the Yard, but as a way of moving the case forward, of getting the faces of the mediums out to the Press and on flyers, it was not really a helpful move. Reluctantly, because he could do with a cup of tea and a sit-down as much as anything, he turned to make his way back to the Yard, another half an hour's walk, at least the way his feet were throbbing.

Before he could cross the road, he heard someone call his name and turned to see Thomas emerging from a side door.

'Hello, Detective Sergeant,' the tea shop proprietor carolled, with only a slight trace of irony. 'What brings you here?'

'I don't know, Thomas, to be honest,' Crawford said, scratching his head. 'Feet. Exhaustion. Desperation.'

Thomas laughed. 'You've come to the right place,' he said. 'I've just been up to the Prof's room with a top-up of garibaldis but she's on her way down. I've got a batch of Chelsea buns coming out of the oven and she was tempted. Why don't you pop over and join her – you know she's always pleased to see you. And I wouldn't mind a chat either, now you're here.'

The thought of Thomas wanting to talk to the police on purpose rather tickled Crawford's fancy and, apart from that, he could almost smell the Chelsea buns. But he really should . . . 'Oh, all right, Thomas,' he said. 'You've twisted my arm.'

They approached the kerb and looked both ways; the traffic was murderous as always. They darted across, taking opportunities when they could.

'In my old dad's day,' Thomas observed, 'the crossing sweepers never had to contend with all this. They had all the time in the world, the odd cab, a dray perhaps. But now, you take your life in your hands every time you step off the pavement. You lot ought to be doing something.'

'There is a man on point duty,' Crawford said, quite reasonably. 'If no one takes any notice of him, it's hardly his fault.'

'There should be rules,' Thomas grumbled.

'There are,' Crawford said, 'and same as before, they only work if people take notice.'

They pushed open the door of the Jeremy Bentham and were immediately enveloped in the warm, tea-scented ambience that Thomas had made his own. For an old lag, Crawford thought, he has a lot of taste and discernment.

'I assume you didn't want to talk to me about the traffic arrangements in London,' Crawford said.

'No.' Thomas looked serious. 'Let's go into the back parlour. The prof'll know where to find us.'

The back parlour was known only to a special few. It was discreetly lit and only Thomas and his most trusted staff served there. At the moment, it was empty.

'I wanted to ask what's happening with poor old Adolf,' Thomas said, sitting down at a table in a corner, making sure he faced the door.

'Adolf?' Crawford was at a loss.

'Adolf Beck. He was arrested in connection . . .'

'I remember,' Crawford said, apologetically. 'To be honest with you, Thomas, I had quite forgotten the poor man. I would imagine they let him go.'

Thomas looked at him with as near to dislike as he ever showed on his face. 'You would imagine, would you?' he said, drumming his fingers. 'You would imagine. Well, that's all right then. He'll probably be walking in any minute.' He craned his neck theatrically, looking at the door. 'No. No sign.'

Crawford started to worry. The last he had heard of Adolf Beck was that he had been arrested. But he didn't usually deal with the paperwork involved in setting anyone free. Surely, he wasn't still in the cells? Although, if he were, that could be a good thing. He tried to sell that point of view to Thomas.

'I don't think he is still in custody, Thomas, but if he is, that could be a good thing.'

'Oh ar? Tell that to the marines.' Sometimes Thomas delighted in letting his veneer peel away a little. 'Banged up with God knows what lowlife and thinking he's going to be in there years, like he was last time. It's all very fine and good for you to say it would be a good thing, but I doubt Adolf would feel the same. Why would it be, anyway, a good thing?'

'Because,' Crawford said, aware he was about to share with a civilian things which currently only the police knew, 'it would mean he couldn't possibly have committed the latest murder.'

'Another one?' Thomas was not surprised as such, because murders in London were not really that rare. But he assumed, rightly, that it was another in the series. 'Another medium?'

'Yes,' Crawford nodded. 'Last night, just off Pall Mall. Florence Rook.'

Thomas furrowed his brow. 'Don't I know that name . . .?'

'You might well, but you're thinking of Florence Cook. The victim was somewhat of a follower of the lady.'

'I remember, yes. She was all the rage for a while, wasn't she? Her and Katie King.' He sighed appreciatively. 'We all thought she had it pat. None of us could spring a lay like her.' He doffed a metaphorical cap.

'Well, anyway,' Crawford said, 'Mum's the word. I'll check on Mr Beck as soon as I get to the Yard.'

The door swung open and a diminutive archaeologist stood there, looking at two of her three favourite men in the world. She stepped forward, slipping off her coat into Thomas's waiting hands.

'Andrew! How lovely! I hope you're joining me for a Chelsea bun.'

'Indeed I am,' Crawford said, resuming his seat, out of which he had bounced as soon as he heard her voice. 'I need to chat to you anyway.'

'Ooh,' Margaret sat down, settling herself comfortably. 'More information on poor Miss Plunkett? I have been worrying about the poor dear, let alone feeling rather guilty.'

'Guilty ain't really the word, is it?' Thomas had reappeared with a plate of buns and a tray of teacups. A maid followed with the pot and accoutrements but she left immediately with a courteous bob.

'What a sweet girl she is,' Margaret said, smiling. 'Always so polite. Shall I be mother?' And she poured the tea while Andrew Crawford handed round the buns. 'I know I shouldn't feel guilty, Thomas,' she carried on when they were all settled. 'But I do. Poor Christina was beaten mercilessly in mistake for me.'

'So the only guilty party is the man who did it,' Crawford said. 'Not you. Reports from the hospital before I set out say that she is much better, expected to go home in a day or so.'

'That's good.' Margaret Murray took a bite from a still-warm Chelsea bun and nodded to Thomas. 'Delicious,' she said, with her mouth full.

'I just wanted to show you these,' Crawford said, fishing the pictures out of his inside pocket and spreading them in front of her. She looked at them closely then picked them up and looked closer still.

'They're . . . well, they are all very alike, Andrew,' she said. 'But they're not . . . unusual women, are they? I mean, mousey hair, greyish eyes, even features. If they all had something like a wall eye or a broken nose, but . . . Thomas.' She held out the pictures to him. 'What do you think?'

Thomas looked at them and could see her point. On the other hand, he could see Crawford's point as well. As three women, they didn't really need a second glance. Pleasant enough faces, but nothing startling. Slightly different ages, but they had all aged well. You wouldn't gasp in amazement if they were lined up in front of you. But – and he couldn't ignore it – they had one thing in common. They were all dead. And that had to trump everything else. He put the cards down. 'If they wasn't all dead, I'd say no more about it,' he said. 'But seeing as how they are, it's a bit of a facer, ain't it? My old man used to say there was no such thing as coincidence and I must say, in this case, I agree.'

Margaret Murray sat back. She was being outvoted, that much was obvious. And she was happy to be so. Thomas was right; the fact that they were all dead made the resemblance more than a mere quirk. It made it something important.

'Does it help us, though?' She had to express her doubts. 'We can't go round London warning every medium in her thirties and forties with mousey hair and a nice pleasant face to watch out, she might be murdered.' She looked at the two earnest faces in front of her. 'Well, can we?'

Crawford was the first to speak. 'No, but . . .' He looked rather crestfallen. 'It's a clue that isn't even slightly helpful,' he said, despondently.

'No information is ever unhelpful, Andrew,' the archaeologist said kindly. 'That's why in my line of work, we never throw anything away, no matter how unimportant it may seem. Who knows whether, in the future, the other half of it may emerge and everything will be clear. And so it may yet prove with this. Although we do seem dogged by similarities, don't we? Miss Plunkett being mistaken for me. Poor Mr Beck being identified by Miss Lorne. We need to keep all this in mind and I'm sure something will drop into place. What do you think, Andrew? Thomas?'

The men nodded. Crawford still had to put the pictures into evidence, but he would let that take him where it may. And meanwhile, he was up by a Chelsea bun and a cup of tea, so the day was looking brighter.

Margaret could have watched him all day. The way Kirk Merrington etched the palm leaves and the reeds that fringed the Nile, the way he duplicated the folds in the robes of the high priests. She particularly admired the elaborate top-knot he had given the pharaoh, resting, in an unguarded moment, without his double crown of the Two Kingdoms.

It was the quiet time at the Petrie Museum, a little after lunch, when the hordes of the morning had gone and the hordes of the afternoon had not yet arrived. Merrington had found himself a little corner of Margaret's inner sanctum where the light hit his table perfectly and he was transcribing his rough sketches into the finished article.

'Wouldn't it be marvellous,' she said, 'if they could talk to us.'

'Who?' Merrington was miles away.

'The people we have here,' she said, sitting a little behind him so that she didn't obscure the light. 'In the cases.'

'Oh, the mummies.' He leaned back and put his pen down. 'Yes, indeed it would.' He turned to her, frowning. 'But don't they talk to you all the time, Dr Murray? With your insight into their world?'

Margaret smiled. 'How very perceptive you are, Mr Merrington,' she said. 'And you flatter me. But an archaeologist can know only so much from bones and tomb artefacts. Skin, now, that's different. There is a man named Collins at Scotland Yard – have you heard of him?'

'I don't believe I have.' Merrington got back to his drawing.

'He's a fingerprint expert. I am hoping he'll be able to take the prints of some of our exhibits – with more than usual care, of course.'

'Fascinating,' Merrington said.

'But even so,' she went on, 'it's not the same as actually *talking* to someone from the past. Have you ever dabbled, Mr Merrington, with the Other Side?'

He turned to her again, laughing this time. 'Are you talking about séances?' he asked, wobbling his fingers in the air and making 'woo-woo' noises.

'I am,' she said, 'and I assume from your reaction that you don't believe a word of it.'

'No,' he said. 'I don't. I believe Courtney, my secretary, has occasionally attended. My only experience stems from when I was really very young.'

'Really?'

'It was all the vogue some years ago, wasn't it? Table-tilting, spirit-writing, something of a party game.'

'Indeed it was,' Margaret said.

'It stuck in my mind because it was so silly.'

'What?' Margaret asked. 'Clanking chains, white sheets?'

'Oh, it wasn't as obvious as that,' he said, folding his arms and smiling at the memory of it. 'There was a little group, a Circle, I suppose you'd call it, men and women. And an old harridan who was the medium. Everybody talked in hushed tones and was very deferential to her. I remember how cold it was and I wanted to keep my scarf on, but they wouldn't let me.'

'Did anything happen?'

'Somebody broke the glass; you know, the one they used to spell out messages from beyond – wherever "beyond" is supposed to be.'

'Somebody broke it?'

'Well, obviously. Oh, it appeared to shatter by itself, but you and I, Dr Murray, know enough about the laws of physics to know that that isn't possible. But it was the wall writing that was the most ridiculous of all.'

'Oh? What did it say?'

'God, I don't remember. Something like "Watch me" . . . no, no. "Look at me". That was it.'

'What did you make of that?' Margaret asked.

'What does a thirteen year old make of anything?' Merrington shrugged. 'Somebody turned on the lights and we all went home. My money was on the medium.'

'The horrible old harridan?'

'Yes. Well, she controlled the whole thing. I've read since how they do it. They build up the tension with silence and darkness and ask silly questions and exert just enough pressure on the wine glass to make it move. Others in the Circle aid and abet them – oh, not intentionally, but imperceptibly because they *want* it to happen. In the darkness, a clever conjuror can easily leave her place at the table, scrawl rubbish on a wall and nip back before she's missed. It's all about misdirection. We were all looking at the glass at the time and that was what we all saw.'

'Were there any voices?' Margaret asked.

'Voices? Yes, I believe there were. And that, really, is how I know the whole thing was a put-up job. The voice said "Boy". Well, how many séances have boys at them? The old harridan could see me there. She was working on the sensibilities of those present.' Merrington paused. 'How on earth did we get on to this subject?'

Margaret laughed. 'The people of the past,' she said, 'and if they could only talk to us. Interesting, though, that mediums should be in the news at the moment.'

'Are they?' Merrington was sharpening a pencil.

'Three mediums murdered in London within a three-week period.'

'Oh, yes,' Merrington nodded. 'I read about two. Who's the third?'

'Her name, I believe, was Florence Rook.'

'I'll check with Courtney,' the artist said. 'See if she knew her.'

* * *

'Mother of God!' Flinders Petrie was standing in Margaret Murray's inner sanctum, Kirk Merrington's artwork in his hands. He couldn't believe what he saw. Admittedly, the wretched artist had drawn in his horns from the cartoonish approach of his first efforts, but these sweeping dioramas would put Lawrence Alma-Tadema to shame.

There was only one other person in the room and the great man launched into him. 'You!' he snapped. 'Brooks, isn't it?'

'Er . . . yes, Professor. Jack Brooks. Is something amiss?' He had never seen Flinders Petrie *quite* that purple before.

'Where is Dr Murray?'

'Umm . . . I've no idea,' Brooks said. He checked his half-hunter. 'She's finished her eleven o'clock lecture by now. Her next tutorial isn't until three. Long lunch hour by the look of it.' He was trying to be helpful. 'You might try the Jeremy Bentham.'

'Arthur Evans might actually try to be an archaeologist,' Petrie growled, 'but I doubt it. I had a less than adequate Eccles at the Bentham last week and I'm in no hurry to repeat the experience.' He stood silently fuming, then he stuffed the artwork into a portfolio. 'Should Dr Murray turn up,' he said, 'tell her I wish to see her at her earliest convenience.' And he swept out, leaving Brooks in no doubt at all who owned and ran the Petrie Museum.

'I'm afraid Mr Quaritch . . .' was as far as the hapless girl on the desk got before the hurricane that was Flinders Petrie whirled past her in a profusion of flapping Ulster and wild, white hair.

'Not as afraid as he's going to be!' Petrie misunderstood the girl completely as he took the stairs two at a time. He crashed into the publisher's office just in time to see a pretty little secretary bounce off Bernard Quaritch's lap and into a demure, secretarial pose on a nearby chair.

'Smartly done,' the professor grated. 'Now, do something smarter and disappear.' He waved her away.

'Now, look here, Professor . . .' Quaritch didn't see himself as a tradesman, whatever Kirk Merrington's and Lord Byron's views of publishers were, and no fuddy-duddy from the world of academe was going to . . .

'No, you look here!' Flinders Petrie threw the portfolio on to the man's desk, 'at these.'

Quaritch made great play of adjusting his pince-nez before he gave his erudite verdict on the artwork. 'Ah.'

'Quite!' Petrie sat down uninvited. 'Dr Murray's book was sponsored by Professor Virchov of Berlin, Sir Mohammed ibn Teshufin of Cairo, not to mention my good self. It is a scholarly work of modest length by a woman for whom I have the highest regard but who is, she won't mind my saying, a beginner in such matters. Merrington has turned the whole thing into a circus, a children's picture book.'

'Oh, come now, Professor.' Quaritch was being far more reasonable. 'A little licence, surely.'

'Licence be buggered!' Petrie roared. 'Either you rein in this charlatan with a paintbrush or I pull the whole book.'

'You can't.'

'Oh, but I can. University College has sponsored Dr Murray's work too. That means the whole project is in my gift. Dr Murray will no doubt go on to write many more tomes, but Bernard Quaritch will not be publishing them.'

The publisher reflected for a moment. Sales had not been going well recently; the republication of *The Lustful Turk* had not gone down at all well – with the Women's Social and Political Union on the prowl, times were changing.

'What if,' he said, looking at the drawings again, 'we reach a compromise? Get somebody else to do a few simple, mundane archaeological drawings and leave Merrington with a cover design and frontispiece – to be chosen by you, of course.'

Flinders Petrie hesitated. 'Will he go for that?' he asked.

'There's one way to find out,' the publisher said, crossing the room to get his coat. 'We can ask him.'

The tall studio houses along Ampton Street screamed artist. Long windows, gleaming with art nouveau glass, reached from pavement to sky, and the equally elegant door was opened by a tall, angular woman wearing a man's riding waistcoat and a long riding habit.

'Is Mr Merrington at home?' Quaritch tipped his hat.

'I'm afraid not – Mr Quaritch, is it? He shouldn't be long. Would you care to wait?'

She showed the pair into a large vestibule, where paintings of a dubious nature hung on walls dark with flock. No doubt they all had deep spiritual meaning, but the Bishop of London would have had a coronary had he seen them.

'Would you like some tea, gentlemen?' the secretary asked in her dark brown voice. 'Coffee? Mr Merrington likes his Turkish style.'

'This isn't exactly a social call,' Petrie scowled at her. 'Will he be long?'

The woman looked at him quizzically. 'Where are my manners?' she said. 'I don't mean to stare, sir, but it *is* you, isn't it? Professor Flinders Petrie?'

'I have that honour,' he said. Famous as he was in the world of archaeology, that was a very small world indeed and he had yet to be mobbed in the street.

'May I say – I'm Courtney, by the way – may I say what a profound honour this is. The doyen of the publishing world and another world's leading archaeologist under the same roof!' She clasped her hands together in pure joy. 'Please,' and she ushered them to soft, leather seats.

She sat with them and became serious. 'It's about the drawings for Dr Murray's book, isn't it?'

Quaritch and Petrie looked at each other. 'It is,' the professor said.

Courtney shook her head. 'Mr Merrington has put his heart and soul into those. He is *such* a passionate man. Every project he undertakes, he gives it his all.'

'Well,' Petrie grunted, 'his all, in this case, may not be enough.'

'Enough for what?' Kirk Merrington stood in the doorway, hauling off his scarf and wideawake.

His visitors stood up. 'Professor Petrie here has misgivings,' Quaritch said.

'Does he now?' Merrington crossed to the man. He did not extend his hand. 'We haven't met, sir,' he said, 'although I know of you by reputation, of course. About what do you misgive?'

'The drawings.' Petrie came to the point. 'They are too lavish, too garish, too large and extreme for a book of this nature.'

'Dr Murray rather liked them,' Merrington bridled.

'With all due respect to Dr Murray,' the professor said, 'and believe me, I have that in spades, this is her first book. I, on the other hand, have published . . .'

'But I don't work for you,' Merrington said flatly.

Quaritch opened his mouth to say something.

'Or you.' Merrington stopped him in his tracks.

'But I shall be paying you,' the publisher reminded him, 'or not, as the case may be.'

'Did Dr Murray send you?' Merrington asked Petrie.

'Certainly not.' It was the archaeologist's turn to bridle. 'I am no woman's lackey.'

'Good for you,' Merrington snarled. 'If Dr Murray has issues with my work, all well and good. I have made changes at her request already. But if you'll forgive me, when a mountebank and his zany make such unreasonable demands, I am inclined to say get out of my house before I throw you out.'

It was one of those moments in men's lives, when civilization vanishes in a second and stone-cold aggression stands, threatening, in its place. Merrington was tall and willowy but who knew what Bohemian tricks he had up his sleeve should it come to fisticuffs? Petrie never wrestled with chimney sweeps and glancing briefly at Quaritch, decided that discretion was the better part of valour. He had also glanced briefly at Courtney, standing like an ox in the furrow with clenched fists. He had noticed, somewhat to his surprise, a pair of distinctly feminine breasts standing proudly under her blouse, over the waistcoat. He was a gentleman and wouldn't want to hit a woman but, anyway, her thighs looked as though they could crack walnuts and he was not about to take any chances.

'Certainly,' he said to Merrington. 'But don't let me hear that you have been anywhere near my museum or Dr Murray again.'

'Er . . . I think the professor's in rather a bad mood.' Jack Brooks was making the tea for himself and Margaret Murray.

'It's his age,' she smiled.

'No, he's really gunning for you.'

Margaret paused in mid hat-removal. '"Gunning for me", Mr Brooks? Do I detect a quotation from an American dime novel?'

Brooks was surprised. 'Why, yes, as a matter of fact, it is. Owen Wister. *The Virginian.* Don't tell me you read such tosh.'

'I'm afraid I do,' she chuckled. 'My guilty secret. But,' she took the proffered cup, 'on a different note entirely, was your mother serious about holding a séance at her house?'

'Oh, rather.' Brooks sat down, passing Margaret the ginger McVitie's.

'Well, can you ask her for a convenient date?' she said. 'I've managed to procure one of the most famous mediums in the world today – Eusapia Palladino.'

'Palladino!' Brooks nearly choked on his McVitie's. 'Dr Murray, how do you do it? She is the crème de la crème of mediums.'

'I hope she doesn't disappoint,' Margaret mused.

'Talking of disappointment, Margaret . . .' Flinders Petrie was crashing through the door, barely remembering to open it first. 'Brooks, make yourself scarce.'

The postgraduate student stood up certainly but showed no sign of going. Like all professors, Petrie could be a bullying old bastard when it suited him, but Brooks's innate loyalty lay with Margaret.

'Now!' Petrie thundered, and Margaret nodded at the lad to go quietly.

Brooks closed to the professor. 'When you say that,' he said, 'smile.'

Margaret suppressed a chortle. The Wisterism was lost on Petrie but she and Jack appreciated it all the same.

'Was there a problem, William?' she asked when he had gone.

'That wretched Merrington,' the professor sat down heavily. 'I have, in effect, fired him.' He caught her gaze. 'With Bernard Quaritch's blessing, before you ask.'

Margaret smiled at her mentor, her colleague, her sometime lover. 'That's as may be, William,' she said softly. 'But you don't have my blessing; not at all.'

'Dr Murray?' A tall man with a quiff and a moustache swept off his hat and smiled down at the shortest archaeologist in London that afternoon.

'Inspector Collins?' She held out a hand. 'Delighted to meet you. And thank you *so* much for helping me in my enquiries.'

'That's usually my line,' Collins grinned. 'And I'm not sure how much help I can be.'

She ushered him into an antechamber of the museum where shrivelled corpses stood around the walls, supported by pegs and hooks. 'I assume,' she said, 'that you are familiar with cadavers.'

'All too, madam,' he said, 'though rarely in the state this lot's in.'

'Indeed not,' she said, 'but this lot is between two and three thousand years old, Inspector. What I believe you in the police call "cold cases".'

Collins smiled. 'What can I do for you?'

Margaret scuttled around a desk and slid a drawer open. She held up a mummified hand. 'The digits of what we believe is a high priest of the Old Kingdom,' she said. 'It would be fascinating to know if his loops and whorls, as I believe you call them, are similar to ours today.'

'Well,' Collins examined the wizened brown hand carefully. 'We've never actually taken a corpse's prints before – not as old as this, anyway.'

'You've taken more recent ones?' she asked.

'Let's just say, I am in the process.'

'Anyone we know?'

Collins laughed. 'Dr Murray,' he said, 'I'm afraid I'm not at liberty—'

'Oh, tosh, Mr Collins!' she interrupted. 'You and I are on the same quest in life.'

'We are?'

'A quest for the truth. I, to find out all I can about the past. You, to catch criminals. Especially,' she tapped his Gladstone, 'murderers.'

'You're very perceptive, madam,' he said.

'It helps,' she tapped the side of her nose, 'if you have a friend on the inside. A friend who might well be involved in the investigation of the murders of three mediums in this city.'

'And who might that be?' Collins asked.

'Aha,' Margaret laughed. 'No names, no pack drill. To borrow a phrase from the Yard – "I couldn't possibly divulge".'

'I thought not,' he chuckled.

'Can you work miracles?' she asked.

'It's not very miraculous, a little graphite,' Collins admitted, 'but I'll give your pharaohs my best shot. And then I believe you have some special items in your office; we'll go there next.'

'Thank you.'

'And don't worry,' he said. 'I shan't tell Andrew Crawford you nearly dobbed him in.'

It was almost knocking off time when the telephone rang on John Kane's desk. He looked at it suspiciously. It was always the same at this time of day. A sword of Damocles hung over his head. If he picked it up and it was urgent, he would be up all night, racing hither and thither after what was almost certainly a red herring. On the other hand, if he didn't pick it up and it was urgent, the caller would ring round all the other numbers at the Yard until they found someone fool enough to answer and that would just give Kane long enough to get home and ensconce himself in front of a nice plate of jellied eels or pigs' trotters or something else he had been fancying all day, only to have some beat plod hammer on his door and tell him there was an urgent case back at the Yard. He sighed and picked up the receiver.

'Yes?'

'Is that Inspector Kane?' A pleasant female voice met his ear, a change from the usual aggressive tones of the desk sergeant, that much was certain.

'It is.'

'I was hoping that Detective Sergeant Andrew Crawford might be within earshot. I need to give him a message.'

'I am not Detective Sergeant Crawford's social secretary, madam,' the inspector said with some asperity.

'Oh, goodness, no, I don't want you to misunderstand me, Inspector Kane. This is Dr Margaret Murray, of University College. I don't know whether perhaps Detective Sergeant Crawford has ever mentioned me . . .'

'In passing,' Kane growled.

'Something that we discussed earlier today has been on my mind and I hoped I would be able to talk it over with him.'

'About a case?'

'Oh, very much so. Is he there?'

'I believe he is just finishing off some paperwork in the sergeant's mess. I can give him a message, if that would suffice.'

Like most people talking to Margaret Murray for long, he felt himself getting more polite and helpful. The woman was positively contagious.

'If you would. Could you tell him . . . oh, dear, Inspector. I think you may think this is a social occasion. It isn't though, I assure you.'

'Madam. I would love to go home. If you could just give me the message?'

'If you're sure you won't misunderstand.'

'The message.' The voice was becoming more like its usual growl.

'Could he meet me at the Tambour House Hotel? He'll know where that is. Thank you so much, Inspector. Goodbye.'

And Margaret Murray put down the phone and looked up at Mrs Plinlimmon.

'Is my hat on straight, Mrs Plinlimmon?' she asked, anxiously. 'Only, Inspector Reid is so very picky, dear Edmund, and I fancy I have rather a lot of persuading to do this evening. It wouldn't do to arrive déshabillé.'

The owl said nothing. Friends don't, when it comes to criticizing each other's clothing.

ELEVEN

The Tambour House Hotel prided itself in its hospitality and had several small rooms set aside in which guests could entertain. Some, it had to be said, were a little grim, with the only aspect from the window being the bins in the yard below street level. But the one they always gave to their regulars was very pleasant, at the front just over the portico, so that while waiting, people could watch the coming and going in the street below. So Margaret Murray and Edmund Reid saw Andrew Crawford before he saw them.

'Are you going to tell me why you have called us together, Margaret?' Reid asked as they waited for the policeman to be shown up.

'I won't, Edmund, if you don't mind,' Margaret said. 'I hate repeating myself more than necessary and this is quite a complex situation so I would prefer to say it only once, if that is all right with you.'

'We can ask questions, I assume?' Reid was being somewhat ironic.

'Of course, of course.' The door opened and Crawford peered round. 'Do come in, Andrew, and thank you so much for coming at such short notice. It's just that I have had an idea. Well, it began with a bit of a worry and became an idea.'

Crawford sat opposite the others, with his back to the light. He wanted to be able to assess what the situation was and how much Margaret Murray was going to try and con him into something he didn't want to do. There was that kind of smell in the air, that kind of expression on her face.

'This is nice,' she said, putting her hands on her knees and leaning forward. 'Is it too early for a small sherry, do you think?'

'Margaret,' Reid said, coming to the point. 'I think that Crawford here and I are both thinking the same thing.'

'Yes,' Crawford came in on cue. 'What is it and no, we're not going to do it.'

'Really, Andrew, you wound me,' she said, pouring the sherry. 'I just need to discuss something and you are always the men I would ask any ticklish question.'

The two men exchanged glances. They were on their guard, the glances said. They had each other's backs.

'This morning,' she said, ignoring the display of male bonding in front of her, 'just to recap, Andrew showed me pictures of the three mediums who have sadly been murdered in these few short weeks. I hope I wasn't flippant, Andrew, when I suggested their similarity to each other was unhelpful, it certainly wasn't my intention. Since then, I have been mulling things over and I think we should be taking steps to protect women – and possibly even the few men – engaged in this business.'

'I'm not sure how,' Reid said. 'It isn't as if they have a trades union, is it?'

'They don't, that's true,' she agreed. 'But the world in which they move is small and I think that if we ask one or two Circles to disseminate the need for care, we can reach everyone, after a time. However, I am not sure that time is something we have at our disposal.'

Crawford leaned forward, his finger in the air. 'You're right,' he said. 'The gap between Muriel Fazakerley and Evadne Principal was longer than that between Mrs Principal and Mrs Rook. Also, and this is the worrying thing, the violence is escalating, from a simple poisoning to a savage beating. And we mustn't forget the incident with Christina Plunkett.'

Reid raised an eyebrow. 'A non-fatal attack?' he said. 'That could be important.'

'Not as such,' Crawford said. 'We believe that the attack was connected, but it was on a woman who was mistaken for Margaret.'

Reid's eyes nearly popped out of his head. 'And you're walking around, woman? Without any protection?'

Crawford nodded wryly. 'I know, I know. She insists she is safe.'

'And I am. Look.' She spread her arms. 'Safe as houses. And if Thomas doesn't soon stop popping in with biscuits and other supplies, I shall scream. However, that's not why we're here. I have a moral dilemma I need your help with.'

The policemen, current and ex, looked expectant.

'I have been asked by the Bermondsey Spiritualist Circle to contact Eusapia Palladino and ask her to do a sitting for them . . . us, I suppose I should say.'

'Why?'

'Pardon me?'

'Why you?' Reid liked to have his facts straight. 'You've only just joined. Is it some kind of test?'

'Goodness me, I don't think so. Your time as a policeman has made you a cynic, Edmund. No, it's because they think I know Sir Oliver Lodge.'

'And do you?' Crawford knew the answer but thought he would ask anyway.

'No. But it's possible I gave them that impression. I have managed to find Miss Palladino's address, but I don't feel I should invite her. Despite her looking nothing like any of the departed, I think I would be putting her at risk if I deliberately invited her into the arena, so to speak.'

'I don't think I have ever seen a picture of the lady,' Reid said. 'Is she really nothing like the others?'

Margaret rummaged in her reticule and brought out a pasteboard *carte de visite*. On it, there was a picture of a very forbidding lady of some fifty years old, with a mouth like a rat-trap and thin hair padded out with combings. She proffered it to the men.

'Ah. I see. So she should be safe, surely?'

'I see Margaret's point,' Crawford said. 'She said this afternoon that the likeness between the others is very slight, based on no strong physical attributes, so it may be a coincidence. But this lady . . .' he glanced at the picture again '. . . looks well able to look after herself.'

'No one is safe from a blunt object round the side of the head,' Reid said, with accuracy. 'I think Margaret is right. If she hasn't already been invited, then I think the best plan would be for Margaret to say she has replied and can't come. No point in putting the woman in harm's way unnecessarily, is there?'

'Quite.' Margaret smiled. 'But my PhD student, Jack Brooks, has a lovely mama who is really looking forward to hosting a very grand séance with Miss Palladino in the chair. And I don't want to disappoint her.'

Crawford gave her an old-fashioned look. He could sense that the punchline was only minutes away.

'If you think you're going to take her place,' Reid blustered, 'you have another think coming. Look at yourself, woman, you're five foot nothing in your thickest socks. This woman is known to hurl tables around. Look at her – she's got shoulders like tallboys.'

'I had no intention of taking her place,' Margaret said, calmly. 'For one thing, I know Lady Sylvia quite well and of course all of the Bermondsey Circle would spot the deception immediately. But replacing her is a very good idea, Edmund, well done.'

Crawford could hardly suppress a laugh. Here it came, delivered straight to the jugular in fine Murray style.

'Do you have anyone in mind?' the ex-policeman asked. 'One of your lady students, perhaps? Except that . . . the age differ-ence is tricky. It's not always easy to do, even with clever makeup. And you do need someone the same build. Do we know her height?'

'I would estimate about five feet four, from other photographs I have seen.'

Crawford turned his laugh into a cough.

'Hmm. It will take quite a consummate actress to carry it off. I suggest you just cancel, Margaret. You'll lose a bit of face, but so what? Worse things happen at sea.'

'The thing is, though,' Margaret said, a tad plaintively, 'I was hoping that such a big event might draw out our man. It would be such a shame to miss the opportunity.' She sighed and closed her eyes, then opened one, just a tiny bit, and watched Reid like a blackbird with the morning's fattest worm.

Reid looked at her and Crawford, glancing from one to the other, saw the light dawning. Before the older man could speak, he leaned forward and patted his knee.

'Come along now, Inspector Dier,' he said. 'Just how attached are you to the face fungus? It'll soon grow back, won't it? Come along. In the interests of justice.'

Reid's expression grew mutinous.

'Yes indeed, Edmund. In the interests of justice. And it will be fun. What about it, Edmund? Eh?'

Reid looked from one to the other, like a rabbit flanked by two very determined stoats. 'I'll think about it,' he said.

They continued to hold him with their eyes.

'Well, all right then, in the interests of justice. And I'm not wearing stays.'

'I'm not sure Italian ladies are that enamoured of stays,' Margaret offered, on no foundation whatsoever.

'And I won't do the accent.'

Margaret cocked an eyebrow and smiled sweetly.

'All right, I'll do the accent. But . . .'

'But?' Crawford sounded like the angel on his shoulder.

'If you tell anyone it's me, I'll never speak to either of you again.'

Two hands snaked out to shake his.

'It's a deal,' Crawford said, quickly, before he could change his mind.

Margaret Murray looked at the fob watch suspended from a brooch worn high on her bosom. 'Now,' she said. 'We must get a bit of a hurry on. Angela will be waiting at the restaurant.'

'Angela?' Crawford said.

'Restaurant?' Reid chimed in.

'Yes, indeed. Mama's Trattoria off Baker Street. You need to work on the accent, Edmund, and what better way to do it than while eating linguine?'

'You'd reserved a table?' Crawford muttered as they went down the stairs.

'Of course.' She raised innocent eyes to his. 'Mama's is very busy in the evenings and I would have been foolish to leave it to chance.'

Crawford shook his head and followed her down the stairs, looking at Reid stumping on ahead. He pictured him in the bombazine and lace; he would be the most perfect Eusapia Palladino in the world, possibly better even than the original!

Angela Crawford was waiting when they got to the restaurant and her face lit up when she saw her husband. She had not been at all sure that he would go along with Margaret Murray's idea but one look at him told her all she knew; he was looking forward to it as much as she was. Murder always cast a pall over their home. They had had more than their fair share, even allowing for his calling, so anything to lighten the mood was welcome and she could already see Edmund Reid in full fig.

He gave her an old-fashioned look as the three newcomers were ushered to their seats. 'Nice to see you again, Mrs Crawford. You're looking well. How are the children?'

'And good to see you, too, Mr Reid.' She paused, a smile hovering on her lips. 'I assume as you are here that you have agreed . . .'

'Not to say agreed, as such,' he said, quickly. 'In principle, perhaps. There are still a lot of details to iron out.'

Angela and Margaret looked at each other with the look that mothers often use when their offspring says something clever. No words were needed, nor were any said.

'Did you fish out those things?' Margaret said, obliquely.

Angela reached down and held up a small travelling bag. 'Everything but the wig. Nanny is proud to have all her own hair still. But we can pick up a wig anywhere along Bond Street, I would imagine. We'll get a better fit if Mr Reid would go into the shop.'

Crawford hid his guffaw behind the menu.

'Mr Reid will be doing no such thing,' he said. 'In fact, at this very moment, Mr Reid may well be heading off home to Hampton-on-Sea and never speaking to any of you again.' He shot his cuffs and picked up the menu. 'Any recommendations?' he asked of the table at large.

'I shall be having the pasta primavera,' Margaret said. 'It may not strictly speaking be spring any more, but it is so delicious.'

'I'm having squid ink risotto,' Angela said. 'It's such fun to have black food. Andrew?' She was a little worried; her husband was such a conservative eater and insisted that his packed lunch be kept as simple as possible every day. She was proud of him for having given up his usual bacon sandwich.

'I will have . . . hmm.' He looked down the menu and then chose his usual. 'I'll have the fried lamb chops.' They weren't chops as his father and grandfather would recognize them, but they were close enough to English to pass muster.

'Me too,' Reid said, with some relief. He didn't really enjoy foreign food.

When the food was ordered, Margaret Murray leaned forward. 'It's going to be tricky, Edmund, because I don't want to make a big thing of it, but I would like you to listen to the accents this evening and see if you can pick out some of the main characteristics. You are a performer, after all, and you have sung opera. It should be easy enough.'

Reid couldn't quite see how being a conjuror and having sung a bit of opera learned by rote made him a natural mimic, but he was beginning to be taken up with the idea of fooling a whole houseful of people into believing that he was a middle-aged female Italian sensitive.

'I will certainly try my best not to let you down, Margaret,' he said. 'Whereabouts in Italy does the lady come from?'

Margaret Murray smiled. She had not chosen wrongly – she knew that Inspector Reid would take it seriously once he got into the spirit of the thing, as it were. However, there was such a thing as being too much of a stickler. 'I don't think we have to worry about that too much, Edmund,' she said. 'She won't be known to anyone at the séance, or at least, not intimately. I think we should go for a generalized Italian feel, broken English, that kind of thing.'

She was interrupted by a bustle at the door from the kitchen and two waiters approached their table, carrying covered plates aloft in a theatrical style. They wove their way between the other diners, with many cries of '*Scusi!*' and '*Venendo attraverso*'. The first waiter beamed down at them and proffered the first dish.

'Righto, then. Who's having the rice?'

Reid was startled. 'What part of Italy are you from?' he asked in some confusion.

'I ain't from Italy at all, sir,' the waiter said, deftly placing the risotto in front of Angela in response to her raised finger. 'Hornsey, me, born and bred.'

'What about you?' Reid asked the other man.

'I'm Italian, yes,' he said.

'Thank goodness for that.' Reid was eyeing his fried chops with disfavour. They seemed to smell of cheese for some bizarre reason. 'What part of Italy are you from?'

'Tuscany,' the man said. 'Left there when I was two, mind. Until last Christmas, I've lived in Swansea. That's why my accent may sound a bit strange, isn't it?'

Reid looked at Margaret with a raised eyebrow. 'Perhaps we can work on the accent some other time,' he sighed. 'Meanwhile, let's enjoy our dinner, shall we? If that's even possible.'

The waiters, confused, backed away. There was always one weird table, every night. It was just that it didn't usually arrive until later on, when more drink had been taken.

The little party ate their food with varying degrees of pleasure and called it a night, Reid promising to practise his stage Italian, using a libretto for *Rigoletto* he had handy; he was performing it with the Hampton-on-Sea glee club and was brushing up on his arias. Perhaps it would inspire him.

The Crawfords escorted Margaret Murray home and they sat in her parlour drinking sherry to round the evening off.

'He seemed quite keen, in the end,' Angela said, trying to make the best of a baddish evening.

'He'll be wonderful,' Margaret said. 'He always is, whatever he does. All it needs now is for me to persuade Lady Sylvia she needs to host her séance as soon as possible and let me be in charge of the guest list. That may prove to be more of an uphill struggle, but we'll get there.'

'Before any more murders,' Crawford said, solemnly. He could see the circus element of all this taking over and there were dead women to remember.

'Before any more murders,' Margaret agreed. 'Let's drink to that!'

The next morning, Margaret Murray had an early lecture and was glad that the students were at least arm's length away. She was always rather aware after dinner at Mama's that garlic was never far away, and didn't want to flay any of them with her breath. She kept a small bag of cachous handy, but there was only so much violet-flavoured sugar a person could take. After two hours of holding forth, however, she felt as though she was probably a little less toxic to be near and had the better part of five hours at hand before she had a tutorial. She had galleys to check and a lot of dusting to do. That was something she had never expected to have to do, having trained the cleaners who worked in her rooms to within an inch of their lives, but after Stockley Collins's visit, everything seemed to be covered in a fine dust, even places where Inspector Collins's little badger-hair brush had not been. She was beavering away, her hair tied up in a scarf and a sack tied round her waist, when Jack Brooks opened the door, expecting the room to be empty.

'Oh, I'm sorry.' He looked at the clock. Surely he couldn't have got the time so very wrong this morning as to have slept the whole day away. He looked again at the woman standing there, feather duster akimbo. 'Dr Murray?'

'The same. I'm just cleaning up after Inspector Collins. Such a nice man, but that dratted powder has got everywhere. Fascinating process, though.'

Brooks shrugged. 'Flash in the pan, I call it,' he said. 'How does it help to know what fingerprints are in a place if you don't know who they belong to?'

Margaret stopped and tapped the duster on her chin thoughtfully, transferring quite a large amount of dust down her front. 'I suppose . . . well, I suppose that eventually, people's prints will be on record. Inspector Collins was telling me that they have a very superior filing system at the Yard, based on shoeboxes and very comprehensive cross-referencing.'

'Hmm.' Brooks had narrowly escaped a hefty fine only the previous weekend because the policeman who felt his collar for climbing Eros in Piccadilly Circus didn't recognize him from the exact same exploit from just the weekend before. 'Can't see it myself. Anyway, you'll need to stop that. I come with a message from the mater. She has an unexpectedly free lunchtime due to the indisposition of one of my great aunts. Mad old trout will insist on going on long walks with unsuitable young men and this time has got herself in quite a pickle.'

Margaret pricked up her ears. Gossip was meat and drink to all university denizens and she knew that at least one of Jack's relatives was a substantial donor.

He laughed, seeing her expression. 'It's no one you know, I don't think. She is based in Somerset. Used to have a house on Eaton Square but poor Great-Uncle Josiah had to move her west, out of harm's way. But the devil finds work for idle hands, eh?'

Margaret looked around her. Somehow, her dusting hadn't made much difference to the general look of the place and she was feeling disheartened. She took off her scarf and untied her sack. She patted her hair into place and reached for her hat. 'Do I look presentable?' she asked her student. 'Could you brush me down?'

Brooks hesitated. The last time he had done that, Flinders Petrie had caught them in flagrante and, with the mood the great man seemed to be in at the moment, he had no wish for that to happen again. Margaret read his mind.

'I've just seen William heading off for one of his special lectures,' she said. 'He won't be loose in the building for a couple of hours, so you can make as free with the whisk as you think fit, Mr Brooks. Your mother is always so beautifully turned out, I really don't want to let the side down.'

She turned like a top in the middle of the room while Jack Brooks flicked the dust off her and soon felt ready to face Lady Sylvia Brooks, a challenge at the best of times but impossible with epaulettes of dust on one's shoulders.

'Are you coming?' she said, as she shrugged into a light linen coat, suitable for the beautiful June day burgeoning outside.

'I was going to carry on with the galleys,' he said, but quietly. He would much rather be enjoying one of his mater's lunches, *sur l'herbe* if he knew his mother.

'Come along, then,' she said. 'Is your father at home?'

It struck Jack Brooks that he had no idea. His father was a vague, if pleasant enough figure, but he didn't exactly stand out. 'I don't know,' he admitted.

'But you live there, don't you?' Margaret was confused.

'When you meet the pater – *if* you meet the pater – you'll understand.'

They stood irresolute on the pavement. On one hand, the day was warm and sunny and London lay before them, the breeze from the river bringing a waft of salt to their nostrils. It was a pleasant enough walk, west from Gower Street to Berkeley Square, but Margaret had long ago learned that her little legs had to take two steps to every one of a six-footer like Brooks and she put up her hand for a cab.

'No point in getting hot and grumpy,' she said over her shoulder as she climbed into the growler. Brooks agreed. He had never believed in walking where you could ride; he just hadn't had Dr Murray pegged as someone with the same habits.

The Brooks house in Berkeley Square had a tranquil air, and window boxes of verbena and mignonette scented the air while they waited to be admitted. Margaret was surprised when her companion had knocked and stood back. She began to wonder if she had her facts straight.

'You *do* live here, don't you?' she asked.

'Of course,' he said, bouncing lightly on the balls of his feet, his hands held loosely behind him as he looked up at the façade. 'But if I just walked in, Bennett would have a fit.'

'The butler?' she checked.

'The same. He rules us all with a rod of iron, even the mater. She moved a vase of flowers two inches to the left the other day and he gave notice. It took her ages to talk him round.'

'Does that happen a lot?'

'Not that often. Only when . . .' the door opened and a man who looked very like one of Margaret's more desiccated mummies stood there, looking down his nose at them. 'Ah, Bennett,' Jack said, hopefully. 'Is the mater in?'

'I will enquire, sir.' The voice echoed up from the tomb. 'If you would like to follow me?' He led them at a stately pace into a small anteroom just to the left of the front door. There were some chairs around the walls and some of the less prepossessing Brooks ancestors glared down from dark portraits, scattered about with no attempt at chronology or colour coordination. It was not a room to linger in.

After less than a minute, scurrying footsteps echoing on the tessellated marble of the hall floor told them that Lady Sylvia was indeed at home, and she burst in on a wave of heliotrope and fluttering lace.

'Darling,' she clutched Jack briefly as if he had been away for weeks rather than about an hour. 'Margaret! I do apologize for Bennett. He is an excellent butler in many ways but lacks . . .'

'The brains God gave sheep?' Brooks suggested.

'Discernment.' She smiled at them both. 'Let's get out of this ghastly room. I have a gazebo erected in the garden and we can sit out there and have a nice light lunch, I thought. Just some *amuse-bouches*, nothing too heavy. It's such a glorious day.' She swept out with her guests in her train and Margaret Murray smiled. It was a well-known fact that what Lady Sylvia Brooks wanted, Lady Sylvia Brooks got, but she had never come up against Margaret Murray before. Jack was looking forward to the next hour or two immensely.

The gazebo in the small but immaculate garden was formed of willow hurdles, and placed just so to protect its inhabitants from the heat of the midday sun. The garden itself was based on the one whose acres surrounded the Brookses' country house, and had herbaceous borders crammed with every conceivable flower. As June really took hold, they would burgeon, but for now they were teasing with fat buds of paeony, spikes of lupin and the first signs of hollyhock. Margaret Murray did not pretend to be a gardener – sand and clay was more her terroir – but she couldn't help but exclaim as Lady Sylvia led them to the gazebo, exiting through the French windows from the drawing room.

'That's just beautiful!'

'Oh, Margaret, too kind. We try our best. Come and meet my husband. Or have you already met?'

'I think we may have been at the same function once or twice

. . .' Margaret was looking forward to meeting the pater, putty in everyone's hands, according to his son and heir.

'He won't remember you,' Lady Sylvia assured her. 'Memory like a sieve, poor darling.' They had reached the gazebo and a man with grey hair and a clipped moustache rose to meet them. He was almost uncannily like his son and Margaret smiled just to see them together. Some synapse in her brain told her that it was hardly fair to drag these very nice people into a murder hunt, but she tamped it down firmly.

'Darling,' Lady Sylvia said, touching the man's sleeve with elegant fingers, 'May I introduce Dr Murray. Jack has told you all about her, I know, and she and I have met many times at WSPU meetings. Margaret, may I introduce my husband, Sir James Brooks. He's got loads of other bits to his name as well, but we don't bother with those, do we, darling?'

Her husband shook Margaret's hand and nodded. 'No. Just James will do. I hope Jack is doing his best, Dr Murray. It's all we ever expect, you know. That he does his best.'

Again, Margaret's conscience gave her a kick. She would definitely let him know he had his PhD one day, very soon.

'It's so lovely to meet you,' she said. 'Jack has told me so much about you.'

The man's face lit up and the resemblance to his son grew even stronger. 'Has he? Has he, indeed?' He sat down happily, smiling at the thought.

'Jack, darling, could you roust Bennett and get him to start thinking about lunch. Cook has it all planned. Perhaps in, what shall we say?' She looked from Margaret to her husband and back again. 'Half an hour? Thank you, darling.'

Margaret Murray had worked out how Lady Sylvia got her own way so often. She made everyone think that they were simply doing her a small favour, no pressure, only if it was convenient. And then they went off, to move heaven and earth. She smiled. She knew that technique, though she bowed to a mistress of the art.

'Now, Margaret,' her hostess said, 'the séance. We were thinking, weren't we, James, of a smallish party.'

'That certainly works best with a séance,' Margaret agreed.

'No more than two hundred, certainly,' Lady Sylvia said. 'A

hundred and fifty as a perfect number.' She smiled at Margaret and then looked worried. 'Margaret, is that not enough? Too many? Tell me what you had in mind.'

Margaret didn't quite know where to begin. It was too many by approximately a hundred and forty-one, using the lower estimate.

'Most Circles – that is, the number who meet to try to pierce the veil, as they have it – settle on eight or nine, including the medium,' she said, and sat back to wait for the reaction.

Lady Sylvia blinked. 'Eight or nine?' she said. 'Eight or nine people?'

'Yes. It's not easy to manage more. Except of course, because we have managed to secure the services of Eusapia Palladino . . .'

Lady Sylvia clapped her hands. 'You *have*? Jack said you were trying to get her, but I never dreamed! Margaret, you are a genius.'

As this was nothing but the truth, the archaeologist let that one go and continued. 'Miss Palladino has been known to manage a table of twenty, but I think the nearer we can get to nine or so, the better. For results, you know.'

Jack Brooks returned to the gazebo and threw himself into a steamer chair. Love-all, so far, if he was any judge. He glanced at his father, who gave a sly wink.

Lady Sylvia looked pensive. 'Could we manage . . . a hundred?' she asked.

'Not around the table, no.' Margaret smiled but was clearly not to be budged.

'But we could have more people? We could have . . . oh, what do you think, Jack? Ouija boards around the rooms? Planchettes?'

He shrugged. He had been hoping he could dodge this particular evening, which he had already peopled with old ladies smelling of mothballs and conversations about the Great Divide. 'That might work. Or would it be too frivolous, Dr Murray?'

'If we could arrange a very quiet room for Miss Palladino,' Margaret said, thinking hard. She didn't want to lose this venue for what might be the final act in a maniac's progress. But on the other hand, she didn't want hundreds of twittering old ladies – she had much the same picture in her mind as Jack Brooks had – ruining any ambience there might be.

'We have any *number* of quiet rooms,' Lady Sylvia said. 'The blue boudoir would be ideal, Jack, James, don't you think? We could clear it . . .'

'. . . of your Aunt Sidelia,' her husband said dryly.

Lady Sylvia looked at him, puzzled. 'Aunt Sidelia? Is she still here?'

'Mater, really!' Jack threw her a kiss. 'She's been here since Christmas. She just never seemed ready to go.'

'Goodness.' Lady Sylvia went quiet, a rather unusual event. 'Well, not the blue boudoir, then. But something similar. Would that do, Margaret?' she asked. 'A soirée of perhaps . . . I could get it down to a hundred without ruffling too many feathers, I think . . . yes, a hundred people. And then we could have the séance itself in a quiet room on the second floor. Now . . . who to invite to the séance . . .?'

'We would need that to be largely adherents of Spiritualism,' Margaret said, quickly. 'Real ones, I mean, if I can say that without giving offence. And you, of course, Lady Sylvia, and Sir James.'

'Oh, no, no, no.' The baronet was shaking his head, his hands up to ward off the very idea. 'Count me out. I don't do mumbo-jumbo, as you know, Sylvia. I will marshal the guests with pleasure. Mingle and whatnot. But no table-turning or that nonsense.'

'Ah.' Margaret liked a man who knew his own mind, though she hadn't had Sir James Brooks down as one such. 'That makes it easier. That would leave a few seats. You could choose a few . . .'

'Goodness me,' her hostess said. 'That would be almost impossible. Anyone left out would be bound to take offence. Oh, dear. I'm not sure that this is going to work.' Her whole face fell and her menfolk immediately rose to the occasion. It was as if their sun had gone in.

'What about a raffle?' Jack said.

'A raffle?' Lady Sylvia knitted her brow. 'Is that not a little common, dear? It smacks of a church bazaar.'

'You don't need to call it a raffle,' her husband pointed out. 'You could . . . let me think . . . you could count people in, and every twentieth or a figure you choose, every twentieth has a place at the séance.'

'Or,' Jack was in full flight, 'we could paste tokens under the supper plates, and some have a tick and some have a cross . . .'

'. . . or,' his father said, 'we could put all the invitations into a hat and pull out the requisite number.'

'*Or*,' Jack said, sitting up straight, his finger in the air, 'we could arrange some games, simple things, bezique, loo, snap, even . . .'

'. . . on a knockout system, last men standing – séance!'

Lady Sylvia looked at them proudly and whispered to Margaret, 'They can go for hours like this. Let's just say we can work out some method to ensure that only the right number sit down with Miss Palladino.'

Margaret nodded. All in all, it had been easier than she had expected. Before the plans could change again, a small retinue made its way across the lawn, bearing jugs, glasses and plates.

'Oh, lunch,' Jack said, jumping up to help his mother and Margaret to the table set up in the shade of a cedar tree in the corner of the garden. 'No more talk of séances and Ouija boards, Mater. *Pas devant les serviteurs*, at any event. You know how they worry about living across the square from Number Fifty.'

Margaret Murray pricked up her ears. 'Number Fifty?'

'Haunted,' Jack said. 'Ask me later. The maids . . .' he rocked his hand back and forth. 'Makes them very skittish.'

'Jack, please,' his mother said. 'It's just gossip.'

'But *is* it, though?' he said, leaning back to let a maid deposit a plate of tiny savoury pastries in the middle of the table. '*Is* it?' The maid had turned white. 'I'll tell you later, Dr Murray.' He turned to the table at large. 'Dr Murray has had some very strange experiences, haven't you, Dr Murray?'

And the rest of the lunch went by on a wave of glorious food and Egyptian anecdotes. Murder seemed very far away.

TWELVE

I t wasn't quite an oubliette, one of those ghastly windowless cells they used in the Middle Ages for prisoners they'd prefer to forget; a place in a circle of hell where rats ruled and gnawed at fingers. It was actually a pleasant little room, with a view through grimy glass of people's feet and the spinning wheels of buses as they passed. But it *was* a cell for all that, twelve feet by six, and Adolf Beck was allowed out twice a day to answer the call of nature.

It was not the appointed hour for that when he heard the bolts jar and slide. The steel door swung open and two detectives stood there. One Beck knew well; John Kane, the inspector who had worked miracles for him once before. The other was Andrew Crawford.

'You are free to go, Mr Beck,' Kane said.

The-man-they-couldn't-set-free-for-long stared at him, open-mouthed. He had begun, like the Count of Monte Cristo and the Man in the Iron Mask, to mark off the days on the bricks of his sanctum, using the little pencil stub they had let him have. But in the end, that was too depressing while he waited for the wheels of British justice to grind.

'I am?' he said.

John Kane closed to him. 'You are.' He held out his hand. 'Mr Beck, I cannot apologize enough. It's not my place to say so, but the system – *our* system – has let you down. You have a strong case for compensation – again. Do you have a solicitor?'

'No, I . . .'

'This is Detective Sergeant Crawford. He will see you off the premises. Leave your current address with him and he'll see that someone contacts you.'

Beck shook the inspector's hand. 'Thank you, sir,' he said, his eyes brimming with tears.

Crawford led the man up from the basement. The lift still wasn't working, so they took the stairs.

'Eye-witnesses, eh?' the sergeant tutted. 'It's funny; I'm working on a case at the moment that involves people who look rather alike. It doesn't excuse what happened to you, Mr Beck, but it *does* make life more than a little difficult for those of us pursuing our enquiries.'

At the desk, Crawford took down Beck's address and gave him his card. As he left, he heard Sergeant Nacker mutter under his breath, 'Five bob says he's back inside by Wednesday.'

Crawford ignored him and waved the man off from the side door. The sun was shining on the Embankment, the gulls far inland today and shitting all over Boadicea's statue. People – free people – were going about their business freely and all was right with the world.

'That's *him*!' a woman screamed. She was standing at the entrance to the Yard, pointing at Adolf Beck. 'Help! Help! Police! Why can't you find one when you need one?'

Beck ran, the demons of hell at his back. This was a nightmare and he couldn't wake up. Crawford was at the woman's side in an instant.

'Madam,' he said in her ear, 'I am a policeman and unless you move along, I shall arrest you for wasting police time. The man you have just pointed at happens to be Chief Inspector Wisbech of the Mounted Branch. His record is impeccable and he is as innocent as the driven snow. Are we clear on that?'

When Margaret Murray tapped on the door of Thirty-One Cavendish Street, she knew what to expect, and waited patiently while Agatha Dunwoody went through the motions.

'Is there anybody there?'

'Yes, Mrs Dunwoody – Agatha. It's me. Henrietta Plinlimmon.'

The door was opened, dragged across the scuffed lino as ever, as though it had healed up since it had last been used.

'How lovely.' Agatha Dunwoody looked furtive. 'Um . . . there isn't a meeting today, is there? Only . . .' she glanced over her shoulder, 'I haven't prepared the room at all.'

Margaret had never got the impression that much preparation took place even when the meeting had been in the calendar for months, but said nothing. The relict of the late Alexander Dunwoody seemed to find life difficult enough to manage, without adding to her problems by pointing out the skeins of cobweb hanging from every corner.

'No, no, I have just popped round with some good news. I have managed to secure the services of Eusapia Palladino for our next meeting, which will be hosted by Lady Sylvia Brooks at her home in Berkeley Square.'

If Margaret Murray was expecting a joyous response, she was doomed to disappointment.

'Oh, I'm not sure that the majority are in favour of Miss Palladino, are they?' the woman said, with a down-turned smile. 'I know that Olivia in particular was most insistent that it wasn't appropriate. And of course, poor dear Christina won't be well enough. And I doubt that the colonel would want to travel as far as Berkeley Square. He doesn't like long journeys.'

Margaret felt she had to intervene, making sure to stick to the common information. 'But surely, the colonel has spent years abroad. From Bermondsey to Berkeley Square for an evening surely won't faze him.'

'Colchester,' Agatha Dunwoody said. 'That's the furthest he's been and then only once. I shouldn't really tell you, but he had to confer with my husband once over a paternity suit.'

'The colonel?' Margaret was flabbergasted.

'It all hinged on his being present during a minor derailment in Birtwhistle on a specific evening, and he was able to prove that he was totally unable to undertake such a journey. But please don't repeat it – I was told in confidence.'

'Of course. So . . . who do you think will come? It seems such a golden opportunity, I really thought we would have a full house, as it were.'

'It's a bit . . . well, a bit *exciting* for me, if I can tell you, again in confidence. I prefer my life to be as it was while married to Alexander, completely boring. So I won't be coming.' She cast her eyes heavenwards and counted on her fingers. 'So I suppose that leaves dear Robert and the general. And you, of course. I am assuming you are going?' She peered into Margaret's face, looking for clues. 'We mustn't forget Mr Mortimer, must we? Although I sometimes wonder whether his heart is truly in it. He seems . . . disconnected, somehow. Do you get that feeling?'

'I think . . .' It was hard to answer, knowing what she knew about Mortimer, also known as Archie Flambard, SPR. 'I think in many ways that the Circle means more to Mr Mortimer than any of us could imagine.' That seemed to fit the bill. True, but at the same time a totally meaningless remark.

'I think four is a reasonably polite turnout, don't you?' Agatha Dunwoody said, anxiously. 'I wish I could come, in some respects. I would adore to look inside one of those big houses in Berkeley Square. Have you been inside?'

'I have,' Margaret told her. 'They are very lovely. Very . . .' she sought for the right word, the one which might tempt Agatha Dunwoody beyond the portals of Thirty-One Cavendish Street, 'very lavish.'

'Lavish!' Agatha closed her eyes and clasped her hands under her chin. 'Lots of marble, I expect. And chintz. And huge windows.' She sighed. 'I would love to attend but . . . I am sorry, Henrietta, but I can't. Olivia made her feelings very clear.'

'Who is the hon. sec. of this Circle?' Margaret asked in her most rousing tones.

'Well . . . I am,' Agatha Dunwoody told her.

'Then you can make up your own mind, surely?'

'I did. And Olivia told me that I wouldn't be going.' She turned anxious eyes on Margaret Murray and spoke hurriedly, looking furtively into the corners. 'I know you won't be with us long, Henrietta. We will miss you when you're gone. Alexander told me this morning over breakfast that he could not see a future with you in it, not for the Circle. Alexander is usually very encouraging, Henrietta, so when he makes that kind of prognostication, I tend to listen. He was very sure that Muriel's days were at an end, too, and he was right, wasn't he?'

It was hard in the gloom to see if Agatha Dunwoody's eyes were showing a mad gleam or any other defining feature, but Margaret Murray was grateful that, indeed, the late Alexander was right on the money. She wouldn't be coming back to the Bermondsey Spiritualist Circle. Not even if Hell froze over.

'Can I ask you to tell the members about the meeting in Berkeley Square, though, Agatha?' she asked. 'I don't have their addresses, you see.'

'I can do that, of course,' she replied. 'I am not a vindictive woman, Henrietta, nor a lazy one. I just feel that perhaps you are taking our little Circle out of its real purlieu.'

Margaret turned for the door. She was disappointed in some ways, but she didn't in all seriousness think that a drunken colonel with a travel phobia or the hen-pecked widow of a solicitor were likely to be habitual homicides, though stranger things had doubtless happened. Olivia Bentwood was not quite such an obvious decision to come to. She looked as though she could bend iron girders with her bare hands and her outbursts of temper were really quite intimidating. She decided to leave Olivia Bentwood in abeyance for the moment and if nothing came of the Berkeley Square bunfight, there would be some other way to flush her out, to see if she was a closet homicidal maniac or not.

'As plays go, Andrew, this is a bit of a long shot.' John Kane was tired. The lights were burning blue at the Yard and a fitful moon flickered now and again on the river. Black barges chugged downstream to their havens in various docks and the lightermen were hauling on ropes and calling it a day.

'There *is* a precedent,' the sergeant said. 'Sort of.'

'Is there? Make me a cup of tea while you tell me about it.'

The sergeant obliged. 'Disguises various,' he said. 'If memory serves, Sergeant McNeil posed as a docker and nabbed the Black Deeps mob.'

'True,' Kane conceded.

'Inspector Moser threw a party for Slasher O'Brien and half the East End turned up. Still holds the record for the most arrests in one day.'

'True again,' Kane said, listening to the kettle coming to the boil.

'Inspector Littlechild—'

'That one doesn't count,' Kane interrupted. 'Littlechild had a nice little holiday in America at the taxpayers' expense and did *not*, unlike the Mounties, get his man.'

'It's the principle, though, guv.'

'All right.' Kane watched his sergeant being mother. 'Talk me through it again.'

'I'm pretty sure – and Dr Murray agrees with me – that the medium murderer can be found in one of two Spiritualist Circles – Muriel Fazakerley's and Evadne Principal's. Florence Rook didn't have a Circle as such; she was very much freelance.'

'I'm glad you mentioned Dr Murray, Andrew,' the inspector said, accepting the teacup in its mismatched saucer. 'There's something highly irregular about using members of the public as unofficial detectives. The woman's unqualified.'

'Actually, she's the most qualified woman I know. Mind like a razor. You and I, guv, are taught by the book, aren't we? Procedure, rule of law, all that.'

'We'd be sunk without it,' Kane said.

'We would,' Crawford acknowledged. 'But Margaret Murray *wrote* the book – and it's not one of ours. She has an uncanny ability to see things as they are. Nothing procedural about Margaret.'

'Right.' Kane sighed. Just for a fleeting moment, he thought he could glimpse the future, when women would be allowed into the Force. God – and he shuddered – there might even be a female commissioner of the Met. Then, he pulled himself together – better leave the science-fiction to H.G. Wells. 'So, you and the good doctor intend to invite those people to a séance at a posh house in Berkeley Square at which a world-famous medium will be the guest of honour.'

'Correct.'

'Why?'

'To flush out the killer, guv.' Crawford sat down, stirring his tea with unusual determination. 'All right, so perhaps nothing will happen, in which case, no harm, no foul. People will have had a party, including a few supernatural tricks and we can all think again.'

'Are you telling me that this . . . what's her name . . . Palladino . . . is going to be the target? We can't put a member of the public in harm's way like that.'

'I'll be there, guv,' Crawford assured him. 'Watching her like a hawk.'

Kane was shaking his head. 'You'll need a few bobbies,' he said. 'Incognito, of course.'

'If they can blend well enough,' the sergeant said.

'All right. Who are you inviting?'

'Everybody in both Circles, but I can tell you there'll be absentees.'

'Say on.'

'Let's look at the Bermondsey lot first. Agatha Dunwoody is a possible. Margaret says she's a timid soul, yet mightily impressed with the idea of meeting Eusapia Palladino; so I'm not sure about her. Colonel Carruthers has a drink problem and he's recently developed something of a paranoia about travel. Bermondsey to Berkeley Square – that's the far side of the moon. Poor old Christina Plunkett is still recovering from her injuries, so we can write her off. I doubt you'd drag Olivia Bentwood there with wild horses; she's furious that Palladino, not her, is holding centre stage. The others, I'm pretty sure, will be there.'

'And Evadne Principal's lot?'

'Lucinda Twelvetrees has been well and truly spooked by what's happened. Her minder, though, Veronica Makepeace, might well come along, just to report back to Lucinda. And anyway, it'll increase, as she told me, her clientage.'

'We'll draw a veil over that, Sergeant, if you'll excuse the paranormal pun.'

'Henry Angel we haven't met, but he travels in women's fol-de-rols, no slur intended, so I'm not expecting him. Auguste St-Remy's out of the country; I doubt he'll come back, not even for Palladino.'

'So who does that leave?'

'Hilda Ransom, who won't be able to resist anything so creepy.'

'Agreed,' Kane nodded.

'The *Mail* man, Alfred d'Abo.'

'Opportunity for an exclusive.'

'Exactly. And . . . now, let me see,' Crawford savoured the moment, 'who haven't I remembered? Ah, yes, His Honour, Mr Justice Grosvenor.'

Kane laughed, clapping his hands. 'I'm not a vengeful man, Lord,' he said, looking skywards, 'but please let it be him.'

There was a knock on Kane's door and Stockley Collins walked in. His tie was undone and his magnificent quiff all over the place.

'Sorry to trouble you, chaps,' he said, 'but something rather odd has happened.'

'Take the weight off, Stockley. Young Crawford here's just about to make some more tea, aren't you, Sergeant?'

'Absolutely,' Crawford sighed, swinging into the old routine one more time.

'A fingerprinter's lot is not a happy one, John, as I may have mentioned to you before.'

Kane leaned forward, adopting his best general practitioner persona. 'What seems to be the trouble?' he asked.

Collins hauled a wodge of paper from his satchel and splayed it out on Kane's desk. 'There, on the left, the relevant dabs from

Evadne Principal's. They were all over the furniture, cupboard doors, drawer knobs – as though whoever it was, was looking for something.'

'Neat, though,' Crawford observed. 'The place didn't look as if it had been turned over.'

'Agreed,' Collins said. 'Then, there are those in the centre. They're from Florence Rook's. Same thing. Obviously, we've got no murder weapon in either case, but I'd bet my pension that if we had, said weapon would be covered in them.'

'Clearly, our man doesn't follow the news,' Kane said. 'The Stratton case. I'd have thought there'd have been an unprecedented rush on gloves in department stores across the land.'

'I eliminated everybody I could,' Collins told the others. 'Casual handymen, Principal's maid. The relatives refused to co-operate, but they didn't strike me as the murderous type. Then,' he accepted Crawford's tea gratefully, 'there are those.'

Kane looked puzzled. 'Don't tell me you went to Muriel Fazakerley's?'

'No, I didn't. See that,' Collins pointed to the Principal pile, 'and that.' He pointed to the Rook reference. 'Identical. The same person was in both women's houses.'

'The murderer.' Kane thought he'd better check that he and Collins were on the same page.

'Precisely,' the fingerprint man said. 'Enter Dr Margaret Murray.'

Kane raised an eyebrow at Crawford. 'That name again,' he said.

'She inveigled – and that's not a word I use often – me into taking the dabs of one of her corpses at the Petrie Museum.'

'Moonlighting, Stockley?' Kane tutted and shook his head.

'All in the line of forensic science, I assure you,' Collins said. 'I now know that you *can* take fingerprints from corpses – that will change the course of criminal history and, don't worry, I'll give you boys a plug when I collect my knighthood from His Majesty.'

'I'm happy for you, Stockley,' Kane said, 'but why . . .?'

'The odd thing,' the fingerprint man leaned forward, fixing Kane with his stare, 'is this. Principal. Rook. The Petrie Museum. Identical, matching prints in all three locations.'

Kane and Crawford looked at each other.

It was the sergeant who found his voice first. 'Are you saying that Dr Murray is involved?' he asked. 'That she's our killer?'

Collins leaned back in his chair. 'Either that,' he said, 'or the medium murderer is a three-thousand-year-old Egyptian.'

'The mater is so excited.' Jack Brooks was tapping a pile of papers into some semblance of tidiness before heading home. For once, he wasn't dreading it. Bennett was being kept busy in his pantry, counting and recounting the forks. He had a dread, born of who knew what past trauma, that guests to the house came with one aim in mind, to secrete the silverware about their person and abscond with it. The house was full of bustle, florists arriving with arms full of flowers, caterers buzzing about laying supper tables, much to the annoyance of the cook, who was sure that given the right help, equipment and three weeks' notice she could conjure up lobster *amuse-bouches* to feed at least a dozen people. She was currently in a terminal snit in her sitting room under the eaves. The maids were all rushing about, pink of cheek and shiny of eye. This made a change from constant dusting, and there was a chance that there might be a ghost released or, at the very least, some family skeletons too long in the closet. They twittered to each other every time they passed in flight, like so many starlings in a roost. If a séance ran on emotional energy, then tonight's should end up with record-breaking results.

'Have you met Miss Palladino yet?' Jack continued, then a horrible thought struck him. 'She is *here*, isn't she? She has reached London with no problems?'

'I daresay,' Margaret Murray said, absent-mindedly. She had come across a rather arcane use of the syllable represented by Thoth, from the Third Intermediate Period, and had put the séance from her mind for a while.

'You *daresay*?' Jack Brooks nearly swallowed his tongue in panic. He had rarely seen the mater so excited and even the pater seemed to have caught the mood. 'Surely . . .'

His mentor raised vague eyes to his and seemed to come back into focus. 'Sorry, Jack. I wasn't really listening. I've found . . .' she waved an excited finger to the photograph on her desk. 'It's very intriguing.'

'Dr Murray.' Her student got up from his desk and came round to hers, striking a histrionic pose on both knees, grabbing her hand and pressing it to his bent forehead. 'Please, *please* assure me that Miss Palladino is in London and ready to take part in the mater's soirée. I don't care what else you tell me. Tell me the Black Death has been diagnosed in Hammersmith. Tell me that the Brighton Pavilion has fallen down, having been made of icing all along. But promise me . . .'

She extricated her hand and ruffled his hair. 'Jack, you are a lovely chap, if a little prone to going too far along the humour path. Yes, I can absolutely, without fear nor favour, promise you that Miss Palladino is in London. Indeed, I know the very hotel she is in and will be joining her briefly there as soon as I can sort out this syllable here. Get up, fetch your magnifying glass and tell me what you think.'

He jumped up. He would tell her whatever she wanted to hear, now he knew that the famous medium was at hand.

Andrew Crawford felt a little over-dressed as he approached the reception desk of the Tambour House Hotel. He knew he wouldn't have time to change so had got ready for the evening at about half past two in the afternoon, to the grief of his valet who, despite conditions being against him as far as he could see, tried to arrange things so that his master could find time to go home to be properly kitted out at a more appropriate hour.

'But, sir,' he had said plaintively, tying the bow tie around Crawford's unwilling neck. 'Our shirt front will be decidedly limp by the time the function begins. Is madam accompanying us?'

'Not this time, Fry,' Crawford had said, running a finger around the inside of his collar, trying to get some breathing space. 'We thought that in her condition, a very crowded soirée would not be appropriate. The weather is very warm even for the time of year and we wouldn't want her to get too fagged out, would we?' Crawford found himself falling into the royal 'we' method of communication as soon as Fry came into a room.

'Quite understood, sir.' Fry didn't actually approve of procreation in any circumstances, but saw that perhaps it was occasionally necessary, so as to continue the line, and to keep people like him in employment. Finally, Crawford was tonsured to the valet's liking and was allowed to go. He now struck a noticeable figure in the understated surroundings of the Tambour House Hotel.

The clerk looked at his watch ostentatiously. To be walking around London dressed like that in the middle of the afternoon, the man was either still drunk from the night before – though he looked a little tidy for that – or looking forward to a hell of a long night on the tiles. He placed his fingertips on the counter and leaned forward, a faintly condescending smile on his face.

'I'm here for Mr Reid. Could you let him know I'm here, please?'

'Certainly, sir. May I take your name?'

Crawford sighed. He had been to this very hotel, had stood in this exact spot and had this exact same conversation often enough over the past week or so to be pretty sure that the clerk knew perfectly well who he was, but he told him all over again, nonetheless.

'Of course, Sergeant,' the clerk gushed. 'I just didn't recognize you dressed like . . . that.'

As he hadn't recognized him on any occasion, wearing anything from an overcoat to a sports jacket, this came as no surprise.

The clerk lifted the phone and dialled a number. After a moment, the earpiece squawked and he said, 'Detective Sergeant Crawford to see you, Mr Reid. Will you come down?'

'Squawk.'

The clerk replaced the mouthpiece on its rest and smiled at Crawford. 'Mr Reid has asked that you step up to his room if convenient, Sergeant.'

Crawford smiled too as he made for the stairs. That was an awful lot to get into one rather irate squawk, and no mistake. Outside Reid's door, he waited for a moment, to compose himself. He had an idea that Reid would look not unlike the late, great Dan Leno in pantomime, with rouged cheeks and nose and enormous petticoats. His sensible self knew that this was unlikely – Reid never did anything unless he did it well – but he needed to be prepared, even so. He tapped on the door and stepped back, waiting.

'*Entrare*,' a voice trilled.

That made sense. Reid had got someone in to help him dress and make up. An Italian, by the sound of it, so all the better.

Crawford went in and looked around. Apart from a woman sitting in the window seat looking down on the bustling street below, he was alone. 'Oh, I'm sorry,' he said. 'I thought . . .'

'Don't be an idiot, Andrew,' the woman said in manly tones. 'It's me. Edmund.'

Crawford knew he looked like a pantomime character himself, with mouth gaping and eyes on stalks. 'But . . . that is incredible,' he said when he had got his breath back. 'You look just like . . . well, just like Eusapia Palladino.'

'Isn't that somewhat the point?' Reid asked, waspishly.

'Of course, of course,' Crawford gabbled. 'I just didn't expect it to be such a complete disguise. May I . . .?' He stepped forward and patted Reid's cheek. It was as smooth as a baby's bottom. 'How on earth did you get a shave as close as that? And, against all the odds, you've got a chin.'

'I popped down to Whitcomb Street. In my experience, they have the best tonsurists in London. I got the man to shave me three times, half an hour apart. He thought I had gone mad, I think. But hopefully, I should be free of stubble for long enough. And in the persona I have given myself, I don't envisage Eusapia as much of a kisser.'

'Hmm.' Crawford was dubious. 'She *is* Italian, though. They are a bit that way, aren't they.'

'*Mi scusi, signore. Non sono io.*'

'Crumbs.' Crawford was impressed. 'You've learned Italian?'

'No, of course I haven't. But I've sung enough opera to have picked up a thing or two. It's no good just spouting the libretto. To make it sound real, you need to know at least roughly what you're talking about. I've surprised myself, to be honest. Anyway,' Reid got up from the window seat, leaning heavily on the end of the bed until his back was upright, at which point he winced a little, 'it will have to do. I have decided to be rather aloof, not to meet anyone before the séance. My back is paining me, as I hope you noticed, and I have a touch of gout.' He stuck a foot out from below the hem of his long dress. It was shod in a bedroom slipper. 'I got the dress with no problem from Petticoat Lane, but evening slippers proved impossible with my size nines.

Is the wig all right? I thought it might be a bit frivolous.' He twirled for Crawford, patting his hairline.

'No,' Crawford said, checking carefully. 'No, it looks in keeping. Are you wearing a veil for the séance?'

'I thought so.' Reid reached over to a chair and pulled a length of black Valenciennes off the seat and threw it lightly over his head. 'I can still see all right. How about from your side?'

'You are still visible, just a little fuzzy.'

'Well, that's what we want. Do you know the time, by the way? I've got nowhere for my half-hunter in this gear.'

Crawford checked. 'It's around four. We've got a bit of time to kill. Do you want to order some tea? It will just be silly little bits of things on biscuits tonight, I shouldn't wonder.' Crawford was not a fan of *amuse-bouches*.

'That might be fun,' Reid said. After his original misgivings, he was rather enjoying himself. 'Shall we go out to have it? Test my disguise?'

Crawford demurred. 'I feel a bit of a fool dressed like this at this hour,' he said. 'And my valet almost gave notice.'

'You have a valet?' Reid was staggered. He kept forgetting that Crawford had a rich wife.

'Well, he came with the house, in a manner of speaking. Angela's parents just assumed I would need one. They can't quite get used to the idea that I am a policeman and not something in the City.'

Reid looked at Crawford with new eyes. He had always suspected that for him being a policeman wasn't a job, it was a calling, and now he knew. He shook his hand; it was always good to meet a fellow traveller on life's highway. 'Does your wife mind?' he asked.

'I was a policeman when we met. I don't think she has ever thought of me as anything else, apart from the usual, husband, father, that sort of thing. I even think she may be a bit proud of me.'

Reid remembered how Angela's face had lit up when they had entered the restaurant and patted the man on the arm. 'And she loves you, Andrew. Never forget that. It isn't until you don't have that that you miss it.' He pressed a forefinger under his eye to stop the tear forming there from ruining his makeup. 'Sorry. It's just that sometimes . . . We Italians, we're so, how you say, *emotivo*, eh?'

Crawford smiled. 'I'll order some to be brought up, shall I?'

'Yes, do,' Reid said. 'But before it comes, I think I'll lock myself in the bathroom. It's only two doors down the corridor – check that the coast is clear, will you, there's a dear chap. I don't want to frighten the guests.'

Crawford checked and Reid scuttled to the bathroom and locked himself in. Soon, anyone who was near enough would have heard some Puccini snippets echoing from the smallest room, enhanced by the acoustics, though Reid's tenor hardly needed the help. Crawford went down to the reception desk and ordered tea brought up.

'I trust Mr Reid is not unwell,' the clerk said, probing.

'We just have some business to conduct, of a confidential nature,' Crawford told him. 'Please have the boy just knock and leave the trolley on the landing. Thank you.' And with as much hauteur as a man in evening dress can muster at four o'clock in the afternoon, he swept up the stairs.

The tea was delicious, although Reid had to eat carefully so as to not spill anything down his one and only dress. Crawford was equally careful – he didn't want to give Fry the satisfaction of having to go home to change their shirt.

'Are you quite ready?' Crawford asked, leaning forward and sideways so any crumbs fell on the floor and didn't inveigle themselves behind his studs.

'I think so,' Reid said, sipping his tea. 'I have a few little conjuror's tricks up my sleeve, in some cases quite literally, which I hope you'll like. Margaret has given me a handy list of the members of the two Circles who will make up some of the table. The others, of course, are an unknown quantity, sadly.'

'I wish we could have avoided that,' Crawford said. 'But I think it's quite understandable that Lady Sylvia wanted to give at least some of her friends the opportunity to meet the great Eusapia Palladino. Apart from the seven you know about, there will be Margaret, Lady Sylvia and Sir James Brooks, their son Jack and myself. We have allowed for another eight, chosen by lottery.'

'That's quite a tableful,' Reid said, carefully nibbling a

cucumber sandwich. 'From my reading on the subject, more than twelve is considered quite unwieldy.'

'Yes, I know. But there are two things, really. One is that you are, after all, the wonderful Eusapia. And the other is that the more people we have around the table, the more likely it is that our murderer will be among them and may make a mistake. Not only you will be disadvantaged by numbers.'

'I suppose you're right,' Reid agreed. 'If we don't expand the table, there will only be you, Margaret and me there, and we know it isn't one of us!'

'Funny thing,' Crawford said. 'Stockley Collins has found fingerprints from Margaret's artefacts in common with some found at two of the scenes.'

'Newfangled rubbish,' Reid barked.

'Well, yes and no. It hasn't helped much, because we don't know whose they are. But it's intriguing.'

'How many people can get near Margaret's artefacts?'

Both men paused for a moment – that could definitely have been better put.

'An unknown number, really. Students. Professors. Cleaners, I suppose. It isn't exactly a free-for-all, but it isn't exactly the vault of the Bank of England either. But it's something to bear in mind.'

Reid stood up, rustling his skirts to rid himself of any stray crumbs. 'Just to be sure, who knows that I am me, and not the real Eusapia Palladino?'

'Just me and Margaret.'

'Will John Kane be there?'

'Yes, but only as a guest. We can't be sure that he will win a lottery ticket to the table. And in fact, if he does, he will need to get rid of it, because we don't really want to take up a seat with someone who we know can't be the murderer.'

Reid smiled, but carefully. His makeup was thick and he didn't want it disturbed. 'It will be fun fooling Kane.'

'One thing we haven't been able to find out, and I apologize, is whether anyone can speak Italian.'

'I've thought of that,' Reid said. 'If anyone speaks to me in what sounds like Eyetie, I will just say, "I do notta speak Italian in London. Isa not polite."'

'Good plan. Is there anything we haven't thought of, do you think?'

Reid shrugged. 'If there is, it's a bit late now. I confess to wearing my own drawers under here. I did get some ladies' bloomers but . . .' he sketched a movement which Crawford drew a veil over, 'they left everything a bit too free and easy for my tastes. So let's hope I don't fall over.'

'We'll try and make sure you don't.'

'Also, I can't eat or drink. As it is, after this tea, I'm going to have to touch up the makeup.'

'I think that can be explained,' Crawford said. 'We can tell Lady Sylvia that Miss Palladino prefers to be alone and fasting in the time up to the séance. It's an absolute monster of a house. They must have somewhere where you can go to be alone.'

Reid took up a notebook from the nightstand and slid it into his bosom. 'Just a bit of homework, while I wait,' he said and went over to the mirror, where he touched up his lipstick and redrew some wrinkles on his upper lip. He turned his head this way and that and, satisfied, stood with his arms behind him waiting for Crawford to proffer his coat, a wide-swinging affair with heavily embroidered cuffs and revers. 'Kicksies aside, lad, these clothes are quite comfy.' He turned sharply and went nose to nose with the policeman. 'If you ever repeat that, you'll be sorry.' He extended an arm and Crawford tucked it into his elbow.

'Shall we?' he said and Eusapia Palladino and her escort went off to take the world by storm.

THIRTEEN

Lady Sylvia Brooks never lost her temper, that was a well-known fact. But she could make other people lose theirs and so her son and husband had retired to the study as things got more hectic outside in the rest of the house. One hundred people – the final invited number – were just as a drop in the ocean to the house in Berkeley Square, which had seen parties of many times more accommodated without a moment's pause. But this was different. Lady Sylvia was the first London hostess to give a soirée entirely devoted to the occult, the supernatural, to what went on Beyond the Veil. Very few of the hundred were really that bothered. It was an easy sum to do. The husbands or escorts were none of them in the slightest bit interested. Not every woman had such a thing about her person, so that left about sixty who could be said to be interested. Of that sixty, a good two thirds were just there to be seen with the people who mattered and to be able to casually drop in conversation that they had met the famed Eusapia. Half of that twenty hoped that something really spectacular might happen. A ghostly emanation, perhaps. Ectoplasm running down the banisters at the very least. The ten who took things seriously were in a froth of excitement; they had heard that eight people would get a lucky entrée into the séance itself and, as they arrived and made their way up the broad stairs into the Brookses' London home, they swivelled their heads right and left, to see who else would be elbowing the opposition aside to get the golden ticket.

As people started to arrive, Lady Sylvia sent Bennett to winkle out her menfolk. It was important that every single guest should be greeted and given the discreet little envelope which held – or didn't hold – the magic way in to the presence. Everyone was enjoined not to open their envelope before ten when supper would be cleared and the champagne served. Anyone who had opened their envelope before then would be denied entry, even if they had a winning ticket. Lady Sylvia managed to make her strict rules sound like a kindly suggestion and, so far, not too many people had looked askance.

With her husband and son at her elbows, Lady Sylvia had soon welcomed all but the most tardy guests and only a few envelopes waited to be handed to those latecomers. These she gave to Margaret Murray for safekeeping. The archaeologist was enjoying herself, as anyone can who has not had to arrange florists, caterers and extra staff. Everyone seemed to be in an extremely good mood, helped by a welcoming glass of sherry and a horde of circulating maids in black and white bearing platters of delicious nibbles of food, perfectly nuanced daubs of foie gras with a hint of sour cherry, caviar balanced in curls of buttery pastry, and slivers of aged parmesan baked to crisp bubbles, the last a nod to the nationality of the honoured guest, currently taking the weight off his slippered feet in a boudoir far above the hum of the crowd.

In the anterooms, tables had been set up with Ouija boards and planchettes, but only a few were taking them seriously. Cries of assumed horror soon came from all over, interspersed with 'He didn't!' and 'Well, the board says he did' and 'As for the duchess . . . well!' A few cheeks had been slapped and, all in all, an atmosphere of good-natured excitement was beginning to prevail.

Margaret found Andrew Crawford and took him aside. 'How do you think it's going, Andrew?' she said. 'How is Edmund? Will he pull it off, do you think?'

Crawford smiled down at her. 'I wouldn't be surprised if he starts making a living at it. In the worst case, with Dan Leno dead, we don't have to worry about who will be the next Widow Twankey in Drury Lane.'

Margaret Murray's expression was anxious. 'He hasn't . . . overdone it, Andrew, has he?' she asked. 'I don't want this to be a parody.'

'I think we both know that Edmund Reid never does anything by halves. You asked him to be Eusapia Palladino. So don't be surprised to find he has actually become her. We're in safe hands, I promise. What's the time?' He rummaged for his watch. Fry kept his waistcoat fitting to within an inch of its life and it wasn't easy to winkle it out.

Margaret looked up to the fine old grandfather clock at the top of the stairs. 'It's a quarter past nine. I expect the butler will . . .' But her words were drowned by a gong that sounded as if it were being struck in her head rather than in the hall. When the echoes had died away, the guests began to make their way to the supper rooms, the general twitter being about what could possibly be in these too discreet little envelopes. Who would be the lucky ones? And what would happen at the séance? Who would Come Through? Almost everyone had a relative who had passed over in the last year. One woman, whose nod towards mourning was a velvet shrug over her evening dress, could claim a mother-in-law dead only three months. Another, a grandfather who had succumbed to extreme old age only last week, but she had to concede that he hadn't spoken a word of sense for the last ten years, so he would not be much of an ornament to any turning table.

The food was as spectacular as food always was at a soirée of Lady Sylvia Brooks, and some envelopes were soon abandoned on tables as their putative owners concentrated on their *brandade de morue* and *coquilles Saint-Jacques*. It seemed no time at all before the sound of distant corks popping made all heads come up, and everyone who had put their envelopes down somewhere scrambled to find them again.

Lady Sylvia stood in the hallway between the two supper rooms and beat one palm gently with the fingers of her other hand. The sound it made was minuscule but, even so, every head turned in her direction.

'I hope you have all had a good evening,' she said. 'Miss Palladino is being escorted to the séance room as we speak, so I would ask you now to produce your envelopes. Please display them to your supper partners, so we can be sure no one has tampered.' She gave them a moment and from here and there came a cry of 'You've opened it!' or 'You are so naughty!'

'Dear me,' she said, with a laugh. 'It seems some of you couldn't wait. I hope none of the opened envelopes contained the golden ticket, because if they did, they are null and void.' She looked around and the miscreants shook their heads – all of the broached tickets were blank.

'Excellent. Well, on the count of three, everyone open their envelopes. And those with a golden cross on their ticket, please make their way to the head of the stairs, where Jack will escort you to the séance. Good luck. One.'

Thumbs were under the flaps.

'Two.'

There was a crumpling of stout parchment as some people tore their envelopes, just a little.

'Three.'

There were cries of excitement, happily spread throughout the two rooms more or less evenly, to Lady Sylvia's relief. She wasn't a mathematician, but she had had slight horrors when working out the possibility of having all eight tickets at two adjoining tables! The disappointed majority were soon back at the buffet tables, while the exalted eight made their way up the stairs to where Jack Brooks stood, arms wide. He had promised his mother to be suitably serious, because this was where the proper business of the evening began, so he just muttered under his breath, 'Roll up, roll up. All the fun of the fair.'

Eusapia had been ensconced in her chair before anyone else was let into the room. The curtains on the floor-to-ceiling windows were drawn against the silver of a London twilight, and even the birds outside had caught the mood and were silent. There was a candle burning on each end of the mantelpiece, throwing the medium's face into deep shadow. Her black lace veil was thrown back for now, so she could watch with her deep-set eyes as each person came into the room, allowed in one by one by the ever-vigilant Jack Brooks.

First into the room was General Boothby. This was a deliberate decision by Andrew Crawford. Although Boothby was an outsider when it came to betting on the murderer, he was a member of the Rag which was a stone's throw from the murder site of Florence Rook. This was of no significance as such, but he was also in need of watching when it came to grabbing handfuls of passing pulchritude, so next to Edmund Reid and his size nines was a sensible place to put him.

Because he was General Boothby, he couldn't help but give Eusapia a bit of a once-over but decided immediately that she didn't come up to his admittedly somewhat low expectations. She was deep in the chest and he did like that in a woman, but there was something about the set of the shoulders and the implacable rat-trap mouth which did not entice. Also, there was quite a whiff of pipe tobacco and a man had to draw a line somewhere. He took his seat to the medium's left and looked down the table, to see who might be next, crossing his fingers that it might be a little bit of all right. Or failing that, Margaret Murray.

Next through the door was a woman who was so far from a bit of all right that Boothby almost laughed aloud. She had 'seamstress' written all over her, for the extremely good reason that she was one. Hilda Ransom was in seventh heaven. She had dreamed for so long of meeting a famous medium, a *proper* medium, not just a local freelancer like Florence Rook, although Florence had a certain unschooled talent. But now, here she was, little Hilda Ransom from the Havelock Street Orphanage, about to be within touching distance of the great Eusapia. Jack had shepherded her up the side of the table which would have brought her to sit on Boothby's left, but Hilda Ransom was having none of that. She evaded his gentle guiding arm and positively ran up the other side, to take the chair on Eusapia's right hand. Jack Brooks moved to stop her, but the medium gave an imperceptible shake of the head. No harm would come if Hilda Ransom sat on the right. General Boothby gave a sigh of relief.

The next person through the door was a tall, uncompromising-looking woman who had received one of the golden tickets. She looked less than impressed to be there and, rather to Jack's annoyance, took a random seat about two thirds down the table. This had seemed a simple task when he had volunteered for it; the very reason he had volunteered for it was its innate simplicity. Yet it immediately struck him that making the occult lot – as he thought of them – do what you wanted them to do was a bit like trying to herd cats. He closed the door again and had a muttered conversation with Andrew Crawford, many words of which could not have been repeated in polite society.

In the end, rather than have to wrestle with a rather large policeman in immaculate evening dress, Jack opened the door and announced in subdued tones, so as to not disturb the great Eusapia, 'Please, ladies and gentlemen, one by one and without speaking, please enter the room and take a seat, respecting the reserved ones at this end, which are for some special guests. Thank you.'

When everyone but Crawford was inside, he turned to the sergeant. 'Well, what was I supposed to do? Drag them out of their seats? It will still work, surely? Or does the great Eusapia need her zanies, assuming she is the mountebank?' Jack Brooks was usually placid, but those women had got his goat.

'Darling.' His mother had come up the stairs as silently as a ghost. 'I'm sure it doesn't matter. Now, Papa has decided to sit this one out, so I have brought Bennett up to take his place, as a treat.'

Bennett stood by her side; if it was indeed a treat, he was

keeping the knowledge to himself. He also resembled a phantasm of the dead already.

'We'll all go in now, shall we? Sergeant Crawford, will you close the door to as you come in. Apparently, Eusapia needs a very dim light.'

It seemed to take forever for everyone to stop shuffling, but eventually the room was silent. Margaret Murray was sitting three seats down from Boothby, directly opposite Robert Grimes. She had seen Mr Justice Grosvenor in the newspapers and his hatchet profile couldn't be mistaken. The eight guests who had drawn lucky tickets were easy to spot. For a start, they were wearing proper evening dress, not the nearest they could manage as was the case with the Circle adherents. Veronica Makepeace made an arresting sight, with a décolletage so low it was almost a belt, the corsage she wore all but engulfed by her breasts which jutted uncompromisingly only inches from Bennett's disapproving chin. She was looking rather pleased with herself, as well she might. Tucked into her barely adequate stays were the cards of enough gentlemen to keep her in clover until Christmas, General Boothby's foremost among them.

A long shuddering breath came from the head of the table. Eusapia spoke. The tone was arresting, even if the English was a little stilted.

'Good evening,' she said, her voice seeming to vibrate along the table and up the arms of those unwise enough to be lounging. Everyone sat up that bit straighter. 'I thank you for attending this little soirée tonight and with so many sensitive souls about us, we can perhaps pierce the veil before we are done.' She reached up and flipped her own veil over her face and extended her arms in front of her. 'Do as I do,' she said. 'Put out your hands in front and to the side, your fingers spread, like so.'

General Boothby looked at the woman's hands. God, these peasants let themselves go. The woman had hands like a docker. They looked as if they could squeeze the life out of anything they got a grip on. He felt himself go pale.

'Do you all see?' the medium said, spreading her fingers wide. 'As I do, see?'

All hands reached out and spread their fingers.

'Now, touch the little finger of your neighbour with your own little finger. Just a touch, no more. You have that done?'

She looked down the table, peering in the dim light.

'You have it. Good.'

And with no warning, the candles went out and left them in the warm, beeswax-scented dark. There was a small scream from the far end of the table as one of the ticket holders realized that perhaps 'lucky' was not the right word to describe her situation.

'*Silenzio!*' the medium barked and the woman gave a small sob and was hushed by her neighbour, Andrew Crawford. He sighed to himself. He was supposed to be keeping a watch and there they were, in the pitch dark, and he had a milksop to his right.

'If anyone thinks they cannot keep silent, I must ask them to go,' Eusapia said. 'The spirits are not to be trifled with. A sound, a gesture and pouf!' as she spoke, a small luminescent cloud burst over the table, 'they are gone.'

Edmund Reid gave himself a metaphorical pat on the back. That had given them all a bit of a turn and also had stopped their eyes from getting used to the dark. As long as he kept his eyes shut during the flare, he had a distinct advantage which could prove to be vital.

The medium waited, tapping her slippered foot. '*Cominciamo*, let us begin.' She began a low humming, which began on one note and then, almost imperceptibly, began to rise and fall, like the breaking of oily waves on the beach of an invisible sea. Everyone around the table began to feel slightly mesmerized, out of their bodies and yet still very aware of the slight pressure of their neighbours' little fingers. Even Margaret Murray and Andrew Crawford, who knew exactly what was going on, felt themselves sliding under.

Suddenly, the humming stopped. The candles burst back into life and the medium's face behind the veil was dimly visible. She dropped her chin to her chest and a guttural voice informed the company, 'They are here.'

Every hand stiffened as they waited to find out just who 'they' were. They didn't have long to wait. Slowly, one by one and then in soft drifts, feathers fell from the ceiling. One caught in a candle flame and there was a brief stench of burning, quickly over. The table lay thick with black down before the last feather spiralled from above.

Margaret Murray and Andrew Crawford locked eyes. How on earth had he done that was the first question. And how were the assembled guests reacting was the second. Everyone seemed to be transfixed. Crawford's naïve neighbour was blowing gently, making the feathers move and smiling like a child.

Eusapia drew in a breath that seemed to take an age to end. '*Uccelli della morte*; the birds of death.' She raised her head and this time looked towards the ceiling. 'They have come to me only once before.' Again, the sound of her shuddering breath seemed to fill the room. She dropped her head and her eyes, though deep-set in her head, seemed to glow. 'For one, it did not end well. If there is a liar here, they would do well to leave us, while it is possible still.'

She waited and no one moved, though somewhere, someone sobbed.

'I continue,' the medium said, still staring down the table. Margaret Murray and Crawford felt the atmosphere almost crackle with tension and, at the bottom of the table, Bennett the butler sat as if he were frozen to the spot. Crawford, to his right, could feel him tremble. The humming started again and the tension lessened as everyone began to march inwardly to Edmund Reid's drum. Just when it seemed inevitable that someone would fall asleep, there was an indescribable sound which only Edmund Reid, watching the Billingtons at their work in Wandsworth, had ever heard. It was the sound of a heavy object, falling through space to oblivion, being fetched up short by six feet of hemp and a solid knot behind the ear. There was something about the noise which, though unknown to all but one in the room, still made the blood pound in everyone's ears and made Crawford's right-hand neighbour grip his hand, digging in her sharp nails until he shook her free and resumed the slight fingertip pressure.

'*Chi est?*' Eusapia cried, with all the superstitious terror of an Italian peasant in her voice. Still leaning on the table so she didn't break contact with Boothby or Hilda, she stood and called to the sky, 'Who are you, who are you, *l'impiccato*, the hanged man?'

She flopped back into her seat, her head back, her eyes wide, her breath coming in short grunts.

'The poor woman!' Lady Sylvia was the consummate hostess and wasn't going to have the great Eusapia pass Beyond the Veil in her house, not with a hundred guests downstairs at any rate. 'Loosen her stays, someone. Give her air.'

'No, no.' Eusapia came round with almost uncanny speed. 'I am not passing beyond, do not worry. I have a shock, that is all. Let us re-form the circle. Any who wish to go, go now. I have never known such energy.'

Somewhat rattled, the sitters stretched out their hands again and touched fingers. Crawford was surprised to find that the table surface where his hands had rested was wet with sweat, and he wondered how those not in the know were faring. He had no idea how long they had been in the room. He could hear, in what seemed like the far distance, the hum of the people still enjoying the Brookses' hospitality below but that was nothing to go by. He had known parties like this go on until dawn. He glanced at Margaret Murray, who was looking at Edmund Reid; what was he going to do next? He realized that he had been secretly hoping that she knew, but from the look on her face, he could tell that she was as much in the dark as he was.

The humming began again, but this time, it didn't seem to come from the medium at all, but from all around. There was more than one voice, some higher, some lower. Behind the humming were words, but he couldn't make them out. In the air there were little sparks. Crawford remembered his honeymoon with Angela, an idyllic time on a Greek island, where there was no one but them, a housekeeper-cook and about a million fireflies. This was like that. If you concentrated on a spark, it seemed to go out or move. The air was alive with them but there was no heat and no real light. He tried to concentrate on Reid's face but it was all but impossible now. Suddenly, Reid arched in his chair, the veil falling off his head and the room re-echoed to a boom that was beyond voice. If asked, Crawford would have sworn that no vocal chords had made that sound.

'*Rapinatore! Voleur!* Robber! Thief!'

With a scream, Reid fell forward across the table and everyone pushed their chairs back, eyes wide. All but one. Bennett, the perfect butler, had screamed louder than Reid and, batting his employer aside, had raced for the door.

In the stunned silence, Crawford kept his head.

'It seems that Mr . . .'

'Bennett,' Lady Sylvia told him. She was being helped back into her chair by Margaret Murray who was signalling with frantic eyebrow semaphore to Crawford to bring the whole thing to a close.

'Mr Bennett has perhaps a less than clear conscience. However, I am sure that Eusapia will be happy to continue, if anyone wishes it?'

'Do what?' A voice echoed round the room and everyone looked around puzzled.

'I wonder,' Margaret Murray said, hurriedly, 'whether perhaps Eusapia is exhausted by all this. Are you exhausted, Miss Palladino?'

The medium raised and let fall a languid hand.

'I think we have to all say,' Lady Sylvia said, herself again after the flight of her butler, 'that we have all had a very exciting evening.' She leaned down to Margaret and asked, under her breath, 'Do we clap?'

Margaret shook her head. 'I think if we leave Eusapia to recover,' she said loudly, ushering the people she could reach from the room, 'she may be able to join us in the supper room later. Perhaps she will get some . . . vibrations?'

The medium's head came up an inch or two and a baleful eye fixed the archaeologist through a tangle of hair.

'Well, anyway, we'll see. If you could all just file out . . .' She flinched as someone grabbed her arm.

'Henrietta.' Mortimer Mortimer was clearly moved, but still kept up her persona, to the confusion of Lady Sylvia. 'I have never seen anything so wonderful. The woman is genuine, of that I have no doubt. I will be reporting to the Society forthwith.' To everyone's surprise, he threw his arms around her and hugged her. 'Thank you,' he breathed, '*Thank you* for this unique experience.' He stumbled to the door, like a man finally arriving in Damascus.

'What an extraordinary chap,' Lady Sylvia muttered. 'Why did he call you Henrietta?'

'Poor man,' Margaret said, watching him go. 'He clearly is off his head with excitement.'

One by one, the company melted away, General Boothby the last to leave and trying a final grab at any handy part of Lady Sylvia, promptly had his collar felt by John Kane, waiting on the landing outside. It had been very annoying, listening to all the racket coming from the other side of the door and being able to do absolutely nothing about it. He was going to arrest someone, he didn't care who it was, nor why.

Margaret went to the head of the table and sat down in the chair recently vacated by Hilda Ransom.

'It's all right, Edmund,' she said. 'They've all gone.'

Reid sat up, hauling the wig from his head and blowing out a relieved breath.

'Was that all right?' he asked, in the tones of one who actually knows it was superlative.

'It was more than I could have ever dreamed it would be,' she told him. 'The candles. The feathers. How on earth did you do that?'

'Trade secrets,' he said, a finger alongside his nose. 'The Magic Circle would never forgive me if I told.'

'Oh, surely,' she said. 'Would you tell me if I told you that you persuaded a member of the Society for Psychical Research that you are genuine?'

'No, really?' Reid blushed under his rouge. 'How very satisfying. But no, I still can't tell you, except that everything in magic is misdirection. You were not looking for a trick, because the *result* of the trick was so much something you wanted to see. Feathers falling from the ceiling are far more intriguing than seeing some old geezer in a dress pulling a string and opening a sack propped up on a pelmet. I had cracked the window a tad so there was a draught, so they fluttered.'

'The noise of the hanged man? That gave me the willies and I wasn't the only one.'

'Excuse me.' Reid hauled up his skirts and showed Margaret the rubber membrane wound tightly around an embroidery frame. When he parted his knees, it gave out a funereal twang.

'That wasn't the noise, though.'

'Yes, it was. You heard some of it, imagined the rest.'

'I don't understand the thief thing, though. What was that?'

'Goodness me.' Reid tutted theatrically and cast up his eyes. 'That was the easiest bit, though I confess I didn't have the butler down for a wrong 'un.'

'I would imagine that Sir James will be going through the accounts in the morning,' Margaret smiled. 'But . . . why robber?'

'Because of the poem in Florence Rook's mouth.'

'No. Sorry.'

'A page from *'Twas the Night Before Christmas*. I think that the boffins at the Yard were worrying about the words, but it could have been any page at all.'

Trying to look intelligent, Margaret shook her head.

'Father Christmas. Santa. Saint Nicholas. The patron saint of . . .'

Margaret clicked her fingers. 'Thieves,' she said.

'And murderers, as it just so happens. If the butler hadn't broken up the party, I would have gone on to that. But I think we achieved quite a lot tonight, don't you? We've rattled our lad, if nothing else.'

'We certainly have,' Margaret agreed. 'Now we have to see what crawls out of the cage. For now, though, let's get your wig back on and get you downstairs for a bit of making it up as you go along.' She looked at him, fondly. 'Are you all right, though? You look tired.'

He turned his face to his shoulder. 'Tired?' he said, and the voice boomed round the room, enhanced by the membrane in his wide sleeve. 'Not a bit of it.' He patted his hair. 'How do I look?'

'Exactly like a fifty-year-old Italian peasant,' Margaret said. 'In other words, perfect.'

FOURTEEN

The soirée had finished early for a Lady Sylvia Brooks event – everyone had gone home by two thirty in the morning and everyone who should not have been there had left by four, the usual magic being wrought by caterers, florists and maids so that when Jack Brooks came down to breakfast, it was as if the evening before had never happened. Except for one very significant difference – his mother was sitting in her place jotting down notes for when she interviewed the new butler.

'So, Bennett, eh?' Jack took a piece of toast and buttered and marmaladed it while planning what to have next. Breakfast was, after all, the most important meal of the day.

'Darling,' his mother murmured. 'Please try not to sound so common.'

'Sorry, Mater,' he said, hiding a grin. 'Now Bennett's gone, are you going to be the martinet around here?'

Lady Sylvia put down her pen and sighed. 'It came as a very great shock,' she said, solemnly. 'Your father and I had always put the utmost faith in Bennett, as you know. So to find that he had been . . .' she faltered and put delicate fingers to her brow, 'had been . . .'

'Robbing you blind?'

'As you say, dear, robbing us blind.' She was too much in shock still to remonstrate. 'Your father is checking the accounts as we speak. It won't leave us in penury, of course, but at first glance it looks as though he was skimming off, as I believe the phrase is, some six pence in the pound. Which doesn't sound much until you think of the upkeep of this place, and the country house . . .'

'What was he spending it on, do we know?'

'Before he was turned out bag and baggage at dawn, your father asked him that. It turns out, he has a family in Isleworth, a wife and two daughters.'

'Goodness.' Jack paused with his fork in a sausage. 'I wouldn't have had him down as a family man.'

'And also, a second family in Tooting. Not sure of the details. At that point, your father had some kind of explosion and kicked him out without waiting to hear the rest.'

'Is Pater all right?' Jack was suddenly concerned. His father was the mildest of men.

'As a matter of fact, yes,' his mother said. 'He doesn't like change, we know that, but like the rest of us, he did find Bennett rather hard to live with. He's very grateful to Eusapia for forcing the issue and very impressed that the spirits knew about Bennett being such an out-and-out bounder. He had a little chat with her after the séance and found her very perceptive, he said. Though he wouldn't tell me what they discussed.' She gave a nervous laugh. 'Do you have any idea?'

'Come on, Mater, there's a good chap.' Jack was back in his place with a loaded plate. 'I'm sure Pa has a completely spotless record. But apart from Bennett – and, can I just ask you, when you replace him, choose someone who at least looks alive, even if they're not – did everyone have a good time, do you think?'

His mother smiled. 'Yes, it was a great success. *Everyone* had such a marvellous chat with Eusapia. Even the Duchess of Blaenavon, who is as deaf as a tree, says she could hear every word she said, so that's a supernatural skill in itself! Your father did share something with me, however, which you can pass on or not at your discretion.'

'Ma!' Jack was touched. 'Here I am, two degrees and another pending, and you've never said I had discretion before!'

'I didn't say you actually had any, darling, but if you do, you may use it now. Your father thinks that Dr Murray is a fine figure of a woman. But then, he said the same about Eusapia, so I think we can assume his judgement is a little impaired by the shock of Bennett and his shenanigans.'

Jack spluttered over his poached egg. 'The prof is a little . . . pocket, for Pa's taste. And as for Eusapia – she has biceps like George Hackenschmidt.'

'As I say, dear,' Lady Sylvia picked up her pen again and resumed her list-making, 'it was probably the shock talking.'

'Probably.' Jack went back to his breakfast, but he had images in his head that he wished weren't there and he couldn't manage his fourth kidney at all.

Margaret Murray was not one for late hours and the night before had rather taken it out of her. By the time she had made sure that 'Eusapia' was back at her hotel and had helped her – with eyes averted – out of her bombazine, it had been well past six before she had finally tumbled into bed. She had broken the habit of a lifetime, therefore, and had not reached her desk until nearly ten and found a somewhat disgruntled Flinders Petrie waiting for her when she finally shouldered the door open and threw her capacious bag on to the floor.

'Margaret,' he said, gruffly.

'William.' She looked at him. 'Here to yell at me again?'

'I don't yell.'

'If you want to be pedantic, that's all right by me, but if you are here for social purposes or just to bully, I must ask you to, pardon my French, bugger off, because I am rather busy.' She gestured to her bag. 'As you see, many marked papers to be discussed with their authors, if that is actually the word. Many appear to be the ramblings of baboons, but no doubt things will be clearer after a chat.' She smiled a wintry smile at odds with the glowing June day outside. 'Chats are good.'

Petrie slapped his knees and got up. 'I came to apologize,' he muttered. 'I shouldn't have shouted at you.'

'Correct. You shouldn't.' She edged round to the seat he had vacated behind her desk. 'Shall we give it a while until we have both calmed down?'

'I *am* calm,' he said. He was worried; he couldn't envisage a life without Margaret Murray in it.

'But I am not,' she said. 'I don't need a man to fight my battles, William, and as far as I could see, the battle was concocted from your bad temper. Mr Merrington is a very competent artist, if an odd man taken all in all. Jack Brooks is undertaking the sketches for the actual syllables and all would have been well, with or without your intervention. So, I'm sorry to seem curt, but I need some time and I would like it now. Please close the door on your way out.'

William Flinders Petrie, by some people's reckoning and certainly by his own, the leading archaeologist of his generation if not of all time, stood irresolute in the doorway like a naughty schoolboy. He kept his temper in check, remembering where it had landed him the last time. Before either of the protagonists had time to blink, the door burst open and propelled Petrie across the room. Had it not been for a fortuitous armchair, he would have ended up in the coal scuttle.

'Oh, goodness, I'm sorry, Professor Petrie. I didn't know you were there.' Jack Brooks was covered in confusion.

'Don't worry, Jack,' Margaret said, smiling. 'Professor Petrie
was just leaving, were you not, William? Help the professor up,
Jack, there's a dear. Thank you.'

Jack Brooks watched Petrie go. There was a man who had
just had a jolly good snubbing from Margaret Murray, or he was
a Dutchman.

Margaret looked at Jack with an enigmatic smile. 'Excellent
timing, Jack. And an excellent thesis as well, by the way.' She
opened a drawer and pulled it out, blowing some dust off.
'Congratulations, Dr Brooks.'

Jack Brooks blinked. 'Just like that. No . . . no questions? No
viva?'

'No need. Vivas are just a lot of hot air, where a bunch of
over-inflated egos think desperately of something not totally
idiotic to ask. Probably the best written and presented thesis I
have ever read. Well done.'

Brooks narrowed his eyes. 'May I ask when this was
ratified?'

Margaret flipped open the cover and then closed it again. 'A
while ago,' she said. 'But let's not quibble. You have some
sketches to complete, I understand. Let's get to it.' She looked
up and gave him the sudden smile which made all her students
her slaves. 'But first, tell me – what is the latest gossip about
Bennett.' She looked around, then pointed. 'Pull up a chair and
crack out the garibaldis.'

Brooks pulled up a chair and began. 'Well, it turns out, Bennett
had a family in Isleworth . . .'

'No!'

'And another one in Tooting. It was like this . . .'

And the sketches had to wait for another little while.

Thomas was the only one in the room who wasn't feeling
just a little fragile. Although on duty, Kane and Crawford had
imbibed a little of the champagne which flowed like water at any
of Lady Sylvia Brooks's events, just to blend in, as Kane had
said. All policemen are used to staying up all night and it was
by no means a new experience for any of them, but being Eusapia
Palladino was more exhausting than anyone might think and Reid
was not as young as he was. He had survived the night on a

wave of pure adrenaline and was now feeling a little seedy. Margaret Murray looked as she usually did, interested in everything, ready for whatever life had to throw, but she was having to force her ears to listen and her eyes not to close.

'Well, gents and Prof,' Thomas said genially, rubbing his hands and leaning over them in best mine host fashion. 'What's it to be, this fine summer's afternoon? How about a nice cream tea? A few muffins on the side, eh? Jam? Clotted cream?' Eight eyes turned to him in mute protest and he made himself scarce. 'I'll just bring some tea,' he said as he walked away. 'See how we go on from there, shall we?'

'He means well,' Margaret muttered.

'Still can't get used to being this near a copper and not getting his collar felt.' Kane was a touch curmudgeonly; he usually had quite a soft spot for old lags who went as gloriously straight as Thomas.

Reid was not in the mood for small talk. He had a lovely crisp bed at the Tambour House Hotel which had his name on it, and he wanted to be lying on it as soon as was humanly possible. 'What are your views on last night, everyone? I assume we don't count the butler as a serious suspect?' He looked round as the others nodded in agreement.

'I doubt he would have had the time,' Margaret said, and told them all about the bigamous Bennett.

'My money's on the son,' Kane said.

'What?' Margaret Murray was outraged. 'I've just awarded him a PhD!'

'May I ask,' Kane said, 'how that stops him from being an habitual homicide?'

Crawford wasn't so certain Brooks was their man, but the statistics didn't lie. There were many doctors who had met their end on the gallows, for example; intelligence was no bar to being a raving maniac. Pritchard, Palmer, Cream – they all had form.

'I don't mean that the degree in itself means he is innocent,' Margaret said, crossly. 'You're putting words into my mouth. What I mean is . . . I *know* Jack Brooks. He wouldn't hurt a fly. Just give me one good reason why it is him. Just one.'

'Fingerprints.' Kane spoke with all the certainty of a man who knew he had right on his side.

'What fingerprints?' The archaeologist would be the first to admit she knew little of the fledgling science, but this seemed rather a leap to her.

Crawford leaned towards her and put a gentle hand on her arm. 'There are prints from your rooms and the museum which are also found at the crime scenes, Margaret. I'm sorry.'

'There are many people who it could be,' she said, playing for time.

'I know,' Crawford said. 'We have made a list and I'm sorry, Margaret, but it looks like Brooks is our man.'

'But *why*?' Margaret heard her own voice and realized it sounded plaintive.

'He was the one who suggested the séance at his parents' house,' Kane said.

'No. It was his mother.' It was clear that these men didn't know Lady Sylvia.

'How do you know that?' Kane was relentless.

'It . . . it's the sort of thing his mother would plan.' As a reason, it sounded weak.

Reid cleared his throat. 'If I may?' Everyone looked at him. 'I did my best to speak to everyone last night and, by the end of it, I hardly knew who I was. But most of the guests were just makeweights, people invited because Lady Sylvia doesn't know how to give a party for less than a hundred people. Is that a fair summation?' He addressed his question to Margaret Murray as the only one in the room with first-hand knowledge of their hostess.

'Yes,' she said. 'That's fair enough. I would say that there were probably only ten or so people there who could be considered serious suspects, less if, as I think is the case, you think these crimes could not have been committed by a woman.'

'Hold on a minute, there,' Kane said, his finger in the air. 'That's a bit of a wide assumption, isn't it?'

Crawford and Reid shook their heads. 'Surely,' Crawford said, 'no woman could have beaten Christina Plunkett so severely? And look at the savagery of the beating that killed Florence Rook.'

Kane laughed, a bitter laugh of sad experience. 'I can see you have never patrolled the docks on a Friday night,' he said.

'You get two toms down there, fighting over territory, and you'll see damage done that makes what happened to Christina Plunkett look like a goodnight kiss. Besides, I'm not convinced that that is connected.'

Crawford and Reid decided to let that one go. If they sat and argued every point all over again, they would be here until doomsday.

'Shall we go through the people there who might be—?'

'Brooks.' Kane interrupted the archaeologist before she could get going. 'I don't see why we're even talking about anyone else.'

'But let's all the same.' Margaret Murray had honed this particular tone of voice on hundreds of students and it rarely failed. It didn't now.

'George Boothby; groper, but that's the worst you could say. Robert Grimes; nothing known.' Crawford began the list.

'Except that his uncle was hanged for murder.' Margaret let that little gobbet of information float around for a moment before it sank in.

'Murder isn't hereditary, though, is it?' Reid pointed out.

'No,' Margaret said, 'not as far as I know. But upbringing plays a part. Look at Caligula – a thoroughly nasty sadist. And who was his uncle and mentor? Tiberius. I don't have to paint you a picture.' From the look on the coppers' faces, Margaret would have to take a photograph, but she swept on regardless. 'Grimes's uncle was Gregory Grimes, I don't know if you remember the case.'

'I do,' Kane said. 'He killed some woman he was conning money out of. Not even the same thing at all.'

'As far as we know.' Andrew Crawford wasn't all that sure about the murderer being Brooks either.

'And he did stove the woman's head in.' Thomas was back with the tea and, because he couldn't help himself, a tray of scones, clotted cream and jam as well.

'How do you know that?' Kane asked, suspiciously.

'Because I was here when the prof was told by . . .' he glanced at Margaret, unsure whether to share what he knew about Mortimer.

'Go ahead, Thomas,' she said. 'No harm in it now.'

'Well, one of the blokes from that Circle was a ghost hunter. Came here after Margaret and told her all about everyone.'

The policemen's heads all swivelled in her direction.

She shrugged. 'It was something and nothing,' she said. 'But I think we can assume that it exonerates all of the Bermondsey Circle. They're not perfect, but they don't have skeletons in their closet worth killing for.'

Kane looked thoughtful. 'You think that's the motive?'

'Why not? It's common enough. That or gain. There seems too much method in these killings for them to be motivated by madness.'

'You can't legislate for the loonies,' Thomas said. 'Why, when I was in Wandsworth, we had a bloke in there—'

'That's a story for another day, Thomas,' Reid said, not unkindly. 'If we can discount the Bermondsey lot, what about the Circle which met with Evadne Principal?'

'I think we really can cross off Hilda Ransom, don't you?' Crawford said.

'Which one's she?' Reid remembered some women but couldn't put names to faces.

'The little one, she sat opposite Boothby.'

Reid furrowed his brow. 'I remember her now, yes. You're right, I don't think she would have the strength. A dressmaker or something, isn't she? Very delicate hands, at any rate.'

'Veronica Makepeace,' Crawford said, suppressing a shudder. 'She's quite . . . statuesque.'

Margaret Murray smiled. 'You're always so polite, Andrew,' she murmured.

'That's one word for it,' Reid said, also smiling. 'She looks as if she could crack walnuts between—'

'That's quite enough of that, Edmund, thank you.' Dr Murray thought she should keep things on the right side of decorous. 'I understand she was there on behalf of another member. Lucinda something, was it?'

'Lucinda Twelvetrees. Very nervous disposition,' Crawford said.

'Is she also hefty?' Reid chose his descriptive word with care.

'I don't know,' Crawford said. 'She wouldn't open the door.

She could have been crouching down, but she didn't seem very tall.'

'There's always Mr Justice Grosvenor,' Kane said, hopefully.

Reid clicked his tongue. 'You have to keep your predispositions to yourself, John,' he said. 'None of us like old Let-'Em-Off Grosvenor, but I don't see him as our man, sadly.'

'No.' Kane was reluctant but had to agree.

'There's what's-his-name, Alfred d'Abo, the *Mail* man.'

'I wouldn't have thought a postman was a typical Circle member,' Reid said. He was more a *Police Gazette* reader when he had the time.

'No, I mean he's a journalist,' Kane explained. 'And he isn't a Circle member. He was just there covering the last séance that Evadne Principal gave, for his paper. Bit of a scoop, it turned into, of course. He was only invited to the séance last night so no one was inadvertently missed out. He was very rude about Mrs Principal's skills, to the point of suggesting she was killed for being a really bad sensitive. But he was being flippant, as journalists so often are, of course. But you can't arrest someone for being flippant, more's the pity.'

'Did Eusapia notice anyone else suspicious?' Crawford asked.

Reid rubbed his eyes and groaned. 'So many people to remember, and some I hope I never think of again. There was a duchess, deaf as a frog, she started to tell me some long story about something that happened in the woodshed when she was a girl – it turned me up, it really did. So I told her that the gardener was in the ninth circle of hell, my spirit guide could see him planting out salvias for all eternity and she seemed to like it.' He gave a retrospective shudder. 'Sir James Brooks, of course – we mustn't forget him. He backed out of attending the séance. Why?'

'He's got alibis up to his armpits,' Crawford said. He turned to Margaret. 'Sorry,' he told her. 'I haven't checked on everyone connected with Jack, but it has to be done.'

Margaret gave him a sour smile. 'It's nice to think that someone has a clean bill of health, maniac-wise. Was there anyone else?'

'Veronica Makepeace told me about someone at the Principal séance who she didn't really know. Hang on . . .' Crawford fished out his notebook. 'I jotted it down . . . here it is. Valerie Exeter. She wasn't a regular, but Miss Makepeace got chatting with her.'

'Not like Miss Makepeace,' Reid said.

'Do you know her?' Kane was surprised. Veronica Makepeace didn't seem Edmund Reid's usual cup of tea.

'No. But I know her sort. She was using the séance as a sort of . . . well, sales opportunity. You have to give her credit where it's due, she's going to be a busy lady for a while, I think. I even saw her slipping her card to young Jack, though I shouldn't think he is her usual clientele.'

'There you are!' Kane was triumphant. 'They're working together!'

'No grasping at straws, Inspector Kane, please.' Margaret could still not believe that Jack Brooks had anything to do with the murders.

'So to take time to chat with a woman is not what I would expect of her.'

'She was being nosy, I think,' Crawford said. 'And besides, women do have brothers. Fathers. I don't think Veronica would baulk at husbands. But Veronica seemed to think that this Exeter woman was a true believer. She didn't say otherwise, anyway, and I think she's quite a shrewd judge of character.'

'True. Do you remember this Exeter woman, Edmund?' Kane asked. 'Was she there last night?'

'I shouldn't think so,' Margaret said, interrupting. 'She wouldn't have been on the Circle's list and she certainly wouldn't be on Lady Sylvia's.'

'A gatecrasher?' Thomas suggested, giving up and sitting at a nearby table eating his own scones.

'Was anyone on the door?' Reid asked.

'Bennett,' Kane said, with a sigh. 'Brooks and his pa, handing out the tickets to get them in to the séance. So, no one we can trust, really. My boys were only there incognito to make sure there was no rough stuff.' He looked at Margaret Murray with a glare that brooked no argument.

'So she could have been present,' Crawford said, hurriedly defusing the situation. 'Tall, quite broad in the beam, according to Veronica. Lots of makeup.'

Reid said, in the tones of one who had found out through sad experience, 'That describes practically every titled woman over forty there last night. In London, probably. Some of them have got handshakes which would faze a collier.'

'We may need to re-interview the people at the séance itself,' Margaret said, finally taking a sip of tea. 'Thomas,' she called over her shoulder. 'My tea's cold.'

Thomas, the perfect host, hauled himself out of his chair and set off for the kitchens.

'No need,' Kane said, getting up. 'It's Jack Brooks and I'm going off to finalize the warrant now.'

The ultimate damper being placed on the party, everyone went their separate ways, Crawford popping back for some scones and a paper bag. He had his homeless to feed and he had been busy lately.

Margaret Murray let herself in to her office high under the eaves in University College that June evening and dropped into her chair, unpinning her hat and skimming it on to the shelf where the newly re-instated Mrs Plinlimmon sat, overlooking the room and the rooftops of Bloomsbury from her lofty perch. She liked a change of scene and Margaret had moved her from the museum that day, after she had awarded Jack Brooks his PhD. The owl had been badgering her for weeks to tell Jack the good news, so it seemed only fair that she could now share a landing with him, now that he was a doctor and eligible for a desk crammed into the corner of the room set aside for the chosen few.

The archaeologist leaned back in her chair and closed her eyes.

'Mrs Plinlimmon,' she said, 'I do believe I may be getting too old for this. My trouble is, I get attached. I shouldn't, I know.' She opened her eyes and looked across at the owl. She was not the bird she had once been. Some feathers had gone from the back of her head, never to return, and her beak had once belonged to a barn owl, but she still looked pretty spry and her wisdom had not lessened with the years. Margaret smiled. 'You're right, of course,' she murmured. 'What's the point in knowing people if you can't get attached to them. It's pointless.' She put the heels of her hands over her eyes and pressed them lightly. After a moment, she cleared her throat and sat up, giving herself a shake.

'Mrs Plinlimmon,' she said, firmly. 'Today has been quite a

roller coaster. I think before the sun goes down, I must find William and say I'm sorry. His apology was not exactly fulsome but perhaps I was feeling fragile after my long night. When does the sun go down tonight, by the way?'

Mrs Plinlimmon thought it was probably about half past eight.

'I have an hour or so, then, to have a small sherry, tidy myself up and have a bit of a snooze. I'll put my "Do not disturb" notice on the door and with luck, anyone still in the building will actually read it and take notice of it.' She rummaged vaguely on the top of her desk but couldn't find the notice. Instead, she settled for setting her alarm clock, usually used to time tutorials, for an hour hence, and stretched out as best she could in the armchair. The last thing she thought, before sleep took her, was that there was nothing like an almost all-night séance to make a person tired.

FIFTEEN

The alarm shrilled through the air and made both Mrs Plinlimmon and Margaret Murray jump. She grabbed the clock without opening her eyes and held the clapper with one hand while clawing for the lever on the back to make it stop. She would probably be still all right for time if she had another twenty minutes or so.

Soft hands removed the clock from her clumsy fingers.

'Here, Dr Murray,' a gentle voice said. 'Let me do that for you.'

Suddenly, Margaret Murray was wide awake. She knew the voice and yet she didn't. She struggled upright in the chair and opened eyes still sticky with sleep to see a tall, upright form walking away from her, to resume the seat behind the desk. Because some sixth sense told her that she had not been alone for quite a while. The room had an underlay of patchouli and neroli, but there was also a faint whiff of fear.

The curtains had been drawn over the low window and the sun, westering fast, came in golden but without much help when it came to discerning detail in dark corners. Margaret peered and tried to lean forward, but couldn't. She felt at her waist and found she was tied to the chair, with William Flinders Petrie's dressing gown cord, of all the ironies. He often left the garment hanging on the back of the door when they had had a late night in his study. Margaret blushed and could have kicked herself.

'Who are you?' she said. 'And why am I tied here?'

'As to who I am, we'll see if you can work it out, shall we?' The voice was almost a purr. But one thing cheered Margaret Murray. It certainly wasn't Jack Brooks. 'You are tied to your chair, Dr Murray, because you have proved to be a very hard prey to dispose of. I really thought I had kicked the living daylights out of you that night by the park railings. I didn't see how you could have survived it. The stupid woman I took to be you . . .'

'Christina Plunkett,' Margaret said. 'She has a name and she isn't stupid.'

'She has a thick skull, in any event. And thicker stays. She should have died from any one of the blows I dealt her. You would have done, I am sure. You don't strike me as a whalebone sort of woman.'

'You're right,' Margaret said. 'A liberty bodice is all I have felt the need for. But . . . why should you want to kill me?'

The shape in the shadows shrugged, the square shoulders lifting and falling with effortless grace. 'Why shouldn't I? You were poking your nose where it wasn't wanted. You and your stupid pet policeman. After you, he's next.' The shoulders shrugged again. 'I may just be a woman, but I can overpower a man if I have to. And I will have the element of surprise.'

'I don't want to appear stupid,' Margaret said, leaning back and not struggling against the cord, 'but I assume you are the habitual homicide preying on mediums?'

'Habitual homicide?' The shadow laughed throatily. 'I think that is to give me a label which I don't deserve.'

'Why don't you?' Margaret asked. 'You have killed three women to my knowledge. In the eyes of the police and most right-thinking people, that makes you an habitual homicide. Three, habitual. Bodies, homicide.'

'But you don't under*stand*.' The voice cracked and the shadow leaned forward, showing a curve of cheek and extravagantly long lashes for a moment. 'I didn't set out to kill three people. I didn't set out to kill anyone. If the first one had been the one I was looking for, and if she had not . . .' there was an intake of breath that sounded like a beast about to paw the ground and charge '. . . defied me, then no one would have died.'

Margaret sat for a moment. Hopefully, give this woman an inch and she would tell a story a mile long.

'But no.' She couldn't keep quiet now she had started. 'No. I went to see her. I was reasonable. She claimed she didn't know what I was talking about, though I knew she did.' There was a silence and the voice, when it resumed, was slower, quieter. 'Or, I thought she did. I put some poison in her soup.' Long nails rapped on the desk top. 'She died.'

'I don't understand how you knew she wasn't the right one. Or when you would know when you had found the right one.' Margaret Murray could never leave a puzzle unsolved, even when her life depended on it.

'Of *course* you don't know,' the woman spat. 'Why should you? And yet, not knowing, you still poked your nose in. You inveigled yourself in to the Bermondsey Spiritualist Circle using the insane name of Henrietta Plinlimmon.'

Margaret could almost sense the owl bridle on her high shelf.

'Of course, George had you pegged almost from the start. He's a bit . . . handy, perhaps, but he isn't a stupid man. Except his belief in all that beyond-the-veil nonsense; that's ridiculous, of course.'

'George? George Boothby? How do you know him? Are you a member of the Bermondsey Circle?' Margaret asked. Her eyes were getting used to the dark and she could almost make out the woman's features. But it couldn't be Agatha Dunwoody or Olivia Bentwood. She could have kicked herself for not asking about other ex-members. In her naivety, she had thought that everyone had been there for ever, but of course that wasn't necessarily the case.

The guffaw was anything but ladylike. 'George and I go back years. I know several of that Circle. Robert and I have known each other since . . . well, goodness, I can't remember how long I have known Robert.' A throaty chuckle came from the shadows.

'Man and boy I have known George and Robert. But you didn't think to ask, of course, and neither did the police. That's the trouble with the police these days and, if I may say so, Dr Murray, with the academic mind. You see one thing and you assume the rest. Sometimes, if it quacks like a duck and walks like a duck, it isn't actually a duck. It's a pelican doing a darned good duck impression.'

The researcher rose in Margaret Murray's chest and nearly burst out, snarling. 'I beg your pardon, Miss . . .?'

'You don't get me that way,' the shadow laughed.

'I beg your pardon, but that is not what I do. When I research anything, whether it is a mummy or a murder, I do it with the facts to hand, not the facts as I would like them to be. I made no assumptions. I have just come from a meeting with the police and they are sending men round to the Brooks house in Berkeley Square to arrest Jack.'

'Oooh,' the woman purred. 'What a worry for you.'

'Not really,' Margaret said. 'They don't have a scrap of evidence against him and the family solicitor will have him out of the Yard before they have had time to make him a cup of tea.'

'You seem to have such a strong belief in the law,' the woman said.

'It has never given me reason to not believe in it.' It was the simple truth.

'Ha! Let me tell you something about the law.' She stopped. 'Or not, perhaps. Not yet, at any rate. I shall be making you a nice drink in a minute. Sherry is it, your tipple at this time of day? I hope it's a nice nutty Amontillado, so the cyanide goes well on the palate. I have no reason to dislike you, Dr Murray, but I have the feeling that if I leave you much longer to mull all this over, you will find out who I am and, although I am open to all kinds of experiences, I am not ready to hang, not just yet.'

'Who is?' Margaret remarked.

'True. Now, where is the sherry?'

'It's in the bottom drawer. There are some glasses there, too. I prefer the one with the green spiral in the stem. Take care with it, it's very old.'

There was a chuckle from the deepening shadow. 'I think I will give you . . . let me see. I will give you this rather clumsy little tumbler, which I suspect is a piece of Roman glass. It would amuse you to drink from it and also, you wouldn't trust anyone else not to drop it.'

Margaret inclined her head, to an intellect close to hers. 'You are very clever, Miss . . .?'

'I don't think we need to repeat this, do we, Dr Murray. I am really not likely to fall for anything that obvious.'

'No, Miss Exeter, I don't think you are.'

There was a palpable silence in the room, but a silence with an edge on it which could have cut diamonds.

'Miss Exeter?' the woman said eventually. 'I don't know any Miss Exeter. Are we back to the duck analogy again?'

'I'm sorry if I have mistaken you for someone else. It just seems to me that there is a missing piece in every puzzle and, in this case, it is in the shape of Valerie Exeter.'

'And what shape is that?' The question was rhetorical, but Dr Murray answered it anyway.

'Tall, quite broad shouldered. Wearing rather a lot of mascara.'

'That could be a lot of people.'

'Eusapia agrees. I was talking to her earlier and she says that many of the women at the séance last night could fit that description. But I think she exaggerates; she has quite a wicked sense of humour, for an Italian peasant.'

'Robert tells me we have you to thank for bringing Miss Palladino to London. I am only sorry I couldn't have been there.'

'But I think you were there, Miss Exeter. There is something about you which I recognized and I think that is because you were sitting around the table last night, opposite me, a few seats down from Hilda Ransom. By the way, how did you end up with a golden ticket? Did you steal it?'

'As a matter of fact, I didn't. I actually got one fair and square. Though I would have stolen one had it been necessary, as I am sure you can imagine. I had some money, in case I had to bribe someone, naturally. But I thought you professors only dealt in facts.' The voice was becoming waspish.

'I'm not a professor, but thank you anyway. It was hard to tell in the dim light, but I thought I recognized someone I knew and struggled hard to remember what it was. You know how it is, when something is on the tip of one's tongue, so to speak, but you can't bring it to mind. I'm not a woman interested much in clothes, as you may have spotted, but some things catch my eye. There was something about the silhouette that struck a chord and it is a chord which has only just begun to make sense to me. Like all of these ephemeral things, it needed a little more information, and that has just come to me now, an old piece of information from the mists of time.'

In spite of herself, the woman was clearly interested. 'Mists of time is what you do, isn't it, Dr Murray? Do let me know what little nugget has emerged.'

'Are you sure you want a history lesson right now, Miss Exeter? I thought you were about to poison my sherry.'

'That can wait,' the woman said. 'I do love history and also love to learn. So let me be your last ever student, Dr Murray. It would be such an honour.'

'If you insist. When I was a girl – I was born in India, you know – my education was somewhat piecemeal, to be polite to it. I went to live with my uncle, who was a vicar in Rugby, and I had a governess but she wasn't the greatest intellect, lovely woman though she was. However, my uncle was friends with some of the masters from the school and they would come round after church on a Sunday. One or two of them were kind enough to talk to me.'

'Lovely for you.' The sardonic voice came low and menacing. 'Get on with the lesson.'

'I'm just letting you know where my information comes from. All good researchers know that provenance is all.'

'Just tell me this amazing gobbet. You're right, I really should be getting on with poisoning you.'

'One of the assistant masters, the Reverend Percival, liked to teach me little bits of church history, which you may well think was probably not that exciting. But of course, the further back you go, the more church history is mixed with the history of the country and so in the fifteenth century, families who provided, as it were, the incumbents of bishoprics were very important people indeed.'

'Nice to know. You have a minute to come to the point.'

'And so, in the reign of Richard III – a much-maligned king, but that may be a lesson for another day – I just happen to remember, for no particular reason, the name of the family which was very connected with the See of Exeter was Courtney. I'm not sure of the spelling – I was only a little girl and not given to researching as I am now – but then, I'm not sure of your spelling of it either.' She smiled in the gloom. 'Shall I call you Miss Exeter still, or should I call you Courtney?'

There was silence for a while. Then, the woman spoke. 'Do you know, Dr Murray, you may be the most intelligent woman I have ever met? You tell a darned fine tale as well. I would imagine that you are going to be a difficult lecturer to replace. I understand that yours are the most popular classes in the whole college. Even William Flinders Petrie would probably agree with that.'

Margaret chuckled. 'Oh, dear me, no. William would never give me that accolade. He believes, and quite rightly, that he is the best lecturer in this or any other university. But I do flatter myself that my students and friends will miss me when I'm gone, Miss Exeter. I have decided, as you will have noticed, to err on the side of formality.'

'What gave me away?'

'Well, it has taken me the best part of twenty-four hours to work it out, so it wasn't a giveaway as such. But you are far too fond of the hunting attire as a look. It suits you, it really suits you, and I don't criticize your taste. But it's very memorable. You wore it the day you came to the museum, do you remember? You brought Mr Merrington's easel over for him and we just met, very briefly, in the corridor. You were wearing it then and I was struck by it. Very . . . unusual.'

'I don't dress like the common herd.'

'And why should you? You should do as you wish, Miss Exeter. Unless, of course, that runs to killing people. In that case, I think you should perhaps stop this side of the law.'

The room was almost completely dark and the woman sitting in Margaret's chair had a suggestion. 'Do you think we could bear to have a little light on the subject, Dr Murray? Now you have, as it were, unmasked me, then it doesn't really matter, does it? Nothing bright, just the kind of light to have a final chat by.'

'I think that would be splendid.' Margaret leaned forward, forgetting the dressing gown cord tied around her waist. 'There are matches in the top left-hand drawer and a candle stub on the shelf behind you. There is an overhead light – no expense is spared here, even up in this eyrie – but that will be a bit harsh for the business we have yet to transact.'

'Candlelight,' Miss Exeter said. 'How romantic. Is that for your little trysts with William Flinders Petrie?'

Margaret smiled. 'A fond memory for my final moments. That's very kind of you, Miss Exeter. William and I are not that fussy about the ambient light, to be honest. We just enjoy each other's company.'

'As fine a euphemism as I could wish from a woman of your intellect, Dr Murray. You don't ask how I know.'

'Please don't make mysteries where there are none, Miss Exeter,' Margaret said, sharply. 'I should imagine everyone in the college knows by now. I made the mistake of telling Maurice "Blabbermouth" Burton of the Human Physiology department about it in confidence at the Christmas party a few years ago and I might as well have taken out an advertisement in *The Times*. But no one is hurt by it, so where is the harm?'

There was a scrape of a match and the candle flame sprang into life, lighting the cheek and some curls of auburn hair of the woman who, even as she blew out the match, was planning to kill Margaret Murray. 'That's the thing that annoys me, Dr Murray.' The lips were stretched in an angry crimson line. 'You speak of not hurting anyone, you and your paramour, and yet you are horrified by the deaths of three pointless women.'

Margaret Murray had heard some hubristic statements in her time, but this had to take the garibaldi. She hadn't really been angry until now, because she had little to be angry about. True, she was being threatened with death by cyanide. But that hadn't happened yet, and she was quite comfortable in her favourite armchair, and she even had an atavistic hug from William from his dressing gown cord. Mrs Plinlimmon was at her back, wishing her well. So there were worse positions to be in. But now, this woman, this *evil* woman was comparing her relationship with William to killing three innocent women and making them the wrongdoers. This she would not tolerate. She leaned forward again but the woman just chuckled.

'Don't forget you're tied down, Dr Murray. I don't expect you to feel as I do, so don't try to talk me round. One of those women, or at least, I thought it was one of them, has something belonging to me. All right, I was wrong about it being one of them, but it is one of their evil kin, that's certain. And I will keep killing them until I find what I am looking for, my inheritance, my birthright. Then I won't have to work for people who don't know anything about art, about style, about anything that matters at all.'

This was confusing to the archaeologist. She wasn't a great adherent to the Flippant School as followed by Kirk Merrington, but the man did have talent when pointed in the right direction. Her putative murderer was being a little harsh and she said so. 'I should think that there are many women in London who would be pleased to be Mr Merrington's . . . helpmeet.'

'Ha! Don't cast me in that role. If you think that that worm and I are anything but employer and employed, you must think again, Dr Murray. We don't all climb into bed with the boss, let me tell you. No, if anything, Kirk Merrington is led by me. *I* am the arbiter and he the follower. He tells me everything and then I have to do his dirty work. I take the risks. He gets the accolades.'

'Miss Exeter . . .' The last thing that Margaret Murray wanted was for the woman to get excitable. If death had to come, let it be by cyanide in a nice Amontillado drunk from a glass from the second century BC, not by being clouted upside the head with the poker.

'What?'

'What is this birthright? You're going to kill me, so I may as well know.'

'Hmmm. Why not? It would be good to get it off my chest, to tell you the truth. I was orphaned quite young and went to live with an uncle. Much like your good self.'

'Oh, no,' Margaret was quick to distance herself. 'I wasn't orphaned. I was simply sent home from Calcutta, as most English children were.'

'I see. It doesn't matter. My uncle was a little . . . unusual, in the way he made his money. But money was made, oh, yes, and most of it spent as well. Uncle G was not a frugal man. But whenever he got what he called a windfall, he would buy bonds with at least a quarter of it and he kept them in a strongbox, always kept in his desk, wherever we were living.'

'And were you his heiress, according to his will?'

'There was no will,' the woman said shortly. 'But everyone knew about our relationship to each other and his solicitor said there would be no problem. There is another relative living but . . . well, he is unlikely to make old bones, let's just leave it at that.'

'And so, I assume, in the fullness of time, your uncle died.'

'Died. Yes, you could say that. Some might say murdered.'

In the light of the candle, guttering now in a growing pool of melted wax, the woman's eyes burned.

'By you?' No questions were out of bounds now. Even Mrs Plinlimmon held her breath in excitement.

'No. By the law. He was hanged for a crime he didn't commit.'

'Goodness. There's a lot of it about, or so I understand from the gutter press.'

'That's so like you,' the woman spat. 'Secure in your little world of mummies, and owls and professors in your bed. What about us, the orphaned, the dispossessed, the robbed!'

'So, why do you think a medium has your uncle's bonds?' It was imperative to get the conversation back to calmer waters, if any waters were calm in this maelstrom of emotion.

'Because all his life, my uncle was obsessed with séances. He would take notes and, at first, I thought he really believed. But of course, what he was really doing was noting down details of the dearly departed, so he could go round later and make friends with the widows.' A harsh laugh almost blew out the candle. 'That's what he used to call it. "Making friends". It was only when I walked in on him one day, "making friends" with a fat widow from Hounslow, with his hairy arse in the air and her blubbery thighs round his waist that I saw him for what he was.'

'That must have been a shock for a sensitive girl.'

'Don't say that word! Don't say "Sensitive". That's what he used to call those women, as gullible as the ones he took for every penny, stupid, *stupid* fools. But, towards the end, when he was starting to lose his looks and the women didn't fall as easily, he began to believe, I think. His housekeeper – I had moved out by then – said he would have them round and would be strange

for days when they had been. And then, when he . . . died, I
went to the house and the box in the desk had gone.'

'Given to a medium?' It seemed the only obvious answer.

'Given to, or taken by. It makes no difference. His housekeeper
described the last one to the house. My God, you have no idea
how many women there are in London who look like that! Why
couldn't he have taken up with one with auburn hair, a squint
and a wooden leg?' Again, the harsh laugh broke out, halfway
to a sob. 'Then, only one would have had to die. If that, if she
had seen sense.'

Margaret Murray sat quietly. There was a lot to take in.
She knew instinctively that what she did and said in the next few
minutes could have an irrevocable effect on the rest of her life,
mainly whether it was going to be long or unbelievably short.
She breathed deeply, using her abdomen as she had been taught
by her ayah, who had learned about yogic breathing. She felt
calmer and only wished she could pass that feeling on to her
companion.

'So,' Valerie Exeter said, 'that's my story. Now, I think it's
time for a nice little drinkie, don't you?' She reached down to
the bottom drawer of the desk and brought out the Amontillado.
Margaret noticed with surprise how low the level in the bottle
was. She made herself a mental note that, should she survive
against all the odds, she must reconsider the wisdom of having
a little nip of an evening before going home. She seemed to be
getting through the alcohol at an unseemly rate. The cork came
out with a satisfying plopping sound.

'I do like that noise, don't you?' she said, in a friendly tone,
pouring about half a glass. 'So convivial, I always think.'

'It is a very comforting noise,' Margaret agreed. 'Makes me
think of old friends.'

'That's nice.' Miss Exeter smiled and Margaret saw the thin
lips stretch again over her slightly prominent teeth. The lipstick
was too dark for her colouring and her rouge was applied very
thickly. Margaret waited for the *coup de grâce* as the cyanide
would mingle with the sherry. The woman rummaged in a pocket
in her skirt and came up empty. There was a moment's shock in
her eyes and then she laughed. 'Forget my head if it wasn't
screwed on,' she said, as if talking about a train ticket or lost

handkerchief. 'It's in here.' She slid her hand into the front of her jacket and, after a little fiddling about, came out with a tiny vial, which she held up to the light.

'You'd hardly imagine, would you,' she said, 'that in here is enough cyanide to kill a horse. I'll use it all, I don't like carrying opened vials around with me. I prefer it to be safe behind the chemist's wax seal until I use it.'

'How do you get it?' Margaret asked, interested in everything to the last.

'I go to different chemists, around London,' she said. 'Depending on the time of year, I say it's for rats, or wasps. This one was to dispose of a wasps' nest in the butler's pantry. As long as you make the setting fairly upmarket, you can get away with it nine times out of ten. And of course, if they ask questions, you just go away and say you'll check and never go back. This one,' an elegant hand swam into the candlelight and turned the vial to the light, 'was apparently bought by Florrie Winters, to kill wasps. I've got very good at forging signatures that don't look like any other I have used. So you see, Dr Murray, I think of everything.'

'I didn't expect otherwise,' Margaret replied. 'An eye for detail, not something everyone has. Tell me, why the feather, and the card, and the page from the book?'

'Artistic licence, dear Dr Murray. A bit of flippant fun. It was a bit of a facer when Eusapia came out with them, though. And the St Nicholas. I never thought anyone would get that.'

'Eusapia is a cunning old soul,' Margaret said. 'She sees things others don't, that's for sure.'

'She almost made me believe in the tosh,' the woman said. 'We've had such a lovely chat.' She was getting up, having added the cyanide carefully to the glass. 'I take care not to inhale,' she said, lifting the glass in a toasting gesture. 'I made the mistake of breathing in the fumes when dear Muriel passed Beyond the Veil and very nearly joined her.'

'You could have asked your uncle first-hand where his bonds were,' Margaret said, still intent on lightening the mood.

'You can't take it with you, though, can you?' the woman said pensively, coming round the corner of the desk.

'So they say,' the archaeologist said. 'Although I think the pharaohs would have a word or two to say on that particular subject.' She grabbed the ends of the arms of the chair and braced her back, turning her face away from her oncoming doom. She could almost hear the celestial clock ticking her last few moments away.

'Please.' The woman sounded almost sad. 'Don't struggle. Let's just make this as peaceful as possible, shall we? You can talk to all those musty old mummies as they were when they were alive. You can ask them why they thought having their brains pulled down their noses would make them live for ever. You'll know everything, won't you? That will be good, surely?'

With her head still averted, Margaret Murray took a deep breath and lunged forward. The knot on the dressing gown cord gave way as she knew it would. There had been many very memorable mornings when William had brought her her early morning tea, his dressing gown parting as he entered the room, all due to the silk cord not holding a knot worth mentioning. It was a risk, but with a glass of cyanide heading her way, a risk worth taking. Her head hit her assailant at about navel height and the woman folded in half like a deckchair.

The crunch as her head hit the floor and the hiss of the air leaving her lungs sounded like the purest music to Margaret Murray as she lay for a second prone across the angular body. As the woman fought for breath beneath her, she sat up and straddled the skinny hips. She reached forward and pulled the wig off the lolling head.

'Oh, Mr Merrington,' she sighed. 'You nearly fooled me, you really did.'

Working quickly and definitely not using William Flinders Petrie's dressing gown cord, she tied the artist up. Jack Brooks, on a very hot day the previous week, had conveniently left his old school tie looped over the arm of a possible priest of Amenhotep and she used that for the ankles. A belt she had bought on a whim and decided made her look like a cushion with a ribbon round it was rescued from the back of a drawer and that sorted the wrists. She toyed with a gag, but that didn't seem necessary. If Kirk Merrington decided to shout for help, it could only be to the good. Once she was sure he was well trussed, she went to the top of the stairs and called for the nightwatchman, who she eventually heard slouching across the hall.

'Ooizit?'

'It's me, Dr Murray. I wonder if you could do me a favour?'

'I carn leave me box.'

'I do understand. Do you have a police whistle in said box?' She wished she didn't get arch when she had just knocked out a murderer, but it was just a little character flaw she would have to live with.

'Yers.'

'Well, can you pop your head outside and blow it, quite hard. And when the policeman comes, send him up to my room. Can you do that now, there's a good chap?'

Going back into her room, she was aware of a strong smell of almonds. She wasn't a scientist and had no idea how dangerous or not that could be. It was a problem. Merrington was tall and was half-trapped under her desk. She wasn't sure whether she could drag him out. On the other hand, she needed him to stay alive. She quite wanted to stay alive herself. So she settled for opening the door, the window in her room and the window at the end of the landing. Then she sat in the doorway and waited for the artist to come round.

She hadn't long to wait. He came to slowly, turning his head from side to side, trying to work out how he was suddenly looking at the ceiling, when moments ago he was on his way to deliver a fatal dose of cyanide to the annoying little woman now sitting on the floor a few feet away.

'I hope you're all right, Mr Merrington,' she said, kindly. 'But I'm sure you can see that I had to do something. Cyanide is not a favourite tipple of mine.'

'How . . . how did you know?' He licked his lips and turned his head, wincing. 'How did you know it was me?'

'I didn't, not for a long time. Your compulsive neatness, of course, explained why the scenes of crime were so tidy. And I had noticed, subliminally, if you like, that you and your receptionist were of similar builds. In fact, I wondered if you were perhaps siblings, because there was even a superficial facial resemblance. You reminded me of someone else as well, but I couldn't remember who. This whole sad business has been fraught with resemblances, one way and another, hasn't it? Then, as you talked, telling me of your uncle and his missing money, his reliance on mediums for his victims, it reminded me of the story you had told me about going to a séance as a child. And that in turn reminded me that Robert Grimes had told a similar tale. His uncle was Gregory Grimes, the conman, who was hanged for murder a few years ago. And that's when I realized that it was Robert you reminded me of. He's much better looking, of course, possibly by dint of not being an habitual homicide of unusual cruelty, but the look is there.' She waved her hand across the top half of her face. 'It's the eyes, I think.'

'Him! He would have been next.' Merrington said, bitterly.

'I would imagine so. Poor Robert, such a nice man and not really deserving of the kind of relations he was dealt.'

Merrington wriggled, but his ankles and wrists were tied too tightly for him to get out of their toils. 'I thought of everything, though,' he whined. 'I even engaged Courtney purposely because I knew I could pass for her in anything but a bright light. If I had had to, I would have sacrificed her, you know I would. I made sure she was doing filing or cleaning alone in the studio when I was killing those worthless women, so she had no alibi.'

Margaret had heard enough. The man had not got the conscience of a sea urchin. She turned her back – even the sight of him, squirming in his bonds, sickened her. A tear, for all dead things, crept down her cheek. She struggled to her feet. She wasn't really built for sitting comfortably on the floor and certainly not for getting up with any grace.

Just as she managed to become upright and was tucking in her blouse and tidying stray wisps of hair, there was a sound of feet like the trump of doom echoing up from the hallway below.

'The police are here,' she said, over her shoulder. 'Please stop struggling. It only makes an appalling situation that much worse.' She turned to explain to London's finest as the landing was suddenly full of large men, mostly wearing blue coats and enormous boots.

All but one . . .

Later that evening, sitting in Flinders Petrie's study on the second floor, an untainted sherry in her hand, her feet on a footstool and her head on his shoulder, Margaret Murray sighed with contentment.

'So, it was my dressing gown cord that saved the day?' The deep voice above her head was all she wanted to hear at that moment, so she forgave the egotistical subject of the speech.

'More or less, William,' she said. 'It would certainly have been a different story if you had had a sensible cotton one, as I have suggested many times.'

The arm encircling her squeezed a little tighter. 'You do give us frights, Margaret,' the professor murmured, kissing the top of her head.

'Frights, William? Call these frights? I've got many more where these came from. Just wait and see.'

The real Margaret Murray

Margaret Murray was born in India in 1863, in what was then the Bengal Presidency. Her father ran a paper mill and her mother was a missionary. Her education was sporadic, largely because women of her social class were not expected to work for a living. She did train as a nurse, however, during India's cholera epidemic and carried out social work in England.

From 1894, despite having no qualifications, she enrolled in the newly opened Egyptology department at University College, London. Here she stayed for many years, lecturing and encouraging the students of her 'gang' and working with William Flinders Petrie, one of the foremost archaeologists of his generation. The work took her to Egypt and led to her publishing a number of works.

On the outbreak of the First World War, Margaret volunteered as a nurse in France. Exhausted by this, she went to Glastonbury in Somerset and became immersed in the Arthurian/Holy Grail legends and her archaeology morphed into folklore and anthropology. She was given an honorary doctorate in 1927 and she travelled extensively before retiring seven years later.

As president of the Folklore Society, she fascinated thousands and shocked several with her publications on witchcraft and demonology, on which she had controversial views. She remained alert, adept and still writing into extreme old age, publishing her autobiography *My First Hundred Years* in 1963, the year of her death in Welwyn, Hertfordshire.

Her legacy lives on today in the writings of H.P. Lovecraft and the whole modern Wicca movement. She was a determined feminist, striking a blow for emancipation in a world dominated by male privilege.